BENEATH THE DIRT

N.J. WEEKS

Copyright © 2024 by N.J. Weeks

All rights reserved.

This is a work of fiction. Any names, characters, places, and incident's either are products if the author's imagination or used fictitiously. Any resemblance to actual persons, living or dead, events or locales is entirely coincidental.

No part of this book may be reproduced in any form or by any electronic or mechanical means, including information storage and retrieval systems, without written permission from the author, except for the use of brief quotations in a book review.

ASIN: B0CW1BXBJ8

Cover Designer: Pia @crimsonsdesigns

Editing: Renee Polkinghorne @ReneePolksReads

Proofreading: The Cauldron Author Services @thecauldronauthorservices

Formatting: N.J. Weeks

Author's Note

This book is very different than my previous works, in that it is **NOT** romance...at all. Beneath The Dirt, is a psychological horror/ thriller. It is meant to creep up on you and likely, nothing will make sense... until it does. Don't expect a romantic, neat bow ending. That's not what this book is.

To grasp the full effect of the story, it is best to dive in blindly. However, your mental health is of the upmost importance to me, so if you need more of a layout of what to expect in this book, please continue reading. If not, the truth that lies beneath the dirt is waiting for you...

Please be aware that this book deals heavily with religious trauma, specifically pertaining to Christianity. Bible verses, bibles, religious artifacts and religious symbols will be referenced/used in varying ways that can be offensive to some. Again, this is a horror story, not a romance, it is not meant to be comfortable. It's crafted to have you guessing and questioning things until the very end. Your mental health as well as the faith system you hold dear to yourself, is important, and I don't want anyone to sacrifice that just to read one of my stories. As always, I urge you to do what's best for you, even if that means passing on this book.

With that being said, the following are some of the dark elements/themes to expect in Beneath The Dirt:

Religious trauma, manipulation, abuse of power, mentions of physical abuse, physical abuse (briefly on page), SA mentioned in passing (and in flashbacks), gaslighting, heavy drug use, overdose, hallucinations due to drug use, suicide, explicit sexual scenes, heavy degradation, suicidal ideations, self-harm (mentioned in passing/alluded to on page), grief, violence, claustrophobic scenes, snakes, and use of religious artifacts not as they are intended to be used.

"Horror is like a serpent: always shedding its skin, always changing. And it will always come back."
— Dario Argento

For those who want their mind to be fucked just as good as their other holes.

Playlist

I'm So Sick - Flyleaf
Fear - Disturbed
Voodoo - Godsmack
Hemorrhage (In My Hands) - Fuel
Blasphemy - Bring Me The Horizon
Going Under - Evanescence
Under the Graveyard - Ozzy Osbourne
Halloweentown - Dark Divine
Prayer - Disturbed
Dethrone - Bad Omens
Bone Church - Slipknot
Miracle - A Day To Remember
Dead Memories - Slipknot
It's Been Awhile - Staind
Monster - Meg & Dia
Pissed - Saliva
Another Life - Motionless In White
Ricochet! - Shiny Toy Guns
Make Me Wanna Die - The Pretty Reckless
Hopeless And Beaten - Korn
Walk With Me In Hell - Lamb Of God
Judith - A Perfect Circle
Slow Burn - Jack Valentine (feat. Baby Goth)
Coin For The Ferryman - Nickelback

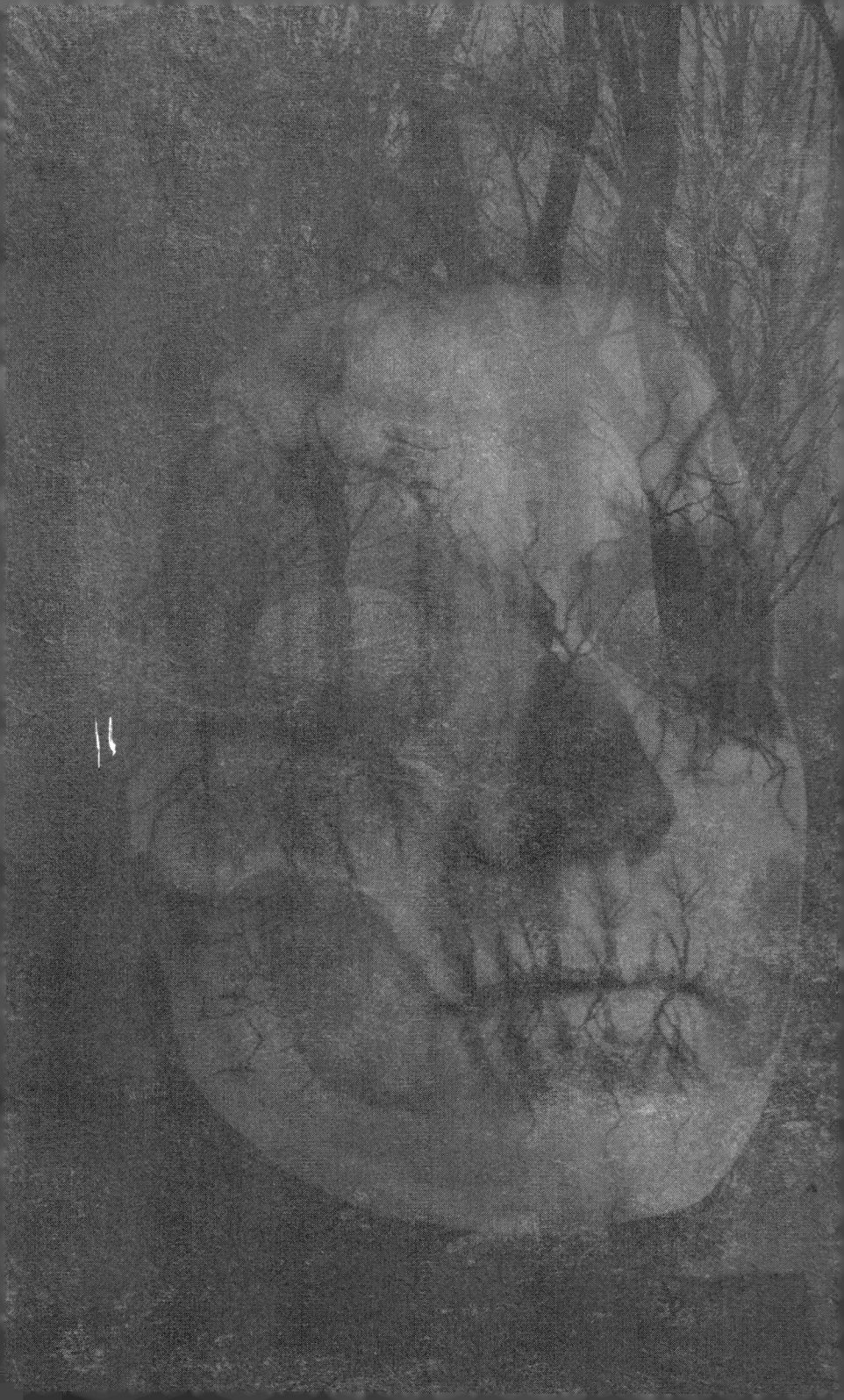

Prologue

Harlan

Blood for blood. Eye for an eye, I hum to myself as I stare at the loaded dump trailer parked in front of me. The control buttons, with their bold crimson hue, the same shade as the blood staining my fingertips, call to me, beckoning me to press them.

My hand lifts, hovering over the up-arrow control. The skeletal design permanently etched on the top of my palm that spreads its black and gray trail along each of my fingers, is just one of many reminders of how far I've fallen from the person I used to be. The old me would never muddy my skin with ink. Hell, the old me wouldn't have had the fucking balls to do a fraction of the things I've done this evening alone.

But the fact remains, I'm here…finally. *I'm so close.* So damn close that I can feel the finish line nearing. *Fuck.* I can practically taste it. The adrenaline rush is all-consuming, and as my inked hand glides to the control, eagerness embeds itself in my fingers, causing them to buzz in anticipation.

Though, as I stand here, with rows of tombstones cluttering my periphery, a part of me wonders if I've taken this too far. Even with the plummet my conscience has taken, the consequences of what I'm about to do isn't lost on me. Not even I can deny what will happen once I press that button. The aftermath that awaits us both is as permanent as the scars she left me with. Which should frighten me, but I'd be lying if I said that kind of destruction isn't what I've been a fiend for since she corrupted my heart, my body, and my fucking mind with the poison that is her existence in my life.

"Harlan, please!" Araceli whines. The desperation in her voice is impossible to ignore, but it doesn't deter me like it should. All her pathetic cry does is solidify my decision.

Ignoring the onslaught of her cries, I slam my finger on the red button with the up arrow. "Sorry," I grunt loud enough that she can hear me as the machine roars to life. Rocks and loose debris buried within the dirt-filled dump box click and clack against the metal basin as it makes its slow but steady ascent upward. "You asked for this."

What did she think would happen?

Did she seriously think after all this time I'd simply forget the promise she made?

That I'd let her escape me?

Escape the truth?

All without consequence?

Absolutely not.

Never.

"You can't do this!" Araceli screams.

Wrong. Yes, I can, and look at that... I'm doing it.

"Shut up," I quip, now standing over the pronounced ditch made special just for her.

This is all her fault, and now, in no time at all, the dirt will begin to pour directly into the six-foot-deep hole in the ground where she lay, giving her no-where to go without any option but to submit to me because I make the rules now... not her.

"You're sick, Harlan. Fucking sick!"

Her eyes meet mine, and her facial expression betrays the exasperation of her words. She looks scared... she should be. All her plans are now in disarray. Her destiny, something she foolishly believed she had control over, now hangs in the balance. All those hopes and dreams are now a pile of loose strands waiting for a puppeteer to pick them up and manipulate her fate. I am her destiny. I am the sailboat granting her passage. She's just a pawn, a measly passenger whose time has run out.

"Want some company?" I tease her, lifting my boot off the ground, moving it side to side, her gaze following it like a pendulum as I hover the open pit.

The usually bright cognac shade of her irises now reduced to a tormented and harrowing plea.

"Fuck you!" she spews. Adorably so, with a scrunch of her nose that's practically begging me to take my foot and pull it back, and to add to the spillage since the trailer is pouring it out too slowly for my liking.

"Soon," I bellow, stifling the imagery of how good she will feel, one last time.

"This isn't you." Her argument is mooted the second my boot drags back and forth on the ground, adding to the assortment of dirt piling into where she lay. An inescapable grin curls my lips, watching the broken fragments of earth shoot out from the sole of my boot. Anger dances on her face as dust wisps her way, forming debris-filled clouds around her. She can pretend this isn't what she wants, but no amount of huffing and puffing can distract from the secret thrill that I know this is giving her. This is everything she wants. Her perfect ending. Gifted to her in a dirty, brown, deep gaping hole in the fucking ground.

Stubborn as ever, even as her face is being pummeled, her gaze is unwavering. Searing into mine with the same dark stare that has tempted me as many times as it's deceived me.

"Please." Another whimpered plea, this time breathless with a hint of surrender that she and I both know is a farce. This is what she does. She manipulates anything and anyone in an attempt to get her way. But giving her what she wants has never benefited me, and sure as hell won't do either of us any favors, not now at least —it's too late. *She made sure of that.*

Ignoring her piss-poor acting skills and the pain she has so conveniently forgotten she caused me—*yet again*—I take hold of the bloody knife and jump into the open grave plot. Becoming one with the earth and grime, I land right on top of her. Araceli squeals from the impact of my bones crashing onto her, and the whimper that follows, leaking from those pouty lips of hers, is like music to my ears.

"Hurry," she pants. Strength suddenly finds her limbs as her hand taps at my waist. Her trembling fingers find my belt.

"You want it don't you?"

She shakes her head. *Yes.*

"How badly do you want it?"

"So. Fucking. Bad."

I shift to my knees, giving myself the room I need to undo my belt and lower my pants. Once my cock is freed, I reposition myself over top of her. Reveling in the fact that I can feel her body and willpower dwindling by the second. She's too weak to fight this—or *me*. There's no stopping this. This needs to be done. It's the only way to move on. To heal.

An irritating symphony of scoffs and whines fill the air as she turns her head to the side, away from me.

"Oh no you don't. Eyes up here. You look at your big brother when he's talking to you." I redirect her attention to me, this time prodding her chin with the tip of the knife. Her breath hitches, fearful that I'll let the blade slip and that's the only reason she obeys and cranks her neck back to face me.

With our gazes glued to one another, I lower the blade as I embark on a slow descent from the column of her throat to the swell of her breasts and continue the sadistic trek until the sharpened edge hovers her torso.

I keep it there, applying some more pressure. Not hard enough that it'll cut her but enough that those pesky fucking clothes of hers—or what remains of them—stand no chance at remaining intact or on her body. I already did a number on her pants, shredding the fabric to make access to that cunt of hers easier.

"There we go," I beam with pride as I tear off the remaining barrier separating me from naked skin.

I didn't go through Hell and back to get her to come here again, to the only spot on this property that brought her peace—the fucking graveyard of all places—to waste our precious time in the grave our flesh will soon rot, to be clothed. Her bare flesh, bloodied and writhing beneath mine, is a sight I not only want, but deserve after everything she's put me through.

Keeping the knife handle clutched in one palm, I skate my free hand to her breasts and cup one in my hand, kneading the perky, full flesh in my palm.

A moan slips her lips, finally accepting that I'm not letting her go. There's no fighting this. No escaping one's chosen fate. Might as well lay back, spread those legs wide, and enjoy the performance before the show comes to an abrupt and suffocating end.

I do her a favor and guide the snake off her legs, freeing her of its stronghold on her limbs. The audible relief she has as she sighs is laughable. I didn't free her from it to ease her fears. I did it to make accessing that greedy sinkhole she passes for a cunt easier for me to dip into.

Her hips lift, bucking and humping at the air in need. Waiting for me to put her out of her misery and fill her with the last cock her warm cunt will ever have.

I know she wants this just as badly as I do. Yet her will hangs on like an impenetrable fortress, as soon as her mouth opens to speak. "Why are you doing this?"

A pointless question.

"Because I have to," I deadpan. I tug at the edge of my mask near my jawline, wanting to pull it up onto my head, so I can clamp my teeth down on her erect nipple, but it won't budge. The heat penetrating my entire body acts like a glue, adhering the mask to my skin with no hope of letting me go. The uneven and cracked plaster of my mask scratches my face becoming one with my skin. Transforming me into the role I was destined to play. Her Ferryman.

Fatum enim eligimus. A familiar voice whispers from within. Reminding me that my fate and hers has already been chosen.

"Fine," she surmises. "Don't bother, it won't come off."

I know. No thanks to you.

She navigates her hand through the dirt and latches onto my wrist. Guiding my knife-laden hand up to her throat.

With our connected grip, we fight for dominance with two differing goals. Hers is to have the knife pierce through her flesh, swift and steady and on her terms. While my goal is to grant her that desire when I see fit. She owes me. Therefore, all her breaths, even her last, are on my time. Not hers.

"Almost time," I try to reassure her, but the added force we share on the handle, moving back and forth, causes the blade to nick her skin, drawing a thin line of red. Relief loosens her shoulders as she relaxes her hold on the knife handle, giving me full power over it and over *her*.

I drink her in. It's impossible not to. Every inch of her is a canvas dying for my claim. No amount of resentment I harbor towards her could change that. There's no denying her serpent-like charm. She's as exquisite as she is diabolical. A curse with no remedy.

Knowing what's coming next, accepting what has to be done, she parts her legs, spreading them wide. Laying in willing silence, with knees bent high, waiting for me to take back what's mine.

Soil continues to fall, clouding the air around us, reminding me we're running out of time.

I release a wad of spit onto one hand, wetting it enough that I can glide it on my shaft, lubricating it. My other hand, still with the knife in it, lifts so the blade hovers the column of her throat.

We exchange a heated look. One that says a thousand words without muttering a single syllable, and I lose all willpower. All. Fucking. Control.

I slam my cock into her, eliciting a screech from her that's both inviting as it is damning. Thrust after thrust, the force I plunge in and out of her needy, tight cunt synchronizes with the pressure I increase on the blade. The tease on her flesh draws a smile on her face that I've never seen from her. It's enough to make me come right now.

"Why now?" A ravenous groan vibrates against the knife hovering her airway. "Why after all this time?"

"Because you made me who I am."

"A villain?" She pants as I continue to thrust into her, rough and attentive.

"No, little sister. The ending you deserve."

PART I

THIRTEEN YEARS AGO

"The oldest and strongest emotion of mankind is fear, and the oldest and strongest kind of fear is fear of the unknown."
— H.P. Lovecraft

"Memories are like quicksand. They suck you in with their nostalgia. Giving your heart something to cling onto. But eventually the lie fades and reality takes you hostage, making you a victim of the truth you spun, just to live another day pretending to be whole."

— A.H. Charon. The Horrors We Endure. New York: Charon Press, 2024.

News Report

"Good evening, I'm Joan Lantz reporting for Channel Seven News here with my colleague Victor Price. Reports have come in about a missing person who was last seen making a purchase at the Halloween Shop on Main Street. You can find their name as well as what they were last seen wearing on the bottom of the screen and on our website. Please, if you have seen or have any information that can help local authorities locate them, don't hesitate to call the number provided. As many of you know, our small town of Mort, New York has been the decade-long target for a string of unusual disappearances. With yet another disappearance, it is not ruled out yet that it could be linked to the Samhain Killer. The pattern appears to be the same, and since it's been a year since the last disappearance that sadly turned into the discovery of Pastor Rainey's wife, found mutilated in a cornfield near their home, authorities are asking that if you are out celebrating, please be extra cautious of your surroundings."

"Yes, and to add on to what Joan has just reported, I would advise against any and all travel near Summerland Drive, while you're at it. Call me superstitious, but if we are to admit that our town is cursed, I think it's safe to say that place is the epicenter of our undoing."

"Sadly, Victor, I would have to agree with you. Stay safe everyone, and for those brave enough to still celebrate, have a Happy Halloween and Samhain."

One

Harlan

"Stay away from her," Dad warns, handing me a set of keys. "I mean it, stay the hell away from her," he reiterates his point, unknowingly aware of how his warning torments me. I wish it were that easy. I wish staying away from the girl whose room is across from mine—who took on our last name when her mom married my dad—was that easy. But nothing with my step-sister is ever easy; not dealing with her and certainly not avoiding her.

He glances at the keys he just gave me. "And she's not to have access to those under any circumstances." There's more venom in his voice than there usually is when he's talking about Araceli. I wonder what she did this time to have him practically vibrating with anger—not like that's a difficult task. Whenever Dad is outside the church walls, he's anything but the godly and jovial pastor he pretends to be. Unlike Araceli, I learned early on that to exist under his roof and to avoid his temper, it's easier to die unto oneself. Kind of how he preaches about what we should do towards God. Except he isn't God. He's a tyrant. Which Araceli would argue to be the same thing.

But in order to survive in this house, I learned a long time ago that you must deny yourself of whatever it is that makes you something he can't understand. The wrath that comes with his fear is a punishment most could never wrap their heads around, so it's best to play his game, if for nothing else, but to gain some semblance of peace. Something I clearly need to teach Araceli.

"Got it." I slip the keys into my back pocket.

A whiff of tobacco blazes past my nostrils as Dad moves past me. A slew of bad memories filter through a part of my mind I've tried to keep suppressed, but the stench is too strong, and the wounds, incapable of healing, make my mouth move faster than my mind can stop it. "Back to smoking?"

Dad grabs his bible, chuckling at my question. "Something like that," he replies, cryptic... *cold*. His boots thud against the floorboards as he heads to the front door, though he stops near me first. "I wouldn't be forced to pick up bad habits again if you kids had an ounce of respect for me."

More words—obscenities mostly—swirl through my mind, wanting to be let out of the floodgates of my mouth, but I keep it closed. It's not worth it. So, I suppress it. Just like I do every fucking thing in my life.

Suppress my thoughts.

My words.

My needs.

My *desires*.

All of it is kept locked inside the torture chamber that is my mind and body. All so I keep this man in front of me happy. All so I continue to feed into the illusion of being the respectable pastor's son that I'm tired of being.

"I mean it. She isn't to get ahold of those keys or access to—" he's interrupted by his phone ringing, and the shift in his demeanor as his thumb slides on the screen to answer is striking.

The confident line his shoulders made as he stood upright just moments before are now stiff and full of apprehension. "Yes?" he answers, voice stern and uncomfortable. "That's impossible, it's my property." Confusion mars his face as a sigh leaves his lips. "I can't tomorrow; it's the—" he stops talking, abundantly aware that I'm listening. He clears his throat, adjusting his tone. "Just hold on one second," he says to whoever is on the other line. He places the mouthpiece to his shoulder, averting his gaze back to me. "I mean it, Harlan. Over the next few days, it's paramount that we don't feed into the cries of the enemy."

My eyes strain from how hard I'm trying not to roll them. For a second, I'm not sure if the enemy he's referring to is the Devil or Araceli.

He continues talking to me through a hushed whisper, clearly not wanting whoever he has on the phone to hear. "Stay away from her. Don't give her the keys and don't you dare allow her to fill your head with her lies."

I nod, this time mouthing to him, "Got it," but Dad's attention isn't on my face any longer.

His gaze has traveled down to my wrists. The healed white lines burn beneath his judgmental stare, even as they are concealed under my long sleeves. "She's done enough damage already," he scoffs with disgust. It's comical how he thinks Araceli's presence in our family is capable of causing such damage —as he puts it. He blames her for everything, ranging from why I resorted to inflicting pain on myself to why I got kicked out of college. None of it, with the exception of the getting kicked out part, is her fault. She may have asked me to get her the pills, but I was the one who agreed. She didn't force me to do it, and it wasn't her fault that I went about it wrong, got caught, and then expelled before I could drive back home and give them to her. I was broken long before she came into our lives. Now, he just hates that he has two broken souls to deal with and has to put his theology degree to work.

"Whatever," I mumble, knowing he can't hear me. His attention is back on his phone conversation. He resumes speaking, hushed, into his phone as he leaves to head to the church he had built on the other side of what is now our property. For years, the lot on the other side of the graveyard that separates the desolate acreage we live on remained abandoned. Until Dad found a way to scrounge the funds to purchase it, turning our home into the birthplace of his pride and joy. Sacred Promises Church.

Relief spreads through my every vein, just like it always does when he leaves. Finally, I can breathe. I stand and wait for his silhouette to disappear as it blends in with the dusk skyline before I head to where I know Araceli is.

It's where she always is if she isn't in her room or soaking in the tub.

The graveyard.

Blades of overgrown grass and piles of fallen leaves tug at my boots the further I walk through the sea of tombstones. Alternating glances between where I'm walking to and what I'm walking on, I continue up to the part of the cemetery my dad leaves unkempt. He says it's because it's on a hill, and maintaining it is difficult, but I know that's not the reason. My mom, just like Araceli's, are both buried in this section, which he hasn't stepped foot on after either of their funerals.

A chill runs down my spine, and I wish I could blame it on the brisk October air or that I'm outside without a jacket but I can't. This is how it always is when I come here. The palpable shift in the air, no matter the time of day or year it is, when I walk on these death-filled grounds. It's impossible to ignore. It's why I avoid coming here at all costs, unlike Araceli, who frequents the graveyard like one would their favorite store or retreat. Especially around Halloween—the time of her mom's passing... and ironically, the same as my mom's.

My steps halt once I catch sight of Araceli off in the distance. I slow my stride, backtracking a bit so I can use the grave keeper's shed on the top of the hill as my shield. I crouch down low enough that she can't see me but not too much that I can't see her.

With dusk no longer lingering, the full moon now hanging above us acts as the perfect spotlight. The small of her back sways back and forth, over and over, drawing my gaze to her dark-as-night hair that cascades in long waves past her shoulders and down her spine. Her hands are outstretched to either side, and each time she moves, her hands dig deeper into the dirt around her. The repetition of her movements makes her appear hypnotized... or high. I can't tell.

Suddenly, my dad's warning from before rings in my ears loud and clear as if he's here warning me all over again, *"Stay away from her."*

Though, the more I watch her rotate her hips around, clawing at the ground like something possessed, the more I become entranced by her erratic behavior, finding myself wanting —*needing*—to move closer to her.

So, I do just that. Like an out of body experience, I shift from my crouched position and fall to my knees. Slow and steady, I crawl, using the tall, weathered headstones to camouflage myself. The closer I crawl to her, the more the wind picks up, shifting the scattered leaves around me. A foreboding sense ruptures my conscience, pleading for me to leave. I ignore it, despite my better judgment, and select a random headstone to hide behind. A patch of moss brushes against my face as I peer around the uneven limestone to get a better view of Araceli. Still on her knees, she drags her hands once more in the dirt before she lifts them upward. Palms open to the night sky, fragments of broken earth fall down the sleeves of her dress as she begins to hum.

It's low.

Hair-raisingly eerie, but sultry all the same. Each chord travels through the air for a brief moment before it stabs at my dick. Vibrating it with the reminder that she—my stepsister of all people—has the power to make me this fucking stiff from the simple act of her humming.

Guilt and fear toy with me as a surge of blood rushes to my groin. This is ridiculous. *Sick.* She has no idea that I'm watching her, let alone getting hard from the view she's unknowingly giving me.

My lids fall shut. Shame washes over me, begging me to leave before I do something I regret. The creepy melody continues to fill the air and somehow my dick is thickening the longer my ears bear witness to whatever she's humming.

This is why Dad said to stay away from her. She's a temptation. One that will get me in trouble... again.

Knowing that I can't keep doing this—watching her when she thinks I'm not and getting caught up in her web—my knees begin to scoot back. My body urging me to move and to head back home.

I start to scoot back, my eyes still closed as a familiar verse taunts me. Matthew 26:28 *"For this is my blood of the covenant, which is poured out for many for the forgiveness of sins."*

Except it doesn't make things better, and it doesn't ease my guilt; it intensifies it. Suddenly the blood that I should associate with forgiveness for my sins—like the sin I'm committing right now by lusting after my fucking stepsister—isn't just rushing to my cock; it's painting my irises with a crimson tint. Distorting my vision. Corrupting my mind.

It's all I can see even with my eyes still closed.

Dripping from the tombstones. Dripping from Araceli's body.

It's everywhere.

Foolishly, I open my eyes blinking twice, three times, then four. Certain that my mind is playing tricks on me, but it's not. It's all I can literally see or want to see.

I shake my head. Scared. Wondering if what she's been humming is some kind of magic, a dark spell, and it's affecting more than my cock.

Bile lines my throat, threatening my mouth. My movements are no longer smooth and stealth but quick and hurried as I run on my hands and knees until I'm far enough that she won't see or hear me.

I switch to my feet, about to run back home to take care of this stubborn ache that's embedded itself in my cock, but her voice has graduated to words. A chant. Still melodic and this time even creepier, but it's louder. Clearer. The distance between us merely makes her voice echo over to me at a deafening octave.

Fighting the pull I have to head back home, I remain still and listen.

"... has to go, has to go so no one knows."

The wind picks up once more, shuffling the fallen foliage I stand on, compromising my hearing, forcing me to take a step back and closer to her.

"... eye for an eye." She stops singing and turns her head in my direction.

My heart stalls and the bile that threatened my throat is rising to the surface. Not sure if she can see me and no longer caring, I swallow it down and run. The vines and debris on the ground tripping me in the process. I lose my footing, the keys in my pocket jingling as I crash to the ground. I don't bother to pick them up. I don't have time. I need to get the hell away from her. Gathering my wits about me I stand back up, navigating the uneven terrain, I run back down the hill.

My feet stomp onto the porch steps and I make a beeline for the bathroom. Vomit spews from my mouth, almost missing the toilet.

What was that?

Her.

Me.

All of it.

What the fuck was that?

And why am I still hard?

Painfully so.

Clearly, this isn't going to take care of itself, so I have to do it.

A slew of rehearsed bible verses and phrases I've been conditioned to say to appease God and alleviate my guilt consume me as I unzip my pants.

They grow louder in my head as my erect cock bobs free. I grip it with a tight, needy fist. The vomit in the toilet that hasn't been flushed yet burns into my periphery, yet somehow, also adds to the sick rush I have in this moment.

My lips purse and spit falls onto my shaft, lubricating it as I beat it. Not with my usual steady pace that I jerk myself off with. No, this is different. It's fast. Incessant. Violent. It's everything I shouldn't be feeling and everything I shouldn't be enjoying. But as I increase the speed and pressure, I'm transported back to the graveyard, back to the view I had of Araceli on her knees, worshiping whatever god or gods she deems worthy of her submission. Fisting myself harder, I envision the way she tore at the ground with angry, clenched fists, wishing they were on my cock instead of my own.

Her violence.

Her witchy fucking violence and that eerie chant now engrained in my mind as I stroke myself. Summoning my release from me as my whole body locks up and I cum in my hand.

Without hesitation, I bring my cum soaked hand to my mouth, sucking my fingers pretending it's her release instead of my own.

The fantasy drives a painful ache in my chest, or maybe that's the guilt trickling back in. I'm not sure which, but with the front door to the house slamming in the distance, I don't have time to decipher my feelings. Panicked that I will get caught, I reach for the box of tissues on top of the toilet and clean myself, tossing the tissue in the bowl and flush it down with my puke.

I scramble, pulling up my pants, already reciting the rehearsed prayer in my head, just like I do every time I watch porn or do something I know God will be mad at me for—which lately has been a lot.

Footsteps sound on the other side of the door. It has to be Araceli, back already from the graveyard. The footsteps are light like hers, not the distinct stomp of my dad's. I wait until they dissipate before I head to my room. My phone vibrates just as I close the door.

It's Dad. Looking down at my phone, I open my messages to see it's from our group chat between me, him, and Araceli.

> Dad: Reminder that tomorrow is Devil's Night service. Both of you are expected to attend.

I type back first.

> Me: Got it.

> Dad: Good.

> Dad: Araceli?

Three dots appear then disappear just as fast. This continues two more times before she responds. My heart jumps at my chest at the sight of her name in the thread and the nausea returns reading her response.

> Araceli: You aren't going to get away with this, you sick bastard.

Who is she saying this to? To my dad? To me? Guilt for what I just did floods me in painful proportions. I blink, confused. Already afraid of how my dad will react. Sure enough, my mind is playing tricks on me. Her message is there, but not the one I could've sworn I saw.

> Araceli: Can't wait Daddy *overeager smile emoji*

I should be relieved by her sarcasm and that the response on the screen wasn't actually there, but I'm not. It's happening again; the voices, the seeing things that aren't fucking there. Everything my dad tried to beat out of me all those years is flooding back. It never used to be like this. Things were quiet—*peaceful*—until she came into our lives and ruined me all over again.

Two

Araceli

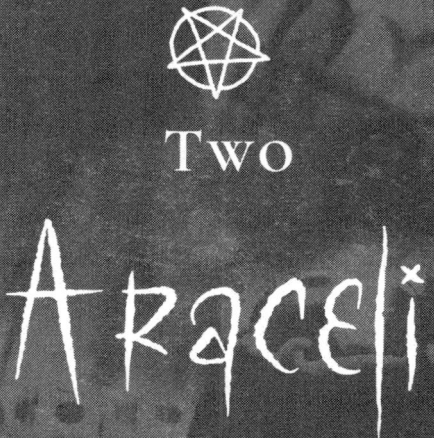

The next day...

"Open up, you stubborn fucker," I murmur in frustration. The rusty door handle scratches my palm, mocking me with each failed attempt. Light illuminates past the stained windows on either side of the most stubborn door ever created, indicating that The Last Stop, the oddities shop I frequent behind my stepdad's back, is, in fact, open. Yet, here I am, staring at the weathered sign on the front door that reads '*We're open, all welcome,*' unable to open the goddamn door. "Fine, have it your way."

Taking a step back from the entrance, my gaze shifts to the arched window to my right, immediately drawn to the vibrant shades of amber and crimson that seep past the mosaic design. Pretty as it looks, it makes it damn near impossible to make heads or tails of what's on the other side. I squint, trying to get a better look inside, but all that meets my vision aside from the glistening patchwork is my silhouette staring back at me.

I glance at the time on my phone. My stepdad, Pastor Rainey's infamous Devil's Night service, will be starting soon. Frida knows this, which is why she told me to get here when I did since she also knows what will happen to me if I'm late or not in attendance. The same thing that happens anytime I do something that he deems disrespectful to his god—he punishes me. I've grown used to it. Oftentimes, I find myself acting out or doing things on purpose, not only to get a rise out of him but to ensure that I will be reprimanded. At least then, I can feel something without having to run to the drugs—even if it means having my skin burnt or beaten. I've given up on peace; it's too fleeting. Pain, as harsh and destructive as it is, has become the only reliable thing I can cling onto in this life. So I embrace it, even if it's slowly killing me.

Still, even though I accept the torment that comes with being his stepdaughter, I know that the repercussions will be more severe tonight if I miss the service that has replaced his Christmas Eve and Christmas Day sermons in importance. I may be a glutton for punishment but even I know my limits.

The crowds of parishioners that tonight's service draws has become such a moneymaker for him that it's imperative to him that our family—or what's left of it—maintain the illusion of a happy, God-fearing family unit. It's that very lie that makes parishioners open their minds and their wallets in appreciation of each service. Without those funds, he wouldn't be able to keep the lights on and the fine-oiled machine of deception he calls his church afloat. Anything that puts his business model at risk brings with it a level of punishment that even I, as stubborn and thickheaded as I am, don't have the desire for. Not today, at least. Not on the anniversary of my mom's passing.

Impatience gets the better of me as I take a step forward to knock on the glass, ignoring the sign that explicitly says not to touch. My knuckles tap at the windowpane. The time between knocks becomes less. One after the other, my knuckles pound on the glass, wanting a reprieve from the chokehold the bitter October air has on my skin, lining it with raised bumps so harsh, it feels like my dress can tear at any moment.

Logic sneaks past my desperation, tempting me to give up and walk over to the church. But if I do that, I won't get what I came here for. A grimoire of sorts, but in journal form, that I've been waiting for Frida—the shop's owner—to obtain. Before my mom married Pastor Rainey and converted to his biblical nonsense, she and each of the women in her family were all given a journal on their eighteenth birthday that they would call "el libro del destino"—*a book of destiny*. Since my mom has passed and I don't have the luxury of turning to my stepdad for his support in my beliefs and tradition, I have to rely on Frida. To keep tradition alive—and to piss off my stepdad, of course—Frida helped me to find my own journal for my eighteenth birthday, which was earlier this month.

"Frida!" I call out her name, though it'd be a miracle if she could hear me over the sound of my incessant knocking. I continue this pointless attempt to get her attention a few moments more, until it dawns on me there is a back entrance to the shop.

Gathering the draping hemline of my dress, I lift it so I don't lose my footing on the mess of moss-covered vines poking through every exposed crevice of the porch as well as the limestone steps.

Just as I lift my platform Doc Marten up to take a step, the unmistakable groan of aged floorboards sounds inside, stopping me in my tracks.

I turn my head, my eyes hone in on the distorted shadow through the decorative stained glass. The creaking continues now paired with the distinct thud of hurried footsteps. As the competing sounds reach a crescendo, I inch closer to the entrance, hoping it's Frida on the other side finally ready to let me in.

"Have you been smoking again?" a voice shouts to me—Frida.

Hinges in dire need of oil grate at my eardrums as a bell sounds. The sound is abrupt, though the lingering percussion has the same effect as a gong, ricocheting its way from the doorway as it latches onto my spine, vibrating every vertebra.

Standing in front of the open door, my hands shoot upward in playful defeat as I shrug.

"What gave it away?"

"Oh, I don't know, could it be that you forgot how to open an unlocked door?" She waves her wrinkled hand, motioning for me to come in.

Frida knows that I smoke weed often. Though, she doesn't know that whatever strain I choose is almost always tampered with, lacing it with whatever I have accessible. I'm sure she assumes it's just a phase. That I'm a cliche teenager trying to act cool by smoking the 'Devil's lettuce' as my stepdad calls it. I'll let her think that. It's easier that way. She doesn't need to be burdened with what drives me to numb myself day after day, or that weed and all the fun ways I can alter it is my second choice since my go-to pills are no longer an option. Not since my fuck-face stepdad took that away from me too.

I move past the threshold and immediately have to stifle the sneeze I have coming on from the strong scent of earthy patchouli mixed with what smells like a fucking heap of nutmeg.

"Besides, you have a key to get in here anyway. No excuses missy." Frida's voice trails as she turns over the welcome sign—another whimsical saying etched into the wood that reads, *'Sorry, we're closed. Better luck next time,'*—before closing the door behind us and locking it.

"Closing early?" I ask, but my question is ignored.

She gives me a blank stare. "Something like that. Anyway, follow me this way," she hums, leading the way through the thicket of odds and ends that fill the small, arguably cramped space. As my steps trail Frida's, I feel the tension that stiffens my shoulders daily start to soften just like it does every time I sneak off here. It's here amongst the peculiar trinkets and items whose existence tests the hands of time, that I feel like I can be what my stepfather fears most... *myself*.

Silence lingers between us, but I don't fight it. Instead, I indulge my eyes in what makes "The Last Stop" the most unique oddities shop I've ever been to.

Walls cluttered in an assortment of taxidermy hung on plaques with displays scattered all throughout, housing items that range from bones to antique masks and even some vintage torture devices, fill my heart with joy. Every detail is vivid and beautiful.

Now stopped in front of the glass display by the register that holds the small macabre themed books, I wait for Frida to say something. She doesn't. Instead she mutters something to herself while she takes inventory of what's inside the case.

Impatience and excitement dance within me though I can't say the same about Frida. The stern expression on her face is anything but a mirror of my own anticipated demeanor.

"Soooo," I drag as Frida crouches down behind the display, flipping on the light switch that illuminates the rare books she keeps inside.

"Do you have it? Did it come in?" My enthusiasm overpowers me, as I rattle off one question after the next.

Straightening her spine, she offers me an apprehensive look.

"He's going to kill you." A dramatic and cryptic warning. "Especially if he finds out that Harlan was here not too long ago, and now you are back after he forbade it."

Harlan... was here?

I'm about to ask her when Harlan was here, a place I'd never expect him to be, but she continues on, stealing my opportunity to ask.

"You have to be more careful. The last thing I need is for your stepfather to burst in and disrupt everything I've built here."

"Don't worry he can't kill me. Isn't that a rule or something? Thou shall not murder?" I joke.

A sigh slips past her pursed lips as she remains unconvinced. "You don't strike me as someone who would have the commandments memorized." Her tone is ripe with disappointment. If there's anyone who despises the church and all it stands for as much as I do, it's Frida.

"I'm not," I reassure her, "I just have a good memory. Plus, it's fun using the shit he preaches against him."

"That's my girl," she clicks her tongue in approval, though her playful demeanor vanishes as quickly as it appeared. In its place, another foreboding glare.

"Let me rephrase, he's going to kill you if he finds..." her voice trails as she lifts her hand, exposing a sliver of the cracked leather spine I've been impatiently waiting for, "... this, mi brujita." My eyes light up as her hand shakes the palm-sized book in her grip for emphasis.

Restlessness settles in my bones, causing my fingertips to buzz with eagerness to have what I came for—*what I've waited so long for*—in my possession. Reaching into my crossbody purse, I fish for my wallet. Sliding the cash, I've been saving for months out, I place it on the countertop and extend my greedy palm out ready for our exchange.

One second bleeds into five, and by the ten-second mark of her just holding it within arm's reach, not giving it up, I go to snatch it.

"Araceli," she scolds, jolting her hands back. "I'm serious."

"So am I," I snap, eyes glued to the weathered black leather she's holding captive. "I promise he won't see."

Frida maintains distance between the book and me, unconvinced or moved by my words.

Adjusting my tone, I continue. "Besides, it's just a book." The words escape me and immediately I feel the weight of them hanging in the air. It's not just a book. It's anything but. Regret fills me. Suddenly, the shop feels ice cold, as if I insulted every object in here, and the violent chill wreaking havoc on my spine is a collective reminder.

No, you fucking dumbass, it's not just a book.

Mumbles in Spanish flee Frida's lips in long streams, were too fast and too low for my high to decipher, despite me being fluent.

"No estás lista," she says, clear as day, and indignance causes me to stomp my feet like a child.

"I am ready." I defend myself. "You know I am."

"Are you?" She places the book on the glass countertop. Her index finger points to the title. Gold, embossed lettering shines before my eyes. "*Fatum enim eligimus,*" she reads the title. "It means—"

"For we choose fate," I answer for her, familiar with its Latin translation.

"Exactly. So no, brujita, it's not *just* a book. It's *your* book—your journal. It's a beginning, and if your mother were—"

"Alive?" I cut her off. "Well she's not, *Frida*. Hence why I'm here so you can give me the book that I would've been gifted had she been alive." A lump lodges in my throat as my voice lowers. The words preemptively sting before they pour out. "Or if she didn't abandon the Pagan roots my birth father introduced her to thanks to—"

Frida snaps her fingers, stopping the spiral I was about to go down.

"Enough, Araceli." She tilts her head in the direction of the book she placed on the counter, signaling me to pick it up. "Let's not focus on any of that and instead focus on why you're here. Go ahead." Her words nudge me to pick it up, and the moment the worn leather meets my hands, a surge of warmth floods my body.

"Jesus Christ," I blurt as my palm glides over the title before opening to skim the pages.

Her tongue clicks, correcting me. "He isn't welcome here."

"Oops," I say through a half chuckle. Skimming the pages, I'm surprised to see that all the pages are empty. Completely blank, aside from a picture on the left-hand side of the cover. Confused, I study the picture. My gaze falls to the curved edge of a wooden sailboat. A man with a stare as blank as the pages that fill the book bore into a woman whose begging expression reeks of pain. I angle my head, trying to take in every detail, but before I can study the rest, Frida's hand emerges and closes the book. My money, trapped between the cover and her palm.

"What is this a beginning to? There's nothing inside."

"Fatum enim eligimus," she reminds me again of the title. *For we choose fate.* "It's the beginning of whatever it knows you need."

I look up at her, confused. "But I have to write it and as the title implies, don't I get to choose?"

She giggles, amused by my inquisitive nature, which is nice to see for a change since my stepfather detests it.

"If only it were that simple. Fate is subjective. It's up to us to choose which of the many stories already written and waiting for us in the stars will be our beginning, so then we can determine how we can impact its end."

Church bells ring in the distance. Their sound is the equivalent to poison saturating the air. Even with the favorable distance the shop is from the church property, Pastor Rainey has made it so anyone within a fifty-mile radius can hear the church bells 'rejoicing' as he foolishly calls it. His hope is that it will bring more parishioners his way since Sacred Promises is the only church in town. Man's got a monopoly on the holy game. If only he embraced his business side more instead of the piss-poor acting he does within the church walls, maybe he'd be happier. Or, at the very least, more honest.

"You better get going, don't want to make Pastor Rainey angry. Not on Devil's Night Service." Her fingers wiggle for dramatic effect.

"Yeah," I scoff.

I grab the book off the counter clutching it to my chest. Peering down at my newly acquired journal, I stew on her words.

"... we can determine how we can impact its end."

"Are you sure you don't want me to pay you?"

"No, Araceli, of course not. It's your gift. Oh, and Araceli," Frida begins but pauses for a moment as if to catch her breath.

"Yes?"

"It's important that you keep that to yourself. Your story is yours and yours alone. If anyone gains access to your path, consequences will arise."

"Okay," I drag. "Got it. I have to go." I thank Frida and walk towards the door. Opening the flap on my bag, I place my journal inside—or try to. I should've chosen a bigger bag today. This one is already jam-packed. Not paying attention to anything but trying to get the book secured, I startle when I hear footsteps stomping behind me.

"Wait!" Frida calls out.

I turn around and Frida is half bent on the floor picking up something that must've fallen out when I tried to stuff the book inside.

Frida rises to her feet, though her attention is on the paper.

My brows furrow, not sure what the fuck she is even looking at. Half the time I just shove shit in my bag and forget about it. It isn't until she turns it over and I see the Petrine cross that my memory is sparked.

"What's the big deal? It's just a haunt." I hold out my hand for her to give it to me but she doesn't.

She holds it close to her chest. Her eyes full of warning look into mine. "The big deal is this isn't just any haunt. It's Heathen's Cross." Her nostrils flare in synchrony with her widening eyes, waiting for me to put together the pieces of the puzzle she thinks she's laying out for me, but her hesitancy is only making me more confused.

Heathen's Cross is one of the only haunts in the area that honors what Halloween actually is about. It's a celebration of the veil between this life and what lays waiting on the other side at its thinnest. From everything I heard about Heathen's Cross, it's the perfect mix of spooky and spiritual. It was originally founded by Lucien Suárez, a leader in the Pagan community that once existed in our small town before my stepdad built the conglomerate that is Sacred Promises Church. I've seen pictures that Frida shared with me from her visits there back in its heyday. The whole vibe seemed so freeing, and from what I've seen in the picture Frida showed me, she looked so happy there. Something I haven't seen often from her anytime I visit. She lost her husband quite a while back, and she said it changed her. I can understand that. Grief does that to a purpose. It steals small parts of us as it transports us to an alternate reality, one where we can go on through our day-to-day fine one second and distraught the next, out of nowhere. It's why I run to drugs when all the feeling and remembering becomes too much of a burden.

I leave my hand stretched out between us with my palm opened and flat waiting for her to give the invitation back.

"I'm going to be late," I remind her, hoping that will be the nudge she needs to hand it over.

Reluctantly she does. "I know how much you hate your stepdad. Gods knows I hate him just as much, if not more, but people have gone missing from there or even worse..." she pauses, looking uncharacteristically frightened.

Fuck, there's something worse than going missing?

Frida's throat clears to finish her thought. "They've come back and never been the same. It's not what it used to be. Trust me."

What she's saying should scare me but it doesn't. What actually scares me is where I have to go after I leave the comfort of The Last Stop, where I have to fake a smile and sit—*and suffer*—through an hour of pretending to be something I'm not. "Saved." I don't want to be, not if it means being like my stepdad.

No. Fucking. Thank you.

I stash the flyer back in my bag. "That makes no sense. How is it worse to come back changed than it is to not come back at all?"

She swallows thickly. "Who gave that to you?" she asks instead of answering me.

"No one. I found it outside after I went to the costume shop in town the other day."

"The one on main street?" she asks just as the church bells ring again in the distance letting me know that I'm really late.

"I gotta go."

"Araceli, please." Frida's hand reaches for my wrist. Stopping me from moving, forcing my attention to her cold and dark stare. "If you insist on going, I can't stop you, but make sure you wear your necklace." She lets go of my hand and points to my pentagram. "It'll protect you."

"I know." I nod in agreement, bringing my attention back to the door. My hand now on the padlock, flipping it first before moving to the handle to open it.

I look at the tripping hazard of steps before me. "I know the door got me, but my high has settled. I think I can manage the steps even though they are a death trap. You really should get them fixed," I joke.

"¡Ten cuidado!" she calls out.

"I know, I will!" I shout as I shut the door behind me, knowing that she is referring to Heathen's Cross. Her warning, though creepy as hell, only makes me want to go more, so I can experience it for myself.

Hurrying my stride over to the church, dread seeps within my gut the closer I get. I hate it there. I hate how everything in that collection of beams and sheetrock judges me for not believing what I'm told I'm supposed to. Inside its walls lies true horror because it's a deceitful entity that looks inviting and is anything but. I'd be lucky to come back changed after attending Heathen's Cross. Hell, I'd be lucky if it took me and never brought me back. Anything is better than the reality I'm forced to live.

Approaching the church entrance, I brace myself for the hour of masking I have ahead of me. Pretending to be the perfect pastor's daughter everyone knows I'm not. My lids fall shut and a wave of lightheadedness consumes me, just how it always does, when my high wears off. I remain still with lids shut, waiting for it to pass and once it does, I inhale and begin to count to four. *One, two, three, four.* I hold for a second, before exhaling, counting to four again, except this time I will open my eyes on the count of four.

One.
Two.
Three.

My lids open preemptively. It's like a force I can't explain wants me to look before it's too late.

Four. This time I count out loud as my gaze falls to the wrought iron handle in my grip.

I squint in confusion because my nail beds are soiled in what looks to be dirt. Wind whips around me, my hair falling out of place. I tuck it behind my ear just as another gust of wind comes, this time bringing a swarm of golden and rust colored leaves with it as the wind spins around me relentlessly.

"*It's your gift.*" An internal whisper grips me, mimicking what Frida said to me back at the shop, but it's not her voice. It's unrecognizable. Unsettling.

Ignoring it, I pull the door towards me, still hung up on the word "gift."

Gifts are subjective because whatever ailment—as my stepfather refers to it—I inherited from my birth father, isn't seen as a gift to those trapped within these holy walls I'm about to walk into. It's seen as a curse and every time I walk and feel what I feel, which is the opposite of the peace that surpasses all understanding I'm told I'm supposed to feel. I'm reminded just how cursed I am.

Jokes on him though, I'd pick being cursed or haunted over being saved any day. It's more fun that way.

Three
Harlan

Where are you? My jaw tenses as I crank my neck to stare at the clock above the sanctuary doors. She's going to be late. Just like I knew she'd be and just like my dad warned her of.

Fuck, Araceli, not tonight of all nights. My gaze ping-pongs up and down from the door to the clock. Service is about to start and of course, Araceli is nowhere to be found. Thoughts run wild in my head, conjuring up one scenario after the other, trying to think of what the fuck trouble she's gotten herself into now and whatever mess I'll get sucked into this time because of it.

But that's Araceli; warnings, rules, really anything that reeks of convention means nothing to her. She's forever unfazed and forever getting in trouble, which arguably is her problem. However, with this newfound role I've been forced to take on as her stepbrother, I now have the uncanny ability and need to make her problems mine—to protect her. If I'm being honest, it gives me a common ground with her or, at the bare minimum, something we can talk about...to spend time together. Ever since Araceli's mom died, she's become more erratic and numb all at once. Building walls that create a fortress she can escape to, and when that isn't enough, she usually finds herself in trouble with drugs or anything she can get her hands on.

Heat spreads down the lower half of my body, and for a moment, my mind tricks me into thinking my cock is the epicenter of the added warmth. It wouldn't be the first time I get a thickening blood rush to my cock stewing over Araceli's poor decisions...and behavior. But what would be the first time it is happening while I'm sitting in the fucking pews. Guilt trickles in, as it always seems to do, stealing my focus and pulling me and my focus abruptly back to reality.

With my eyes now on my leg, I see the source of the added heat. A petite palm with white manicured fingertips squeezes my thigh.

"Are you okay?" a feminine voice whispers.

Dark hair waves in my periphery, similar to my stepsister's, but not quite as dark, as silky, or as tempting to touch by swirling around my finger...or pull.

The image of Araceli in the graveyard from last night suddenly invades my mind, causing the blood to increase, painfully so. *Ah.* I hate her. I really fucking do.

In dire need of a distraction from the Araceli show playing on a continuous loop in my mind, I turn to face Tori, one of my dad's best friend's—and wealthiest congregant—daughter. Ever since I got caught trying to buy drugs for Araceli at university at the beginning of my junior year—which led to me being expelled—Dad's been trying to set me up with Tori. He's always going on about how she's the pinnacle of a God-fearing woman and 'wife material in the making,' as he likes to put it, since she never misses a service or youth group meeting. But looks can be deceiving. I wonder how my dad would react if he knew the only reason she likes to be here and volunteers at church functions is because her favorite thing to kneel to is *me*. There's something about sneaking around and sucking off the pastor's son that really gets her going. Probably because she falls into the delusion of thinking any sexual act outside of sticking a cock inside a warm, tight hole doesn't count as sex. I'd beg to differ. But who am I to judge, she gets to feed into her delusions while I get off, fantasizing about whose lips I actually wish were wrapped around my cock.

Tori's grip tightens, sliding ever so slightly closer to my groin, and suddenly the thought of Araceli on her knees sucking me off flashes in my mind.

My cock twitches in response.

Ah, I can't do this now. Araceli's your stepsister. You're in church. Get with it, Harlan.

"Yeah, I'm fine," I deadpan, adjusting my posture and shimmying my leg over to the side so she can get the hint and get the fuck off me...and hopefully this boner in the making can diffuse itself.

A soft giggle irritates my nerves as Tori flutters her eyelashes at me. Her lips part, but the boisterous and unified "amen" sounds silencing her. I'm grateful for the interruption, for once, even though it means Araceli is officially late and another service is upon us.

"Welcome, my faithful friends." My father speaks into the microphone as he walks onto the stage that he had built like he's a rockstar not a pastor. He waves a thank you to the parishioner who led the opening prayer, that I was completely zoned out for, and raises his hands to wave at all of us sitting in the pews.

I don't wave back or acknowledge his presence. It's bad enough he forces us here to save face, me especially, since he hopes one day this will all be mine—it won't. The property, maybe, but the church will end whenever the good lord decides to take him. Hopefully, sooner than later.

I look back one more time, but of course she's not here. Thankfully, my father is too busy buttering up the people to notice that my neck is contorted, looking back and all around to see where the fuck Araceli is.

"Can you feel it?" Dad roars excitedly.

People clap and coo in response as if they're at a rock concert. I face forward, surrounded by the abundance of parishioners. All of them look ahead in eagerness awaiting my father's annual Devil's Night Service to commence. I don't know how he does it, regurgitating the same tired spiel every year on the eve of the Holy Harvest. It's an event he created shortly after my stepmother was found murdered in a cornfield just up the road, with a satanic branding on her skin. He's used our family's tragedy as a way to not only spread the 'good word' as he calls it, but as a ploy to get more people attending Sacred Promises. More people means more money. How God fits into the equation, I'm not entirely sure. It's something that I've questioned, secretly, for as long as I've been able to string together a coherent thought, but unlike Araceli, I won't say it out loud. Questioning the beliefs he's chosen to shove down our throats isn't worth the violence and threats that come with it.

"Can you feel his presence tonight?!" Another roar erupts, this time cueing the band behind him to start playing the dramatic instrumentals my dad requires to begin each service so he can get into character. As soon as the drummer takes the lead and the guitarist follows, everyone around me becomes entranced, feeding into my dad's schemes. Everyone is so enamored by the music, I'm sure all of them don't pay attention to the focus he has on the clock above the sanctuary doors, as he notes that Araceli is now five minutes late.

A sadistic scowl washes over his face as quickly as it vanishes. I doubt anyone staring at him would even notice—but I do. I know that look all too well. The one he gives when his pastor mask slips, and we're blessed with who he really is. A monster. A cruel, relentless, manipulative monster.

"Well, I hate to break it to you, but he's here tonight. Watching us all." Another dramatic pause. "So, I will ask you one more time, do you feel his presence?"

The convincing tone of my dad's voice has me and others looking around but, as always, all we see is each other.

"That's right, you may not see Him with your eyes, but you can't tell me you don't feel Him in your heart."

Oh, for fuck's sake Dad, get on with it.

"He is watching over all of us." More clapping erupts. "Protecting us all. Especially today on this day that the unsaved call Devil's Night." He forces a dramatic shiver to visibly run throughout his body and somehow that gets everyone amped up.

It's such bullshit. Theatrics. All of it. Yet jealousy, even if it's fleeting, nips at my conscience. Sometimes, I wish I felt the way they all feel. Maybe life would be easier and less painful, but I don't. No matter how hard I try, I don't feel or see anything when I'm here. Nothing but my own thoughts and internal questions. Maybe I really am broken like Dad says Araceli is, but maybe that isn't such a bad thing, to be broken like her, because then that would mean we're alike. It would mean there is something that bonds us, and if it's a powerful enough connector, maybe she'll pay attention to me how I wish she would. The only time Araceli looks at me is when she wants something. It would be nice for a change if when she looks at me, she sees what I can be, and not who I'm forced to be.

"But it is on this day, the day before what nonbelievers call All Hallows Eve..." he stops, and suddenly, all that excitement in his face drops as a bang echoes from the outside of the doors that lead into the church.

Adam's apple bobbing, Dad clears his throat, trying to muscle through the disruption. "As I was saying, it's today, the day before the wretched *holiday*," he air quotes for dramatic effect, "that it's essential to stay grounded in our faith. It's why..." Another pause. This time, the hinges on the sanctuary doors squeal, filling the vaulted ceiling with what one would assume to be an ear-piercing cry judging by the look on Dad's face.

Necks snap to look back as footsteps squeak against the marble floor, taking their sweet *and bratty* time stomping their way over.

I don't need to turn around to see who it is. I can tell from the tension spreading along my father's jaw to his shoulders that Araceli is here. The already pale skin on his face vanishes, reducing itself to a ghastly white. It's amazing how, just seconds ago, he was talking about being grounded in faith, and here he is, practically trembling at the sight of an eighteen-year-old girl who terrifies him, all because he doesn't understand her. Neither of us do. Her differences, jarring as they may be, compared to the illusion of holiness my father tries to maintain for our family, don't scare me like he warns me they should. It intrigues me. *Tempts* me even.

"I apologize. Call it old age, but sometimes I lose track of my thoughts," Dad jokes. A rumble of forced laughter follows as he fumbles through his tabbed bible, looking for the passage he wants to read from.

I pay no attention to what he's saying. I can't. My attention —*my entire fucking body*—is distracted by notes of cinnamon and pumpkin as she nears where I'm sitting. Araceli's signature scent no matter the time of year.

The aroma intensifies the closer she gets. Instead of filling the air with subtle notes of perpetual autumn, it's overshadowed by the earthy musk of Marijuana. Relief entangles itself in my core. I've grown to prefer the smell of weed hanging off her. At least then I know she settled for a high she didn't have to achieve by swallowing or injecting something worse.

Her silhouette burns in my periphery as she takes a seat in the pew on the other side of the aisle. The urge I have to turn my head and fully take her in is immense. I can feel my father's gaze searing its way onto me as he fumbles and fails to get his wits about him. It's like he can sense my torment, and it gives him the push he needs to continue.

"As I was trying to say. I feel compelled to read from Corinthians." His voice bleeds through the expensive speaker system he recently had installed. "1 Corinthians, 10:21 in particular." He takes a purposeful pause to stare into the souls of each attendee, Araceli in particular. "You cannot drink the cup of the Lord and the cup of..."

Araceli interjects, clearing her throat and it's all the invitation

I need to abandon my self-control—that's hanging by a thread as it is—so I can finally look over to her.

"Yes?" Discomfort lines my father's voice.

Araceli sighs. Her lips move to speak, but I can't process a lick of what she's saying. She consumes my attention. The look of disinterest in her brown eyes. The coy grin spread upon her plum-stained lips. The dress that blends in with her black hair is so fitted to her frame that it looks painted on. The pentagram she wears in defiance around her neck falls perfectly in the line of her cleavage. Sinful. Delicious. All of it is a fuck you to my father.

"... demons too; you cannot have a part in both the Lord's table and the table of demons." She completes the prayer.

Shocked, my father shoots her an apprehensive glance. He's waiting for her to pull the rug out from underneath him and tack on a cunning remark like she usually does.

"That's right," he nods his head, thinking he's in the clear, "very good."

She crosses her legs and a chuckle follows. "It would be if the fucker were more clear."

No she did not.

No she fucking didn't.

I'm used to her challenging—no, fighting—Dad tooth and nail with bible verses but during service... not even I thought she had it in her. Judging by the stunned look on Dad's face, and a few rumblings from everyone else tuning into this disaster in the making, no one else did either.

"I think I misheard you."

"You heard me just fine, so would he, if he existed," she spews with an eye roll to match.

"Excuse me?" Dad's question is rhetorical. His mask is about to slip, and a version of Pastor Rainey that no one in this church other than Araceli and I have seen is about to be unleashed.

"Well, despite the fact that you conveniently found a verse to recite that has the word *demon* in it just to stay on trend with the whole 'demons are lurking everywhere, beware' vibe you got going here, *Dad*." The venom in the word 'Dad' is undeniably ripe and full of disdain. "Who is He to say what a demon is? Are they wicked based on their own accord, or because they don't fall in line with His word?" Her question is also rhetorical but no doubt a challenge.

I turn in my seat, eyes ping ponging between my father and stepsister. He's frazzled while she's calm and collected. Flustered, he doesn't respond. Instead he realizes that we aren't at home where he can yell and hit us. We're in front of the people who keep the lights on, so if he wants to sell the good word he better get back to playing the part and put his mask back on.

He knows this. No amount of anger that Araceli can evoke from him can change that. Turning on his charm, he engages with the crowd, trying to do damage control. "What my daughter meant to—"

"Step," she corrects him.

"No, Araceli, you are my daughter. Just like we are all daughters and sons of His." Dad's argument sealed with a pointed finger to the ceiling.

"Whatever," she mumbles, loud enough for me and others around her to hear.

"What my *daughter*," now he purposely harps on the word, "and I have rehearsed is how the world will tell you that his word isn't true. How every time we read or speak the truth, the demons or temptations, whatever it is trying to pull us from His truth, will be out there. All it takes is one moment of temptation. Just one taste of what the enemy has to offer, and even the best of men, can be transformed into evil incarnate."

Dad's words linger. The weight of them causes yet another rumble of applause to sound but to me, it sounds like freedom.

"Everyone, please give my sweet daughter a round of applause for helping drive home my point this evening."

Like mindless sheep they clap. A standing ovation somehow

occurs and the look on my father's face towards Araceli reeks of 'I win'.

Araceli holds her ground, sitting with the pentagram pendant hanging from her neck clasped in her hand, twirling it in her grip so that Dad is forced to look at it when he looks at her.

Tori's hand kneads my thigh, forcing my attention back to her and away from Araceli. "I'm so sorry you are stuck with her," she whispers her condolences.

Stuck... with Araceli. Now there's a thought.

I peel her hand off my thigh and bring it to her lap. "It's fine," I reassure her.

She glances over in Araceli's direction then to me again. "She'd be fine if she cut the witchy shit."

No, she'd be boring. Like you.

We settle into our seats, and the rest of the hour continues at a snail's pace. Finally, the burden of sitting through another service ends. Conversation buzzes around us, people talking as they file out of the sanctuary. Tori tugs at my arm, saying something, but I'm too busy looking at Araceli's scowl as she tries to avoid my father. A congregant waves at him, forcing him to nod and play nice, but the second he's free, he storms over to Araceli, which is my cue to get over there.

"Dad," I say, loud enough that anyone around us can hear, diffusing whatever he is about to say or do to her.

Stepping in front of her, shielding me from her, and faking a smile, he answers me. "Yes, son?" His voice is calm, but his raised brows are a strong indicator that he wants me to go.

"Everything good?" I ask him.

Araceli steps out of the shield Dad created around her, and it takes everything I have not to let my eyes roam her body in front of him.

"Yep, everything is fucking peachy," she singsongs, ripe with sarcasm.

"Language," Dad mutters to her before turning his attention to me. "Yes, everything is fine. Isn't it, Araceli?"

Our gazes clash before she answers.

"Mmhmm," she hums, unconvincingly.

"I was just about to have a quick chat with Araceli, and I was about to tell you to go help Tori take inventory of the supplies we had delivered today for tomorrow's Holy Harvest." He averts his gaze to Araceli. "I want to make sure everything goes off without incident."

I stand still looking at her, not wanting to move. Afraid of what he'll do to her once I leave and the sanctuary has cleared out.

"I'm fine," she says to me, lying.

Almost forgetting Dad is there, I step closer to her. Feeling the brotherly urge to protect her from him, I reach for her hand, wanting to take her with me, away from him. Despite how ten minutes ago I was fantasizing about her lips wrapped around my cock, or just now wanting to bury my face in her cleavage, pentagram touching my skin and all.

Sensing this, Dad steps in front of her. "Boy, I swear to everything that is holy, you get the—" he stops to adjust his tone, settling on 'heck' and not 'hell' because God forbid he say such profanity like he does at home in church, "—away from her now. I will handle her."

That's what I'm afraid of.

A breath hitches in my throat. My fists tighten at either side. Anger like I've never felt before emerges as I stare into those dark pits he passes as eyes.

"Tori is fine on her own prepping for the Harvest. I can wait until you're done talking to Araceli and walk her home."

"The fuck you will," he laughs through his threat. There he is. The pastor mask fading and prick bag Dad is here to play. He stares her up and down, disapproval ripe on his brows. "She's more than capable of walking alone." His gaze falls to her hands, inspecting them. "And not wander off anywhere she shouldn't be going. Just directly home once I'm done with you, isn't that right, Araceli?"

She turns her head to the side, refusing to answer or look at him.

"Answer me you little—" He begins to point his finger at her, hovering over her collarbone. The way his fingertip bounces back and forth repeatedly it'll be a matter of seconds before he makes contact. He won't hit hard like he has at home, but he'll still find a way to make it hurt.

I puff out my chest, feeling years of suppressed rage boiling over.

Sensing that, Araceli steps between Dad and I. "Stop!" Araceli shouts, a few lingering eyes stare at us. Dad motions to them that it's alright and they move. "Just go, Harlan," she clips, shooing me away like I'm a fly in her presence.

I look at her pleadingly.

"It's fine," she says, softer. Even though it's not fine. It's never fine.

"Fine," I bite back.

"That's a good boy," Dad says with a nauseating amount of condescension. "Now let me deal with her. Tori is already in the basement waiting for you."

"Ooh, who's Tori?" Araceli chimes in, wiggling her hands sarcastically like she always does when she's deflecting or jealous, but in this case, I'd say it's a combination of both.

"Tori is a fine Christian girl. Not like you'd know anything about that. Now that's all you need to know," Dad boasts. "Isn't that right, Harlan?"

Yeah, "fine at sucking dick" is what I want to say, but I don't.

As I walk away to the door that leads to the basement, argumentative mumblings rumble my eardrums between them. Forcing myself to ignore it, I open the door and walk down the steps. As I reach the bottom step, something catches my eye. It moves quickly. It is so quick that I brush it off as a shadow, convinced that my eyes are playing tricks on me since they haven't fully adjusted to the dim space. Though, the faint thud of footsteps rustling on the floor convinces me someone is there. I squint, trying to focus on the inky air in front of me, and I swear that I can see someone tall dressed in all black walk past me, but it's hard to tell. "Hello?" I call out, cautiously I move forward and a voice calls back.

"Hello." Tori appears with a clipboard in hand, doing exactly as my dad told her, and disappointment lodges in my gut at the sight of her.

"You okay?"

"Yeah, I thought I saw something."

"There's no one here. Just you, me and Jesus," she laughs, bending forward to show off her cleavage. The turtleneck she was wearing before is gone, and a lacy bra is in its place.

"Come over here," she whispers, flexing her pointer finger. I follow, looking at her delicate features, wishing they were Araceli's instead. In the same way, I pretend the dark hair grazing her shoulders is Araceli's, and the cross around her neck is a pentagram like Araceli wears.

Tori begins to bend her knees, our usual arrangement obviously on her mind. I click my tongue, pointing to the table off to the side.

"Sure, whatever makes you comfortable."

"Not me," I correct her. "You. Table. Now." I sound like a damn caveman.

"Ooh, this is new." Tori squeals as she walks over to the table. "How do you want me?"

Silent. Every time Tori speaks, her voice pulls me from the fantasy I've thrust upon her, using her as a stand-in for Araceli.

"Just lay back," I instruct her, seating myself in the chair in front of where she is sitting on the table. "Lay back," I demand, repeating myself. She listens, this time spreading her legs for me.

My fingers skim her lace thong from beneath her skirt, gliding it to the side. Her pussy glistens for me.

"Wait!" Tori shouts, leaning over and reaching for her bible. She opens it to a random page while propped up on her elbows and thankfully it blocks my view of her.

Well Dad, looks like that fine Christian girl you wanted me with is about to be my tongue's punching bag. When I have her pussy engulfing my mouth—pretending it's my sister's after what her defiant outburst did to me—I'll be the demon he'll have to worry about, not her.

Four

Araceli

"Stop staring at my son."

Too late.

I can't stop looking at his beautiful and tormented son. Especially not when he's running his fingers through his hair, squeezing the loose blonde strands in pure frustration; his veins practically summoned to rise to the surface from the taut squeeze. I wonder what has him more pissed off—the fact that I got in the way of him releasing years of anger at his dad or that I didn't allow him to swoop in to save me from him.

I don't need saving. Not from God, Harlan, or anyone.

The door to the basement opens and slams within seconds, and the vaulted ceilings in the sanctuary exacerbate its echo as it closes, something flashes in front of my eyes. It happens so quickly I can barely make out what it is exactly, but I can feel the remnants of whatever it was latch onto me. A cool breeze entangles itself on my skin, beckoning me to close my eyes as if that will help me see it. It can't be the drugs. The high I get, even from lacing my weed, doesn't last this long. Whatever I think I saw, whatever I know I feel, is begging me to listen... so I do.

As my lids fall shut, the bitter cold moves past the surface of my skin trickling into my veins and spreading to the top of my head. I wince from the sting it's leaving on every inch of my body. I'm tempted to open my eyes, but just as the soul-consuming chill escalates to an unbearable level, it stops and a shadow appears; dark as the cloak my lids created over my eyes, but it's there. I can sense it moving, blending in with the darkness while still making its presence known to me. Desperate to know what it wants, I stand still, ignoring the onslaught of threats leaking into my ear from my stepdad's mouth and fighting the physical pull his hand has wrapped around my arm.

The shadow moves back and forth before settling in what feels like the center of my entire body, paralyzing me.

"Araceli," a voice calls from deep inside of me, its tone unrecognizable, menacing. *"Help him sail,"* it cryptically instructs, *"help him sail."* It repeats the same phrase over and over. Each time the volume lowers until it dissipates, my lids spring open, and I'm met with a now empty sanctuary space except for me, and Harlan's dad.

"Look at me," he barks, finger snapping at me like I'm a fucking dog.

"You're embarrassing yourself."

"No." I keep my head turned opposing him, secretly hoping that whatever that presence was would come back to tell me what I need to know or to kill him—either or.

"Araceli Rainey," he roars, and the sound of his last name paired with my first causes bile to rise in my throat. "I said—"

I swallow, fighting it from rising to the surface. It's telling that interactions with my stepdad are capable of causing this kind of response within me. Yet, just moments before, I'm pretty sure I encountered an apparition of some sort, and all I'm left feeling is the desire for more instead of the fear I should feel. Since this is a holy place and all, apparitions are the Devil's doing, according to Daddy fuck-face over here.

"I can hear you just fine," I interrupt, and I can tell by the grumble he's making deep in his throat that's not the answer he was looking for. "Or do you demand I look at you because it's your way of establishing dominance over me since you have no control over your pathetic life? All because of Him." My brow lifts in condescension as I point to the ceiling, finally turning to face him. Our eyes clash just like our temperaments. His anger mirrors my own, though we're on two different frames of mind. Still the hatred and resentment linger. A vexed hand wraps around my arm pulling at me. His pulse throbs above my skin as he squeezes me tighter and for once in his dreadful life, he's speechless. I revel in the silence but it's short lived. As more people filter out of the sanctuary, he allows his mask to slip, gracing me with the presence of the monster I'm forced to call stepdad.

Not letting go of me, his free hand travels to my chest. His slimy fingers taking their sweet ass time making their way to my necklace that he's using as his excuse to stare at my cleavage for.

"Like what you see?" I don't bother holding back my disgust.

His gaze finally settles on my necklace. "What did I tell you about wearing this demonic shit?"

Unbelievable. Here he is worried about a piece of metal contorted into a pentagram around my neck, and not the fact that he's alternating glances and so blatantly staring at his stepdaughter's tits—in a church, no less.

You insufferable hypocrite. Apparently, the Devil does walk among us.

I guess I'm lucky that he at least has the decency to keep his hands solely on my necklace while we're in the church. That courtesy only recently commenced at home after Harlan returned from college.

He yanks my chain so hard that it digs into my skin as it becomes a prisoner to his taut fist.

"Let. Go."

Ignoring my seething demand, he takes a step closer, now wrapping the pendant and chain in his palm.

"Where did you get this?"

Two can play this game. If he refuses to let go, then I refuse to answer.

A light bulb illuminates in his small-minded head, his wheels turning in real time. "You didn't..." He fumbles his speech a bit before clearing his throat to strengthen his words. "You didn't go there, did you? After I forbade you!" he shouts in fear. "Witch," his voice trembles, still loud but there's fear there.

Knowing he's referring to Frida and The Last Stop, I swoop in to correct him. "She's not a witch," I correct him. "Just because she doesn't believe in all that you do doesn't make her a bad person. If anything, it makes her smarter than—"

He maintains the hold on my arm with one hand, and with the other that's been playing with my necklace, he proceeds to yank it off. With the pentagram secured under his thumb, he uses the symbol he detests to his advantage as his clammy palm makes contact with my cheek. The sting on my skin is amplified by the pentagram's sharp edge.

"How dare you bring this into my church and on today of all days." His voice trembles, "On the day before she was..."

"She was what?" I interject, dying to hear what brainwashed bullshit he's about to say.

His fist clenches as it lifts upward; he wants to hit me. This time with a closed fist.

"Go ahead," I challenge him. "Do it." I stand my ground, but he doesn't bite. Coward.

Lowering his fist, he looks over his shoulder, remembering that we're in a holy place, and he can't act like the demon he is constantly pretending he's not.

"On the day she went home to Him." He finishes his sentence, and it's just as delusional as I thought it'd be.

"Whatever helps you sleep at night," I mutter. "She was murdered." Slashed to death and found in a cornfield with a Petrine cross drawn on her forehead from her own blood. Last time I checked, that's the furthest thing from a welcome home party, but who am I but a heathen in my stepdad's eyes? What the fuck do I know?

Phony muses of sadness break from his lips as he sighs. I know it's fake since he rarely, if ever, brings it up anymore. It's as if her life and death never happened to him. He's only using it as a tool to punish me for having my own beliefs.

Just as quickly as it came on, the pretend show of emotion vanishes as he settles back into his usual angry self. "None of this witchcraft will bring her back. All you're doing is embarrassing her memory and yourself. Well, and quite frankly, all of us."

"I never said it would, but it represents a part of her that you conveniently forget. Who she was before you poisoned her with your dick."

His head shakes, blown away by the brutal honesty of my words.

"You little fucking..." his voice trails off. The hinges open from outside the vestibule separating the main entrance from where we stand in the sanctuary. He grumbles to himself, frustrated that it's preventing him from going off on me the way he wants to. Another set of hinges whine, this time to the sanctuary itself. He shields me from the door, lowering his mouth to my ear. "The best thing I ever did for your mother was poison her with the truth. The real truth. Not the lies your father filled her head with. She was sick and he made her worse. At least she wasn't as thick-headed as you. She learned real quick that my way is the best way."

My insides twist at the mention of my birth father.

Before I have the opportunity to retort, two men dressed in all black approach us. Their long-hooded trench coats give me a rush of déjà vu to the shadowed figure's presence from before. There's an emblem on the right sleeve of both their coats, but I can't make it out with how they're standing. They are both silent, neither of them saying a word. Their presence alone is enough to make my stepdad's jawline knot from the tension spreading. He waves to the two men, offering them a fake as fuck smile but neither return the gesture. If anything, they seem disgusted to be in Pastor Rainey's presence as he looks to be in theirs.

"We aren't done here," he mumbles to me, keeping his eyes on the men. "I forgot I have a business dinner to attend."

"Business dinner, huh?" I eye the men standing there. The taller of the two has his hand cupped in front of his mouth, mumbling something to the other.

"They don't look like pastors or congregants to me," I challenge him.

"You're right," he answers with an unexpected burst of vigor that contradicts the physical chokehold these two strangers visibly have on him.

"They're here to discuss the Holy Harvest tomorrow. Which you will not be attending."

Relief grips me and I can't help but smile. Little does he know this punishment makes it that much easier for me to go to Heathen's Cross, like I intended to do anyway.

"You will spend the entirety of the day and evening tomorrow in your room. Under lock and key," he tacks on, only adding to my glee.

Though that is short-lived, and as my grin fades, one beams onto his face as he reaches for the pack of cigarettes in his pocket. He takes one out, lighting it, not bothering to miss my face as he exhales. With each wisp of smoke carrying notes of tobacco and menthol, I can feel the scabs on my back start to hurt all over again. His favorite punishment for when I "sin"—using my back as a fucking ashtray. I want to run away or slap him in front of his guests, but the only reason I haven't done either is because I want my fucking necklace back.

"Fine by me." I inhale, trying to remain on an even keel and not give him the reaction he so pathetically craves out of me. I jut my neck forward, holding my hand out. "Necklace," I remind him.

He exhales another stream of nicotine drenched smoke,

ignoring me. "See you at home." He moves towards the men, my necklace still in his possession, forcing me to follow after him.

"But—" I begin, but he whips around, blowing yet another puff of smoke directly in my face. My lids close and flutter, trying to prevent the smoke from burning them. It works, barely.

"Oh I almost forgot," he trails off teasingly, eyeing me up and down with a sadistic grin. "Please, for the love of God, bathe when you get home. You look like you've been rolling around in the dirt."

He slips my necklace into his pocket and mumbles something to the men standing there, resembling obedient mastiffs with their towering size. I blink again as I peer at them because they aren't wearing the black hooded trench coats anymore. They're in suits. "Your hands are filthy," he chuckles, breaking my concentration on the men.

I peer down at my hands, almost forgetting how dirty they were from the book Frida gave me. Standing upright, I wrap my hands around my purse strap, wanting now, more than ever, to keep said book safe so fuck-face doesn't take that too.

"Fine."

He nods, taking another puff of his cigarette, leading the way out of the main sanctuary as the two men follow.

I wait until they've left so I can fish through my bag for my joint case, needing a reprieve, but I open it and it's empty. *Fuck.* The one I smoked before I went to Frida's was the last one I had pre-rolled.

I'm about to head home when I remember that anything my stepdad has ever confiscated from me—with the exception of my necklace he's decided to hold hostage tonight—he keeps locked in his office. Including the pain pills he caught me with, which were prescribed to me by a doctor; a doctor that Frida was able to get me an appointment with because I needed something to take the edge off the physical pain he's inflicted on me—but of course, it's locked.

But I know someone who should have a key, and that's Harlan.

I head to the door that leads down to the basement. My hand curls around the brass knob, and as it glides in my palm, that chill from earlier remerges, freezing me in place. I wait for the voice to speak to me again, but all I can hear is a moan cut through the air coming from downstairs.

The door flings open faster than I'm able to move it myself, and the coldness wraps itself around me as if to push me to move downstairs.

Curiosity fuels me as I make my descent down the steep old staircase. With every step I take, a creek sounds in response, though no noise can compete with the breathy whimpers or the chant-like hum that accompanies them.

The closer I walk down the pitch-black hall—with the only light coming from the inventory room that Harlan was told to go to—the chanting becomes clearer. Nausea strikes my stomach. The voice is feminine, and the chant... the fucking Lord's prayer. Gross. Yet, the nausea is quickly replaced as a primitive and unexpected moan overshadows the repetitive prayer.

A flutter forms in my stomach just as one pulses at my center as I step into the small inlet directly across from the open door. My black dress and hair blend in with the recessed space, camouflaging me. Got to love these old churches, even the ones that have been renovated to look modern. They have so many hidden nooks and crannies that are worth exploring... and misbehaving in.

With my hidden vantage point, I stare through the open doorway. Harlan is sitting down, his side facing me, going to town on this girl—who I assume is Tori. She is lying with her back flat on the small table, with her back arched and her legs spread wide. She has a bible in her hands open to a page that she's reading over and over again, trying to cleanse herself from what my stepbrother is doing to her—and from what she is very clearly enjoying.

Lucky bitch.

Seeing him fucking someone with his tongue in church...is

doing something to me. Something unexpected that's never happened before any time I've looked at Harlan. Not only am I becoming unbearably wet. I'm disappointed that it's not me. *Jealous* even. Which is something I haven't felt before with Harlan. I mean sure, jealous that he is treated better than me in our house, but this kind of jealousy is new. It's festering in my gut, but the more it twists and turns my core, the more I can't look away. I remain hypnotized, unable to look away from the attentive, harsh strokes of his tongue. He's consuming her with such passion... such anger.

So much anger.

I don't blame him. Living as a Rainey is anger-inducing, and vices are the only way to get through that. For me, it's escapism through drugs, and for him, shockingly, it's through eating pussy like he hasn't had a meal in years... or ever.

As much as I want to stay here and watch his little bible thumper finish in his mouth, I've seen enough to aid my self-care session that *I'll need* to have tonight. It's not my pussy being eaten anyway, so I'm getting bored.

Stepping out of the inlet I've been hiding in, I reach for my phone to text him, because, after all, I came down here for him to do me a favor.

My thumbs swipe at the keyboard, my pulse rising as the crescendo of an orgasm echoes around me.

> Me: When you're done eating, be a good big brother and get me my pills from Daddy's office.

A grin hits my lips as I fire off another text.

Five
Harlan

Tori tosses the bible she's been holding onto for dear life just as she announces she's coming. She isn't lying either. I already knew she was getting close, she's been practically convulsing, thrashing against my mouth. But I can't focus on that, nor do I care. All I can pay attention to are the footsteps on the other side of the door that I know are Araceli's. She thinks I didn't see her—of course I did. That dark corner she thought she hid in failed at providing her with the camouflage she needed. Darkness doesn't provide her with the shield she thinks it does. It compliments her, highlighting all the parts of her that she is forced to keep hidden but I wish she didn't, not from me.

I lick up Tori's orgasm, secretly wishing it were Araceli's, and skid the chair back just as my phone pings.

What do you want, Araceli? I know her well enough to know that she isn't trying to small-talk with me, and that she didn't come down here just to watch me go down on Tori. Just like I know when I get a text from her it's because she wants something.

> Araceli: When you're done eating, be a good big brother and get me my pills from Daddy's office.

Knew it. I'm about to text her back when she beats me to it.

> Araceli: Hope she's a squirter and blesses you with her holy water =P

My fingers glide across the keyboard to text her back, but before I know it, Tori is fully dressed in the outfit she wore during service.

"Everything okay?" she asks, standing over to my side.

Her hair drapes over the phone screen, blocking my view. Not wanting her to see the text, I hit the lock screen.

"Yep. All good."

"Okay." She bites down on her lip. At first, I take it as a flirtatious thing, but the longer she stays with her lip trapped and kneaded under her tooth, I see the guilt on her face.

"Are you okay?"

She stops chewing on her lip to answer. "Yeah, but you're not going to tell anyone are you?"

"No," I reassure her.

Satisfied with my deadpanned response, she turns on a smile. "Okay, just wanted to make sure."

I nod, looking around the inventory room. I don't know why Dad told me to come down here. Everything was in order by the time I met Tori here.

"Yep," I drag, an awkward energy filling the room. My mind drifts off to Araceli, wondering what she thinks about what she saw me do. Hoping it turned her on as much as I hope it pissed her off. "Well, it looks like everything is taken care of down here, so I'm going to head home." I move to the doorway, ready to sneak into my dad's office to get Araceli's pills—and hopefully not get caught this time. Patting my pockets, I realize that I don't have the key.

Something jingles and distracts me.

Tori, now dressed, walks past me with the keys to my dad's office. "Thank you," she blushes, placing her hand with the keys on my cheek. "I'll see you tomorrow."

"Are those the keys to my dad's office?" I ask, already knowing the answer but confused as to why she has them.

A laugh erupts from her. "Yeah, silly. Since my mom had surgery, I've been filling in for her as secretary. Well, just on the days or nights that I can since I have to juggle my own job and commuting to campus."

"Right." I offer her a short response while I'm trying to brainstorm how the fuck I'm going to get into the office now with her having the keys. "Are you locking up or do you have work to do?"

"With the Holy Harvest tomorrow, there's so much work to be done." She begins to move through the doorway. "So I'll be here for a little bit still."

Great.

I follow after her. "Need help?"

She pauses her stride, looking back at me over her shoulder. My gaze falls to her lips and the smile tugging at the corners of her mouth. She says something, but I can't focus on what she's saying. Like a pin dropping in the dead of night, something crashes, faint yet loud enough to be heard, behind me. The acoustics linger in my eardrum, causing a ringing to occur. The noise is unbearable. In desperation, I throw my hands up, covering my ears, but it only makes it louder. I look around to see where the noise is coming from, but I see nothing.

Tori walks over to me, fear ripe within her hazel stare.

"Harlan." My name is muffled, but it cuts through the ear-piercing ricochet that is attacking my hearing.

With a yank at my wrist, she breaks the seal I created with my hands around my ears. To my surprise and much to my relief, the sound is gone.

"I was just telling you I don't need any help."

"You didn't hear that?" I blurt, baffled by how nonchalant she just spoke to me.

Dumbfounded, she widens her eyes at me. "Umm, my voice echoed a bit. I, uh..." She fumbles her words, and it's clear she didn't hear what I did.

"You seriously didn't hear that sound? It was so..." Now I'm the one fumbling my words. "It was so..." I don't know how to finish my sentence. Even if I wanted to. I'm too distracted by one of the many core memories embedded in my psyche taking this opportunity to remind me how fucked I am.

My body remains where it is. Where I know it ought to be. In the church basement next to Tori but mentally I'm back home. Younger than I am now by about fifteen years, back to my five-year-old self, curled up in a ball, crying. Begging for the sting to go away on my back from my father's belt.

"It's in your head! You were never there! It doesn't exist."

"No. It's real. I heard it. I saw it. I was—"

Whip.

"You hear that? That's the sound I will continue to make until you stop talking altogether. No child of mine will feed into these delusions. You're just like your..."

"Harlan." Tori breaks the bubble I'm in as she rubs my back, but her touch only drives the trauma further to the surface, and I tear away from her touch.

"I'm sorry, I just wanted to see if you're okay. If you need me to do something I can..."

I lift my hand to stop her. "I'm good." I lie. The same lie I've been telling since I learned my lesson at the ripe age of five, and of what telling the truth to someone who can't accept it means— embarrassment, pain. Neither of which I have time for. Making my way out of the storage room, Tori follows after me.

"Didn't you need something from your dad's office?"

"Forget it," I say, continuing to walk away.

I shake my head, brushing off whatever it was I thought I heard back there. Convincing myself it's in my head, and needing the lie to be true. I continue moving, through the blanket of darkness in the hallway of the basement and up the stairs. I only stop to place my head on the door that separated me from the main sanctuary. Hand on the knob, I go to turn it, and as I do, the uncontrollable urge that I have to look down at the floor overcomes me. I peer down as I open the door, look to the floor, and giant muddy footsteps fill my vision.

I walk around them and the noise sounds in my ear again, forcing my attention back to the floor. This time I see something. A pentagram—Araceli's pentagram—lies on the floor. I bend to pick it up, slipping it into my pocket. A grimy texture brushes against my calluses but I don't have time to look at what it is, not with Tori now standing a few feet behind me.

"Where are you going?" Tori calls out.

My lips part, but something else catches my attention on the floor, dark brown blotches of mud line the floor. The footsteps I saw just moments before are now long, jagged letters. I take a step forward, trying to decipher what it says. Squinting, I can make out the first two words, *'no one'* but it isn't until I move closer that I can see the rest, *'gets in for free.'*

No one gets in for free. What the fuck does that mean?

I blink. When my lids ascend, and I go to read the message again, the writing... the mud... all of it is *gone*.

"Harlan." Tori breathes my name, a question on her lips. "What's wrong?"

I shake my head, heading back to the door. "Nothing," I quip as a vicious chill lodges down my spine.

I have to get out of here. I need air.

"I'll see you tomorrow." I burst through the doors into the October night air. Leaves whip at my jeans, and the weight of the necklace in my pocket becomes prominent.

Araceli probably put some spell on it, or whatever she believes in, and she's fucking with me. That has to be it.

I convince myself that this is the truth, as I walk past the graveyard that separates the church from our farmhouse on the property, replacing one nightmare for another. If she did purposely leave her necklace for me to see in the hopes that I'd bring it back to her and she tampered with it, that means that whatever she did, is real.

So maybe her mom was right, that night that she and my dad were arguing before she was found in the cornfield not too far from here.

Maybe the veil is slipping since tomorrow is Halloween.

That, or I'm cursed for everything I've been secretly wanting to do with Araceli. Nothing brotherly, and everything that makes me the sinner my dad has always feared I'll turn into.

Six

Araceli

My lips pinch together, holding the fresh joint in place so I can light it. The earthy scent drifts my way and the eagerness I have to smoke it only increases as I crave the calm I know it will give, even if I know deep down that it won't be enough. Well, until I get my pills, and Harlan better have gotten them, it will suffice.

A small, controlled flame blossoms from the lighter, drawing my eyes to it. My vision crosses, focusing on the twisted end of the rolling paper as it crackles and burns as I suck in a deep inhale until it's ready to smoke.

One hit becomes another until the joint is reduced to a flameless roach. I lean forward, tossing it into the garbage pail off to the side of the tub, though as I do, the damn dirt that has embedded itself in my cuticles steals my attention. I try rubbing the dirt away with an equally tarnished hand, but it doesn't budge. Grabbing the loofa slung on the faucet in front of me, I dunk it into the water to wet it, hoping it will be able to scrub it away. But its abrasive texture is no match against the dirt that's clung onto my skin like cement.

I toss the loofa into the tub and stare at it. Not even a fragment of the mess on my hands transferred onto it. As I sit back, settling my backside against the tub, I try to think if there was anything on the book when Frida handed it to me. I don't remember there being any, but then again, I was just coming down from the laced joint I smoked prior. Details are always fuzzy when I begin to sober up.

Unable to let this mystery go, I lean over the edge of the tub and grab my towel to dry my hands. I need to see the damn book again so I can figure out what the fuck got on it that is holding my skin hostage to its mess. Grabbing my bag, I reach inside for my journal. As my fingers search—cataloging all the things that aren't the book—Harlan suddenly appears in the doorframe as he barges into the bathroom.

"Araceli," he scolds, startling me. Despite the naturally deep rasp of his voice he still manages to spew my name like a little fucking goody two-shoes.

"You forgot something." His hand stretched in front of me, my necklace his dad took dangling from it.

Water splashes onto the floor as I plunge upward with every intention of snatching it from him, but his gaze derails my plans. I remain propped up on my knees while his eyes are glued to my bare tits. The mix of feral hunger—*and guilt*—injected in his stare is too delicious not to mess with.

My fingertips gently caress my neck, running soft lines up and down, before my hand runs down my sternum. He tries to look away, and he's almost successful, until my palm slithers under one breast, circling it in a tease before making my way over to the pointed peak of my nipple. Absolutely reveling in how bothered he's becoming.

A deep hum fills his throat as he tries to drag his attention from my tits to my face. The moment our eyes meet, the lust that was just filling his gaze disappears. Concern now wreaking havoc on his defined features.

Fuck. Goodbye to the Harlan that secretly wants to touch me, and hello to the Harlan who ruins all my fun, when he gets into big brother mode. Since his attention isn't on my tits anymore, I'm fully aware that he can see the cut his dad left on my cheek.

"I'm surprised he gave it to you," I break the silence, trying to deflect. My chin tilted in the direction of said necklace.

"If by *him* you mean my dad... he didn't."

Confusion spreads on my forehead, crinkling it. His dad took it from me. I watched him leave with it still in his possession. How else would Harlan have gotten it?

Harlan steps forward, twirling his fingers, signaling me to turn around. Still wondering how the hell he didn't get it from his dad, I lower myself back into the water and gather my hair in one hand, letting it drape over my shoulder as I turn, exposing my back to him.

Harlan slips my necklace back on, and the cool chain mixed with the warmth of his skin creates an oddly comforting sensation.

Though as his fingers linger on my shoulder, and slowly trickle down my spine, the trepidation buzzing from his fingertips lets me know that he's only accessing the previous trail of hate that his dad left on my skin. The scene Harlan's taking in is enough to make the most avid of smokers swear off cigarettes immediately.

A breath hitches in my throat. The memories will never fade. Not when my skin heals. Not ever.

"Maybe I have to burn the sinner out of you. Stay still, you wretched little..."

Harlan clears his throat, snapping me out of my daze. "Turn around," he commands dryly-mean sounding—but I like it coming from him. It's so different from when his father acts and talks like a prick. From Harlan, it somehow adds to his allure. It's almost like the invisible halo hovering over his head is slipping, and he's just waiting for someone—like me—to yank it off and give him permission to exist without its confines. To be free.

"Let me see your face. Now, Araceli," he snaps, only adding to the fantasy I have of how I wish he'd be.

"Geesh. Chill your balls." I throw my hands up as I follow his command.

He mutters something to himself as he heads to the medicine cabinet to get rubbing alcohol and a Band-Aid.

"Pills," I breathe, trying to jog his memory of what I asked him for when his tongue was buried in Tori.

Harlan shakes his head, dragging the small stool by the sink over near the tub to sit on. "I couldn't get them."

He works in silence, first cleaning then covering my cut. A disappointed sigh leaves my lips, but it's overshadowed by the one that leaks from Harlan's mouth as he leans over to toss out the bandage backing. The contents of my purse that must've spilled out when he startled me coming into the bathroom are now at the forefront of his attention, and the invitation to Heathen's Cross is in a death grip.

"Where did you get this?" He shakes his head, causing the loose waves of golden hair to cover his eyes instead of frame them as they usually do.

"From the person who invited me. Now hand it over."

"You're not going," he deadpans as if he has the power to order me around. Hell, not even his dad, with his arsenal of consequences he likes to hang over my head, or the man upstairs he subscribes to, has any authority over me. Why would this moment of command from Harlan—unexpected and hot as it may be—be a determining factor in me going?

"Why not?"

He peels his attention from the invitation to me. "He'll kill you." The bold tone in his voice takes me aback.

"You know, you're the second person who has said that to me today. I'm well aware how much your dad hates Halloween. I mean, for fuck's sake, he's built a church and a whole fucking festival around his hatred for the holiday," I remind him. "But it's not enough to convince me not to go. I'm going. Like it or fucking not. You can either stay here and be your dad's good little boy, or you can finally grow a pair and come with me. It's up to you. Either way, I'm going."

Harlan's fist tightens, crushing the paper in his grip. The veins on his hand lift to the surface. Each thick, raised blood vessel telling a story, and speaking for him to let me know that I struck a nerve. Who knows, maybe something I said has what it takes to get that invisible halo to fall like I've been waiting for.

Pushing through whatever his inner quarrel is, he shoots me a conflicted look. Vexation still ripples through his body, and his blue eyes contradict his anger, pleading with me.

"You know why he hates it, Araceli. It's when—"

I cut him off, wagging my finger at him. "My mom died, yes, I know, but clearly that wasn't enough of a reason to make him not slap me, in his church no less, today, now, was it?" I challenge him with my rhetorical question, and my gaze falls to his arm. With his sleeve rolled up to his elbow, the reddish-purple mark on his forearm is impossible to miss. "Didn't your mom die around this time of year also?" I ask, already knowing the answer. It's a harsh approach, sure, but it only proves my point on just how awful his father is, even more.

His jaw tightens, answering for him.

I nod. "Exactly and that didn't stop him from leaving yet another mark on your skin. Wake up, Harlan." I snap my fingers. "Your dad doesn't give a fuck about anything or anyone other than himself. The church, his love, it's all a fucking act. The sooner you realize that, the sooner—"

The stool skids on the tile floor before it crashes onto it as Harlan rises to his feet, immediately towering over me.

"You made your point," he clips, now unrolling his sleeves so they cover the evidence to my point. "Why do you want to go there anyway? Heathen's Cross isn't safe."

I roll my eyes. "How the fuck would you know that? You've never been there."

A forbidding expression captures his chiseled cheekbones, paling his skin.

"Just trust me, Araceli. I need you to promise me you won't go there," his voice, though rough and deep, still quivers just a bit.

"I promise you that if you don't hand me that damn invitation, I'll do something way worse than stepping foot on Heathen's Cross grounds."

"Araceli," he scolds.

"Harlan," I scold back. "Just give me the fucking invitation."

He doesn't move. Not even a flinch.

Exasperated, I let out a sigh that sounds more like a huff. "Listen, if you want to keep being the good church boy, and skip out on the fun of Heathen's Cross to go be lame with the bible thumpers at the Harvest tomorrow, knock yourself out. But it wouldn't kill you to live a little for once. Have some fun with me."

"Stop calling me that." His Adam's apple bobs visibly down the thick column of his throat.

"What?" I coo, egging him on it. "A good church boy?" My lips fall to an exaggerated pout. "Isn't that what you are? A good, God-fearing, willing to do anything to deny your inner demons, suppressed, fucking, church boy?" I taunt him.

Flustered, he crumples the invitation in his hand, about to chuck it in the garbage, but I spring up onto my knees. This time damn near losing my balance in the process on the slippery ceramic bottom of the tub while I try to stop him.

"Go ahead, throw it out. I'll just take it out of the trash."

"Whatever," he grumbles, taking a step back; he nearly trips on my bag. Shit. The book Frida gave me hangs out of it. I'm staring at it, and now Harlan is too. Intrigue trickles into his voice, "What's this?" He crouches down to pick up my journal.

"Give me!" I yelp. Frida's warning rings in my psyche. *It's important that you keep this to yourself. Your story is yours and yours alone. If anyone gains access to your path, consequences will arise.*

Harlan doesn't listen. I reach over and try to grasp the book in his hands, but he takes another step back, increasing the distance between us, too preoccupied with the book than the sudsy view of my tits that captured his attention from before.

"This is cool," he blurts. He doesn't sound convincing, but more hesitant instead.

"My tits or the book?" I deflect with crude humor, hoping it distracts him enough that I can take my journal back from him.

He looks up for a second, and his gaze lands on my tits once more. Red colors his chiseled cheeks as his gaze holds mine, mortified.

Go ahead, church boy, tell me how pretty my tits are. I challenge him silently with a long stroke of my tongue at my lips.

He doesn't take the bait. Instead, he clears his throat and redirects his attention back to the book.

In horrified silence, he studies the illustration, and the visible tinge of embarrassment that was just on his cheeks vanishes as a ghastly white emerges in its place.

"Why the—" he stammers, his voice almost escaping him. "Why the—" he repeats before slamming the book shut, tossing it at me. I catch it, thankful for my fast reflexes; otherwise, it would've been ruined by the water in the tub.

"Why the fuck would you want to keep something like that?" His question is both accusatory and full of disgust. "It's horrifying."

I clutch the leather-bound book to my chest. "Jesus fuck, Harlan, calm down. It's just a picture. A beautiful one at that." I reminisce about the peaceful scene, envious of how peaceful the woman looked, just sailing into oblivion with the man waiting patiently for her. "Besides—" my voice drifts, about to open the book to show him the picture he was studying when he lifts his hand. His large, veiny palm curls around the book's edge, preventing me from opening it.

"No! Please," he begs me. "I've seen enough," he adds, adjusting his tone, lessening it. "Celi, I mean it. If the Holy

Harvest isn't where you want to be tomorrow, then please just stay here."

"I am."

Confused, he looks back at the crumpled invitation still in his possession.

"Then why do you have this?"

"I'm forbidden from leaving my room tomorrow. So what you're going to do for me is sneak away from the Holy Harvest, make up some excuse, work or whatever, I don't care, and you're going to let me out."

He shakes his head, but I continue.

"I'll be back before Harvest is done."

"Nope, not doing it. You need to stay home. Please."

"Will it make you feel better if you come with me? That way my big, strong brother can take care of me?" I pout.

His silence is all the confirmation I need that he wants to go with me. To protect me, or maybe pretend he's free for the evening. Either way, I take his lack of quip or fight as the ammo to solidify our plans for tomorrow evening.

Water splashes as I fully rise from the tub, the soap and bubbles falling from my curves, and he begins to backtrack.

"You're afraid, Harlan." I announce unintentionally sultry, but I don't bother to change my tone.

His gaze lingers on my exposed sex as he continues his slow, backward walk, and I use his attention to my advantage. Parting my thighs, I bend one knee and place my foot on the edge of the slippery porcelain bath. Keeping it there, I dip my fingers into my pussy, dragging them up and down slowly. Coating them in a mixture of arousal and bathwater, I circle over my clit, giving her the attention she's been begging for since watching him eat out that girl in the church basement.

Swirling my digits at the bundle of nerves, I touch myself. "Are you afraid of what he'll do to *you* if *I* disobey him? Or are you afraid that you want to disobey him... with me?"

"No," he growls, turning his head.

"Don't lie, church boy. It's a sin." I remind him through a breathy pant.

"Don't call me that," he grinds out.

I spread my lips wider, pinching my clit, applying the pressure I like with two fingers, suffocating it with my touch. A moan escapes me before I can continue speaking.

His steps halted by the wall, and his head turns away from me, pretending like this is torture, as if he hadn't imagined having this view of me a million times over.

"Stop praying in your head and look at me. Look at how pretty I am when I touch myself for you," I demand, and to my surprise, he listens. Not only that, he starts to lower himself onto the floor.

Edging myself, I extend my bent knee and step out of the tub. Moving over to him, I sink my wet body onto his lap, straddling him on the floor.

"Why are you doing this?" he asks.

"Because if I don't, I may die waiting for you to make the first move." I drop the book on the floor beside us and wrap my arms around his neck. Leaning in, I force my breasts against his shirt. "And because I think it's kind of hot how afraid of me you are."

"No, I'm not," he whispers.

"Ssh." Slowly, I grind my hips on his lap as I lower my lips to his ear. "I won't hurt you. Unless you want me to. Maybe you and I can experience a different kind of pain than the one your dad inflicts on us. Maybe we can hurt each other while making each other feel good."

He stays tight-lipped.

Tough fucking crowd.

Switching up tactics, I move my lips from his ear to his mouth. Deciding to up the fun, I bring my hand to his thick throat. Grazing the protrusion of his Adam's apple before rotating my wrist and wrapping my small palm around his neck as much as it can go.

My lips skim his. Our breath competes with one another.

"Tell me, brother, whose pussy you had to lick this time pretending it was mine?" I press a kiss to his lips and hold it there, reveling in his thrashing heartbeat and the quiver he's trying so damn hard to stifle. Breaking the seal of our kiss, I swipe my tongue at his cupid's bow, humming as I do it. "Stop punishing yourself for wanting to break the rules." I bite at his bottom lip, tugging it.

He groans, lips puckering to kiss mine, but I pull back, just enough that he can see my fingers drop to the apex of my thighs. In stunned silence Harlan watches me thrust my hand deep inside my pussy. A subtle gasp sneaks past his lips as I bring my wet digit to his mouth.

"Sin with me," I hum, smearing my arousal on his lips. He doesn't flinch or fight it like he wants to. *Like he should*. "I'll make it worth the burn. I'll have you begging for it." I take my hand and pat him on the cheek playfully. "You want that don't you? I can feel it." My eyes skim to his cock, thickening under my straddling stance.

Embarrassment stains his cheeks as he deflects my question by looking at the book on the floor next to us, then back at me. His hands land on my sides as he squeezes at my wet hips, lifting me up and placing me down on the floor. He moves to the door, taking the towel off the hook, and wraps it around me. Looking back down at me, he slowly brushes his hand on my cheek—pausing there—before taking the same hand to his back pocket.

I look down at his hand. It's the duplicate key he made years ago from the one his dad uses to lock me in my room as punishment.

He pulls at my towel, securing it enough to stick the key in without undoing the makeshift knot.

"Is that a yes?" I ask, but he's already heading to the door.

"Good night, Araceli." He deflects, back turned to me.

"Good night, church boy," I tease.

Whatever, it's not a no. I'll convince him. I know I can.

I gather my stuff and drain the rest of the water from the tub before making my way back to my room. Harlan's door slams from down the hall. The picture frames and crosses that hang on the hallway walls clatter and shake in response. I walk to my room across from his, and in nothing but my towel, my skin immediately pebbles as I walk through the threshold of the doorway.

I look over to the window near my bed and see that it's open. I never open the windows in this house. They are still original to when the house was built. The previous owners painted them several times, making them damn near impossible to open and close, hence why I never bother.

Confused as to why it's open but too tired to care, I place my purse and journal down on the bed and go to close the window. As it always does, it gives me a hard time. My reflection stares at me from the glass, highlighted by the small lamp resting on the nightstand. As I begin to press down, my silhouette shifts into something taller, darker. It expands until I close the window, and it's gone.

I drop the towel wrapped around me to the floor and walk my naked body to bed, ready to fall victim to the warm cocoon of blankets. As I slip beneath the covers, I notice that the book is open to the Ferryman illustration. The blank page next to it is no longer empty. A bold, crimson circle, reeking of the iron tang of blood, shines before my eyes at the top of the page. Unable to control myself, I feel drawn to touch it. I dip my fingertip in it, swirling it around to create two more circles. It's still tacky and abundant enough that I can use it to write the first thing that comes to mind.

A title.

The Horrors We Endure.

My name is next, though after the first letter of my name, my hand takes over. Smearing one letter after the next, I watch the page as if it's an out of body experience until the blank page is no longer empty. I read the name out loud.

"A.H. Charon."

I don't know who or what that is, but apparently, the story I'm meant to write isn't mine... but theirs.

Seven

Harlan

"Look at it," Araceli coos, pointing to the flashing marquee of the pop-up Halloween shop in front of us. I look begrudgingly. I can't fucking believe she convinced me to come here and go out tonight. Alternating shades of vibrant red and burnt orange burn into my retinas as I stand staring, internally mulling over all the ways this night can, and likely will, go wrong. Anytime I've ignored my gut and gone along with one of Araceli's ploys, it's never ended well. So tonight, with me already on thin ice with my dad, not to mention lying to him, I told him I picked up an extra shift at the movie theater. I can only imagine what will happen if he finds out who I'm with and where I am. But if I'm being honest, a part of me—the part of me that has denied myself freedom my entire life—doesn't care... at all.

I feel my fist tighten at my side, but with a gentle tug of my hand, Araceli weaves her fingers in mine as she leads the way through the remainder of the parking lot. With each step we take, I can feel a shift in Araceli. The usually defiant, grumpy rebel—somehow, in the blink of an eye—vanishes the very moment we step through the automated doors.

Two steps into the shop and my feet freeze on the spot, and my hand locks onto Araceli's, causing her to stumble back.

"You can't be serious?" She looks up at me with a raised brow before rolling her eyes. "Oh my fuck, seriously?" She giggles. "You're afraid?"

"No." I glare at her.

"You should feel comfortable in a place like this... it's no different than The Last Stop, silly," she says teasingly, dragging us down the first aisle by my hand.

"I don't know what you're talking about," I say in defense. It's true. I don't. I have not the faintest clue what the hell The Last Stop is.

Araceli doesn't elaborate more. She simply leaves it at that and leads the way through the grotesque displays. Some are scary, others gory, and all are definitely not my vibe, but I can't help but notice how happy she is amongst the cheesy macabre displays. It's like she's home.

Now at the back of the store she lets go of my hand, spinning around to face me, a floor-to-ceiling wall of masks behind her.

"Well," she motions, both hands to the masks as if I could possibly miss it, "don't be shy, pick one." The feistiness laced within her tone is a challenge, and so is the smirk on her face. She thinks I won't pick one or go through with tonight. I don't feel great about it, but we agreed tonight was a 'fuck you' to my dad. If celebrating a holiday that's been ingrained in my head since birth is a sin, and stepping out of my comfort zone with my stepsister, who seems to find trouble wherever she goes, is my only way to do so, then so fucking be it.

I bite down on my lip, looking past her at the overwhelming display. "Calm down, church boy," she hums her go-to jab. "No one is going to see us here." She takes a step closer, my pulse ricocheting through my veins. "Well, no one except, you know." She teasingly cranks her neck up, insinuating that the god I've been conditioned to believe in will see. I look up pathetically, but all I see is the ceiling.

Looking at me knowingly, Araceli steps forward, closing the space between us. It's as though she can sense the angel that I'm forced to keep on my shoulder is pleading with the devil on the other to come out and play. She places her hands on the leather harness wrapped around my waist that traces and wraps around both of my thighs—that she somehow convinced me to wear—and pulls at it, tugging me closer to her. "Tonight, it's just you and me. No one to stop us..." she pauses to point at the mask wall once more, "... no one to recognize us." She lets go of me, stopping in front of a section of the overwhelming display.

"That's the beauty of Halloween, you have one night to let down your guard and lose yourself in the fantasy of being something you're too afraid to be all the other nights of the year."

Fuck, she's wearing me down.

"I'm not afraid," I interrupt her speech, through a tight jaw.

"It's ok if you are. That's also part of the magic of Halloween." Her voice trails off, waiting for me to complete her thought.

"Let me guess, Halloween is about facing your fears too?"

And here I was thinking it's just about trick or treating in corny costumes.

"Exactly!" She claps. "Except you get to experience your greatest fears in a controlled setting. That way, you can not only conquer them, but find a way to actually enjoy them."

Enjoy? One's fears? Sounds like bullshit to me.

"Jesus Christ, Araceli," I mumble, still processing everything she's saying as I take my time looking at the mask wall.

She moves behind me and leans up on her tiptoes. She attempts to hover over me, but she can't—she's too short. It's not like that stops or limits her from getting or doing what she wants. Not like I'd ever stop her.

"Uhhh, ah," she clicks her tongue, reaching her hand around in front of me, picking up a mask that she drops in my hand. "No talk of God tonight. Just you, me, and whatever devil latches onto us."

"Right," I shoo her off, rejecting the mask she chose for me.

"Oh, all of a sudden a horror aficionado, huh?"

We both stare at the green mask I rejected.

"It looks like Shrek."

A disgusted scoff leaves her mouth as she leans over, pointing at the rubber green neck. "Shrek, Harlan? Really? What fucked up version of Shrek were you watching? Because the last time I checked, Shrek didn't have gills like the Gill-man."

My brow furrows.

"Jes—" she begins, immediately stopping to correct herself. "Nope. None of that," she reminds herself. "Gill-man..." her eyes widen, waiting for me to pick up on her cue. "Fuck, Harlan, the Creature from the Black Lagoon," she says like a question she's waiting for me to answer.

"I don't get it," I shrug, moving to see what my other options are.

"Of course not, they must've forgotten that on Veggie Tales."

A frustrated breath hitches in my throat. I'm so tired of this shit. Here I am once again, doing something she wants to do. Risking getting in trouble like I did months ago, all because of her and her rebellious, arrogant self. She can't set that ego aside for one fucking second to not treat me like I'm a fucking altar boy.

Angrily, I snatch a hooded mask, it's black mesh with just a small hole to breathe through and a long black hood. "How's this?" I ask her.

She fakes a yawn, patting her hand to her mouth. "Boring."

"What's so boring about it? It's the Grim Reaper."

Her hand moves from her mouth, an amused glint shines bright in her dark eyes. "Well fuck me, I guess hope isn't lost on you after all, brother. At least you know who the Grim Reaper is."

"Of course I do. So, what's wrong with choosing this one?"

She looks at me and then the mask in my hand. "I don't know, it's just a tad cliché."

"I thought you said tonight was a night to face our fears?" I remind her.

"I did. Why? Are you afraid of death?"

I put the mask back on the display hook, choosing not to answer her question. The truth is, death is my biggest fear, mostly because I can't believe a word that comes out of my dad's mouth, whether he's preaching or not. If what he claims waits for us doesn't exist, it means that my mom, as well as Araceli's mom—and anyone for that matter who is no longer here—is in a construct. In a realm, or whatever, that we may never fully understand, and that terrifies me.

Deflecting her question further, I move past her, trying to scramble and find a mask so we can get off this topic and get on with the evening. Araceli is still going on about whatever when something on the far side of the mask wall grabs my attention. At first, I thought it was glass shattering, but this is duller, and the noise lingers longer than a shattering of glass would. Panic trickles in my veins, my first instinct is to look over my shoulder to see if anyone is spying on us, but that's just my anxiety. An emotion I've been far too familiar with in my life, but it's something my father insists is a side effect of my lack of true faith. I continue to look around, though nothing but shoppers, busy purchasing their last-minute finds, meets my eyes. Still, the noise persists, summoning me to continue walking to see where it came from. I go until I stop at the end of the display, cornered in by the walls merging. There's nothing there. I'm losing it. About to turn around, I hear the noise again, sounding like it's coming from right under me. I peer down, and again... nothing... is... there.

Fuck. This can't be happening again. Please, not again.

I take a deep breath, closing my eyes. As I do, a mask catches my eye, summoning a surge of déjà vu too strong to ignore.

With eyes forced open, I look at the display in front of me. Two masks, stacked one on top of the other, stare back at me. The shelf pegs that stick out around it are all empty, only adding to the eeriness of the decaying skeleton mask hanging, just waiting for me to grab it.

It's hideous and nothing I would ever think to pick up. Not that I would come here on my own to browse. Halloween has never been my thing. It's never been allowed. Dad forbade it, saying it's a cursed day for cursed souls, and because of that I've never given costumes or masks or anything of the sort much thought. Not until now that is. No thanks to Araceli, and now I feel drawn to —compelled even— to pick up the atrocious mask, not because I want to, because I *have* to.

An onslaught of thoughts roam through my subconscious, all pleading with me to ignore the pull I have to the mask in front of me. I ignore each one, lifting my hand towards it instead. Slowly, I creep my calloused palm forward, and the rush of familiarity increases the closer my hand gets to the mask, reaching a crescendo until my fingers brush against the rough plaster. The cement-like texture reminds me of what the tombstones that litter the graveyard between our house and the church feel like, rough and unwelcoming.

As I take it off the display peg, a molten, tangible heat spreads on my skin. It's so hot that I shake my hand, wanting to toss the mask to the ground, but it becomes relentless in my grip, like it's glued to my palm. No matter how much I try to get rid of it, it won't budge. It's like it doesn't want to let go of me.

Lost in a forced trance, I continue to assess every detail of the grotesque mask in my possession, suddenly realizing why it looks so familiar. I've seen something like this. Just last night... in Araceli's creepy notebook. An inferno lodges itself in my veins as I run my hand over its features. It has the most realistic painted lines reminiscent of decay, rot mars beneath the nose, and all around the exposed jagged, equally rotting teeth. The two eye holes are black, bottomless pits. It's a damn near perfect replica of the mask worn by the Grim Reaper depicted in the illustration. The picture she said looked peaceful, but what's staring back at me is anything but peaceful. It's chaotic. Ominous. Sinful. I hate it and want it all at once.

I go to put it down, but my other hand somehow gets the grand idea to reach for the other mask that was behind it. This one is equally as grotesque as the first. Yet, an odd sense of relief fills me when I see that the second mask is identical to this one.

One for Araceli and me to wear together so we can match.

I lift the masks in my hand to show her. "What about these?"

"Ooh, let me see," she beams, skipping over. "They're awful," she says in a monotone voice I'm not able to read, and an unexpected jolt of disappointment erupts within me. "They're perfect!" she squeals. "I can't believe I've never seen these here." She moves closer, cupping her hand near her mouth, shielding it, as if she's about to tell me a secret, "I love this place, but after a while, seeing the same masks and decor year after year gets old real quick. These are everything," she boasts, still taking in the masks.

"Lucky us." I shrug.

"I'd say so. I wonder what the name is." She eagerly looks at me, urging me to check the tag.

"Ferryman?" I question.

"Hmm, I don't recognize it."

"Me either," I shrug.

She takes both from my hand as she walks past the mask wall to a small end cap of wigs. Picking a split-dyed one, with one side matching her natural black hair and the other a brighter version of my blonde, she tries it on, looking at herself in the mirror.

"Look, hermano, it's me and you. The saint," she points to the blonde side, "and the sinner," she points to the onyx side.

I don't want to be the saint. I want to be the sinner. Your sinner.

Visions of Araceli grinding on my leg in the bathroom last night cause a rush of blood to jolt my cock to life. I clear my throat, trying to snap my body and mind out of this involuntary fantasy yet once again.

"Whatever," I downplay the effect she has on me, opening my palm, "give it to me so I can pay."

She takes the masks and holds them tight to her chest. "None of that chivalrous shit with me. It's a fucking damned miracle I convinced you to come out with me tonight, this is on me."

"Araceli," I urge her, trying to snatch the masks from her, but she only grips them tighter.

She steps towards me. "Harlan," she teases, bobbing her head.

Conceding defeat, I drop my arm. "You're not going to change your mind, are you?"

"Nope," she says with a grin, walking off to the registers.

I illuminate the lock screen on my phone to check the time while I wait for her to pay. We only have three hours before Holy Harvest ends, so we have two hours at the haunt before we have to leave to make it home before Dad freaks out on both of us.

About to toss my phone back in my pocket, it vibrates twice. Two long distinct buzzes, but there's no text. I swipe to my messages, and there's nothing new. As I swipe out of the conversation log, three dots appear by Tori's name.

Fuck.

> Tori: How's the harvest?

> Me: Don't know.

> Tori: How come?

Panicked, I lie.

> Me: Picked up an extra shift at work.

Expecting hesitant typing, I stare at the screen, but to my surprise, she buys it—surprisingly, just as Dad did.

> Tori: That stinks, but it's money. Same. I'm sad I'm missing the harvest but duty calls.

> Me: Yep.

I close my phone just as I get a waft of Araceli's perfume.
That fucking smell could bring me to my knees alone.
"All set?" I ask as Araceli returns.
She holds a short receipt in her hand. "It really is our lucky night." She hands me my mask, ripping the tag off hers.
She walks past me, and I follow behind her to the parking lot as we head to my car.
"Why's that?"
Stretching the mask over her face, she puts the wig on, it's a mixture of colors draping over her shoulders.
I furrow my brow, waiting for her to continue.
"Apparently the masks we got weren't updated in inventory and the girl didn't feel like making up a price, so she just gave them to me. I only had to pay for the wig. That's the cheapest I've ever gotten out of there."
"She gave them to you for free?" I ask, pressing the unlock button on the key fob.
"Free." She slips into the car, and I follow on the driver's side. "And she even gave us these."
My stomach drops. Church boy, as she likes to call me, or not. I know drugs when I see them. It doesn't matter if they are disguised as cutesy squares with pumpkins and snakes on them.
"You showed her your tits, didn't you?" I ask because this wouldn't be the first time she's done it. She's shown her tits for much less.
"Yep, except hers were better," she winks.
I doubt it, I think to myself, looking at how Araceli's tits practically spill out of her tight corset top.

"I'm not doing that. Knock yourself out."

A playful scoff sounds from Araceli as she taps my leg. "Well, if you change your mind... I'll give you the wittle baby pumpkins," she mocks with a pout.

Her comment about the wig rings in my mind. *"It's me and you. The saint and the sinner."* It plays on repeat. Mocking me. Motivating me to stop playing the role I've been forced to play my entire life of the good pastor's son. Well, good enough. Unlike my dad, the full commitment to holiness has always felt cumbersome, too cumbersome. I'm ready to sin with her, like she hoped I would when she was grinding her wet, bare pussy on my fucking leg last night. My heart races. Adrenaline and lust, a lethal combination, moving my arms for me like an out of body experience. I snatch the drugs from her, leaving the pumpkin ones for her and opting for the snakes.

She stares at me, unsure of what to say, but she doesn't have to say that she's impressed. It's there in her dark eyes and it practically wisps around us in the air. I can feel it as my cock jolts and throbs from the rush that comes from her—the sinner's—approval.

"Good boy," she coos, playful and condescending, adding to the surge of warmth flooding my length. "But let's wait until we get there to do those." Araceli takes the sheet back.

"Whatever." I shrug her off, disappointed.

Engine revved, I'm about to get into first gear to get out of here when she taps my leg again.

"Here." She offers me an already lit joint, but all I can smell is cinnamon.

"No, I'm good."

Her eyes roll. "You were just about to drop acid, now a little weed is too much for you? Will it help if I take the first hit?"

"Do what you want."

"Fine, I'll take the first hit." She brings the burning paper to her lips and jealousy strikes me as her plump lips pucker around the edge as she inhales.

She takes another hit before passing it over to me. "Here," her eyes bulge and I can tell she isn't going to take no for an answer. "Have some. This is my special weed. I promise it'll get you right where you need to be."

"But—"

She clicks her tongue. "But nothing." Taking the joint back to her lips she breathes in and holds the smoke in her mouth. She leans over to me, taking her hand to my chin and turning it towards her. Gently prying my mouth open, she exhales a stream of bitter, earthy smoke into my mouth. I leave my lips parted, taking in every last drop until the smoke clears.

"Good boy," she claps, excited. "Now it's your turn."

Against my better judgment, I take it from her and suck in a hit. My lungs burn as I hold it, and unlike the steady line of smoke she poured into my mouth, mine is staggered as I cough it out.

"Good enough." She takes it from me, taking one last hit before chucking it out the open window. "Mask," she reminds me, tipping her head down to my mask that's still in my hand.

"Right." I finish switching gears. Draping the mask over the top of the steering wheel, I rip off the tag but notice a rough, muddy texture coating my hand.

Gross.

I open the window button with my elbow, shaking my hand and throwing the tag out. A wind gust fills the car, and Araceli's wig almost falls off.

"Close the window!" she shouts, voice competing with the wind.

I press the button but as the window takes its sweet ass time lifting, I try to get more of the dirt off my hands, and out the window.

"What's wrong?"

"Nothing there was just dirt on the tag. Must've been stuck in the back room or something."

"Yeah maybe." Her tone is off. She stares at the dirt on my

hand, studying it before she plugs her phone into my car to connect the GPS to the speaker.

"What's the name of the road?" I ask.

"Uh, hold on." Araceli fumbles for the invite in her pocket. "Fuck, the GPS is just spinning."

Of course.

"Well hurry up, I don't know where I'm driving to."

"No shit," she bites at me, sounding as frustrated as I am.

Taking my eyes off the road, I reach over her for her phone. "Give it to me."

She pulls it away from me. "Just keep driving."

Shifting my gaze back to the road ahead, I offer her a glimpse of my periphery. "Where would you like me to drive if I have no idea wherever the fuck I'm—"

I slam on the breaks. The car skids to an abrupt stop, tossing both of us forward, and testing the restraints of our seatbelts.

A stunned silence creeps over us as we watch someone run at lightning speed across the road.

"Did you see that?" Araceli's voice trembles.

My pulse thuds in my ears. "No shit."

The road around us is so desolate it makes it impossible to determine what's around us. "Should we go see if they are okay?" I ask Araceli, keeping my gaze on the driver's side window, trying to see where they ran off to, but it's so dark out, I can't see a damn thing.

"Fuck no! What are you, nuts? That's a fucking death wish if I've ever heard one. Just keep driving. This area isn't safe."

"Then why are we going?"

She's too preoccupied with the GPS on her phone to answer me. "I got the address to load." She shakes her illuminated screen at me, and sure enough, as she presses start, it connects to the speakers. "Also, to answer your question, the unsafe places are the most fun on Halloween. You know since it's all about—"

"Facing your fears, I know," I finish for her, unable to look away from her phone. There's no service since we're in the middle of nowhere. Let alone no Wi-Fi hook up in this beat up car I have, so getting the signal to work should be next to impossible. "Are you sure it's working? There's no service here."

She shrugs. "Well, start driving and we can find out. I don't want whatever that person was running from to get us." She's joking. Somewhat.

"This is fucked. We should..."

Unfastening her seatbelt she wastes no time contorting her body so her lips crash into mine for a kiss I have no time to react to. But fuck, if her lips don't feel good on mine.

Like a jackass—and exactly how she intended—I'm completely distracted by her fucking lips. My tongue slips out of my mouth, ready to crash into hers, but right as I do, she pulls back. Her tongue clicks with a grin.

"Relaxed?" she whispers, softly humming against my mouth.

"Not really." My thoughts spin again.

"Drive, Harlan," she instructs, "and maybe if you're a good boy I'll let you kiss something else."

The thought sends yet another rush to my cock, and like a jackass, I ease off the break and continue down the unpaved road.

"In a quarter of a mile, turn down 333 Summerland Drive."

I follow the directions until my tires turn down the entrance.

"Hmmm," Araceli hums.

"What?"

"Nothing," she trails off, assessing the open lot as I park. "It's just that this place looks familiar."

I throw the car in park, and we exchange a look just as a chill runs down my spine.

"Yeah, I know. I was thinking the same thing."

Eight

Araceli

"Welcome to Heathen's Cross!" a pre-recorded greeting announces, though its mechanical voice becomes lost to the symphony of noises off in the distance. An odd mixture of drums beating, people chanting, and screaming.

Tall corn stalks, most of which are bare, surround us as we approach the haunt's entrance. The path is illuminated by lit jack-o'-lanterns that are scattered throughout; some on the ground and others resting on hay barrels. Though, as we approach the end of the widened path, the remaining corn stalks are decorated. Fashioned into a cross with bones centered on them, complete with decaying skeletons with hands bound by nails and heads drooping, reminiscent of a crucifixion.

I look over to Harlan. He's been so quiet since we got out of the car. He's probably just taking it all in. He isn't used to—or even allowed to indulge in—Halloween celebrations outside of Holy Harvest, so this is a lot for him. The drugs add another element of things he isn't used to, but to my surprise, he isn't fighting it.

We reach the end of the pathway, and a wall made of wooden slats with an arched opening in the middle now faces us. Faux cobwebs line the wood, accompanied by more hay barrels and cornstalks. The drumming is now replaced with loud music and boisterous cheers echoing through the arched entryway.

I step in front of Harlan, holding my hand out for him to grab onto. Reluctantly, he does. The mask is still off his face, with the elastic strap clenched tight in his other fist.

"Your mask," I remind him, tugging at his hand in mine.

A foreboding expression lines his chiseled features as his gaze alternates between the mask in his hand and the mask on my face.

We're so close to being free, church boy, don't quit on me now.

A sea of black consumes my vision as a group of people walk past us. All dressed in hooded black cloaks. The draping fabric brushes against the fallen leaves mixed in with the gravel we're standing on, and the sound creates a storm in my eardrum. I can hear every footstep hit every rock.

"Are you okay?" Harlan asks in concern, but his gravelly voice is just another vibration. Its sound ricochets down my spine.

I laugh.

"Araceli, are you okay?" he repeats.

Squeezing his hand in mine, sweat slicks his calloused palm.

"You're starting to feel it, aren't you?" I can feel his pulse throb in my hand. The drugs are starting to kick in for him too.

He turns his head to the entrance the group of hooded individuals went through before turning his attention back to me. "Mhm," he practically growls, letting go of my hand so he can stretch the mask over his face, and my knees buckle at the sight before me. Finally, my strong, golden boy, big brother, is standing in front of me dressed in all-black from head to toe. The fact he has no cross hung on his neck, and a uniquely terrifying mask covering his face, is an added bonus. He looks like everything his father detests, as well as everything I want to corrupt... and everything I want to corrupt me.

His head shakes and the loose strands of honey blonde hair that escaped the mask's strap mimic the breeze, swaying back and forth.

Closing the space between us he lifts his hand and I expect

him to take mine again in his possession. I reach out to him but he swats my hand away and his large palm settles on my hip, adding to the inferno swarming my body.

An immediate mood shift graces my presence as the plaster of his mask taps against mine. "You're going to regret bringing me here." His vague response excites me.

"Why?"

"This is what I've always wanted."

"Halloween?" I ask, confused.

"No," he quips. He sways slightly, knocking into my side as we make our way through the haunt's entryway. "To be free."

"That's what you want? For me to set you free?" I pout, in jest. Not like he can see it concealed beneath my mask, but he doesn't like that, apparently.

Harlan stops walking so abruptly, our connected stride breaks on impact and I lose my footing.

"Jesus Chri—" I begin, but my words are stolen from me as is my mask. In the flash of an eye my mask glides up my face and onto the crown of my head. Harlan's calloused slick palm squeezing my cheeks, hollowing them in with his unexpectedly possessive grip.

My eyes fire a challenging glance his way. I've been waiting for this version of him to emerge. I know it's always been there. His darkness buried deep, unlike mine. Who knew all it would take are some cheap drugs—I should've done this sooner.

"Don't make me feel like I'm at church tonight or home. I don't want to hear any of that. Not tonight." His voice is harsh but there's still a pleading undercurrent to it. One he's trying so hard to stifle.

"You don't have to tell me twice."

Letting my face go, he slides my mask back down.

A shrill cry echoes from inside the haunt, adding to the thrill, thinking of all the trouble we're going to get into tonight. All of which will infuriate his dad, which makes it that much better. Harlan walks ahead of me, his boots scuffing on the gravel. We walk through the arched entrance and into a tunnel. Purple, red, and green alternate in flashes illuminating the artificial cobwebs that hang from the tunnel's ceiling. We make it to the other side, where two haunt workers stand waiting to greet us. Both of their features are concealed by black cloth masks. Their jackets look similar to the ones the two men were wearing yesterday who came to Sacred Promises to speak to my stepdad.

I shake my head at the thought of anything to do with that place. Like Harlan said—so unexpected and bold—tonight isn't about feeling like we're at church or home. It's about us letting loose. Being free.

Harlan steps to me, keeping his masked gaze on mine, he dips his finger in my cleavage, spilling over my corset. I stand stunned. Wanting more of this version of him. He fishes around, his hand becoming lost between the swell of my breasts.

"What are you—"

"Ssh." He silences me with the invitation now in his possession. I forgot I put it there.

Harlan hands it to one of the workers, who nods for us to walk in.

"Ready?" he asks.

"Si, Barquero."

"Barquero?"

"It means 'Ferryman'. Like your mask, silly. That's what the tag said, or yours did."

"Yours didn't?"

I shake my head. "No. But seeing that yours is the Barquero, I can be your pasajera." I step forward to lower his mask back down for him. "Since what's a Ferryman, without a passenger? I can be a blank slate that I'll allow you to corrupt. Just for tonight."

Hunger echoes beneath his mask in the form of a groan. "I thought you were the one corrupting me."

Be careful what you wish for, church boy. Suddenly the thought of corrupting him, of *breaking* him, is all I want. It'd be the ultimate fuck you to his dad and, if I'm being honest with myself, would satisfy the itch he created in me since seeing him sin between someone else's legs... that wasn't me. Like it should've been.

"You're right, and speaking of which..." my voice trails, taking the blotter sheet out again—also nestled between my tits. The designs on the small squares mesh together slightly from my body heat.

Harlan snatches the acid from my hand, and the glint of mischief in his stare mirrors my own. We remain with our gazes locked until I see him ripping two squares from the sheet in eagerness.

"No!" I snap at him just as he's about to lift his mask to take them. "You've never done this before. Take this much." I take one and halve it.

He scoffs, low and angry. "Stop babying me, Araceli. It's insulting. You wanted me to let loose tonight, remember? So if I'm going to go all out tonight, let me," he grits through a tense jaw, grabbing the sheet from me, "go all fucking out," he boasts, and the level of delusional confidence leaking from him is as hot as it is cringe worthy.

I take the sheet back. The body heat from how I had it stored mixed with Harlan and I handling it in a stubborn tug of war is causing the design to transfer onto my palm.

"Going all out and dying are two different things. Now you can lift your mask."

Another scoff sounds. This one, however, is met with him obeying my directive. Like a good boy, he lifts his mask, and I lift mine. With the hideous plaster resting over our heads, we look at each other, and once again, the apprehension he had in the Halloween Shop returns, holding his handsome features hostage. It's as if all the confidence the mask seemed to give him vanishes when it's off his face. His jaw tightens so hard that a visible knot shows.

I rip a small square from the sheet. My gaze falls to his lips. "Open," I instruct, my free hand squeezing his cheeks as I attempt to pry his mouth open. He wants this. I can see it—fuck, I can feel it, but where was that guy storming in here before? I need him to come back.

"I need your tongue. Stick it out."

He doesn't budge, but he doesn't fight off my touch either.

"Fine," I huff in defeat, loosening the hold I have on his cheeks and instead bringing my hand to his neck, squeezing it as hard as I can. "I liked you better when you were acting like an asshole," I murmur. Squeezing his throat tighter, I take the two blotter squares and place them both in my mouth.

"Then put my mask back on." His deep baritone says, practically begging me to do it.

"I will, after I do this." Without warning, I extend my tongue and dive into his mouth. He doesn't fight my aggressive kiss—or the drugs. Our mouths remain entangled, our tongues sliding over each other until the paper dissolves. I pull back, not giving up the dominance my hand has on his throat.

"What did we just take?" Harlan asks.

I don't answer right away. I let go of his neck, admiring the red marks my hand left on it, leaving an invisible collar on him. Marking him as mine, at least for tonight. I pull his mask down, over his chiseled face, and I do the same to mine.

Eliminating any and all space between us, I get onto my tiptoes. Our masks clacking against each other as I nestle myself near his ear. "An escape," I finally respond.

"Do you promise?" He asks. Scared, yet hopeful, all within the same breath.

"To give you more?" I stare at Harlan, dumbfounded. "Umm, sure."

"No!" He shouts before lowering his voice. "To escape, I mean."

I tilt my head in confusion as he continues. "I don't want to go back home." The admission tempts me as much as it surprises me.

"Please," he pleads. "Araceli, I mean it. I can't go back there."

"Are you suggesting we run away?" I ask, jokingly, though the enthusiastic nodding of his head is anything but a joke. He's serious. "How about we just see where the night takes us? Then we can figure it out."

"You promise?"

"I promise." The words slip out so fast, and Harlan's demeanor shifts to sudden elation upon me saying just those two words. The idea of being free of his father, of that fucking house, is what I've always wanted... alone. Not with him or anyone else. It'll be a clean break from all things Rainey. Harlan included. Not wanting to burst his bubble, I leave it there.

I tuck the drugs back in my corset and can see Harlan peer at my cleavage as I do it. I give my breast a pat playfully. "If you want any more, you're going to have to get past these first."

"Will it make the voices stop?" Another question, this one throwing me off just as much as the first. I'm not sure if he's referring to a possible side effect, or if he's talking about the same internal voices that guide me as 'part of my gift'—as Frida likes to call it. I doubt it's the latter. Even with his hatred for his father, I doubt he believes in anything outside of what he's been told to believe.

"It always does for me," I lie.

"Good." Relief lines his voice as we become submerged in the chaos that is Heathen's Cross.

Everywhere I look is an absolute sensory overload. Every inch of this place lives up to its name. More crosses made of bone and corn stalks surround us, forming a large circle around the fire that's burning in the center of the open area. There are so many people scattered about. Some are in cloaks, like the ones we saw earlier, wearing all black with hoods, while others are completely naked.

I try to see if there are any of the usual haunt-type attractions that pop-up spots like this are known for, but as far as I can see, there's nothing like that. Just an open area of people losing themselves to the night.

A fire burns in the center of the open area with a group of people gathered, dancing around the open flames. My attention is immediately drawn to a woman standing on a podium so high she looks like she's standing *on* the flames. She's completely naked, wearing nothing but a large necklace made of bone in varying sizes around her neck, and some sort of symbol smeared onto her sternum in the same shade of rich crimson that paints her lips.

Is that... blood?

She lifts a cow skull in the air as her lips part, chanting in a language that sounds similar to Latin. The people around the fire begin to sway their arms in the air and chant along with her.

The woman is no longer alone on the podium. A man and woman have made their way on the platform attached to the bottom. They kneel before her, bowing, and she slips the cow skull overtop her head as she spreads her legs in a wide stance. The couple kiss each other once through a heated exchange. Their tongues clash against the other before they move on their knees to be centered at the apex of her thighs. They continue to kiss, this time making out on her pussy, licking it together.

"Are you seeing this?" Harlan asks. He's standing behind me now, both arms draped over my shoulders. Our bodies sway together as one, mimicking the motions of the crowd.

I nod. Unable to look away. My own pussy grows wetter by the second the more I watch.

The wind picks up, and through the chanting mixed with moaning, I can hear every particle on the ground as it's transferred from the small shift in the air.

The woman getting her pussy eaten—who I assume is their leader by the level of power she holds over the crowd—begins to chant louder just as another woman, who is also naked, runs in front of us. A man is chasing after her with a bucket in his hand.

A dizzying rush takes over my head. I turn to look at the running woman, my head falling deeper into Harlan's hold. The iron tang of blood mixed with sweat becomes alive in the October air. The smell is ripe, like the vibrant hue of blood everywhere my eye lands. There's no doubt in my mind that there's blood in the bucket the man is holding. He dips his hand in, swirling it in the red liquid before bringing it to the woman who was just running. He smears it onto her chest.

She doesn't fight it. In fact, she moans louder with each swipe of his hand. He continues to smear the blood onto her until she is covered everywhere in different unfamiliar symbols.

The more I watch, the more turned on I become.

My back arches as my head finds solace in the divot between his broad chest and his shoulder. I can feel his heart thumping at my back.

"This place is..." I begin, practically moaning.

"Amazing," Harlan finishes for me.

"Yes," I breathe.

It really *is* amazing. Frida was wrong about this place. It isn't dangerous. It's freeing.

We remain swaying together, taking in the crowd and the scene before us. The chanting grows louder by the second. So loud my hands spring upward, unintentionally breaking the hold Harlan has on my shoulders. My mind is begging my hands to lift to either side of my head, to create a shield for my ears, but my hands aren't moving up. They're moving down. Skimming past the elastic waistband of my skirt. Traveling with vigor to my throbbing clit.

The sex... the blood... the madness all around me is too much of an aphrodisiac not to submit myself to. The flames burn in my irises, matching the heat coursing through my center. The colors move in synchrony with the motion of my hand rubbing at my bundle of nerves.

Harlan tugs at the hem of my miniskirt. "How wet are you right now?"

Thrown off by his question, a grin spreads on my lips.

"Well?" He purrs.

I go to answer, but all that slips my lips is a guttural moan. The pace I'm touching myself quickens.

"Fine," he clips. There's a sadistic tone to his voice. A confidence that I know surely wouldn't be there if there wasn't an altered state brewing in his mind or a mask to hide behind. "I guess I'll just have to feel for myself."

No longer teasing the edge of my skirt, his eager hand slithers its way to my center, replacing mine. His fingers trace a line up and down my slit, poking through the open holes of my fishnets. He continues this for a few more passes, and each one has me growing more desperate for him to tear at my fishnets and sink his fingers deep inside me.

I throw my head back and my lids close. "What are you…"

"Shhh," he whispers, breaking through the barrier of scattered nylon wide enough that he's able to slide into me with ease.

I clench around his fingers upon impact, and he groans in approval.

One finger graduates to two, as his thumb finds a rhythm at my clit while his fingers pump in and out of me. I grab hold of his wrist, locking his hand in place. Adding to the pressure his thumb has on my sensitive center, I unintentionally drive his fingers deeper inside of me.

"Fuck," he growls. "You're so fucking wet."

"For who?" I pant, wanting him to say that I'm wet for him. Craving, in this moment, to hear that my body belongs to him. "Who am I wet for?" I repeat, desperation entangling my words. "Say it." I grow needy. Distracted, consumed by the noises synonymous with carnal pleasure and euphoria infecting the night air. "Who am I wet for?" I'm practically begging him at this point.

A third finger enters me, stretching me. The added pressure shifts my balance to my tiptoes. He wiggles his fingers deeper. His fingertips prod and poke me, pinching my walls, making me pulse around his hand, suffocating it.

"Oh, I think you already know who this sloppy pussy is wet for." He pumps his fingers inside of me once more. This time even deeper. More aggressive. "Me."

The second word 'me' leaves his lips, he retracts his hand, and my walls clench at the absence of his touch, only adding to the violent pulse at my clit.

Pushing away from me, an unexpected chuckle sneaks past his mask. It's as mean sounding as his edging feels.

I adjust my skirt and shift the fabric back in place, trying to ignore the number the crisp air is doing on my throbbing center. Wanting to pretend that he isn't getting to me, or that our dynamic, within an instant, has changed.

A rush of heat flushes my cheeks, the mask becoming a burden. I lift it up and onto my head.

As I turn around, ready to hurl some church boy insults his way, Harlan charges at me. My senses are aware of his touch, but my eyes process his movements as if he's moving in slow motion. His fingers skim my lips, pulling at my bottom lip to gain access to my mouth. Loving the stares we're getting from those moving past us, I open my mouth so he can sink his fingers in, to feed me the remnants of my own arousal. His eyes roll in pleasure the deeper I suck him in. Sucking his fingers with the same vigor I would his dick, but just like he did to me, just when I can tell it's getting him going, I break the seal of my mouth enough that my cheeks don't hollow around the girth of his fingers. Though, I still keep just the right amount of pressure on them so my tongue can still tease him while I speak.

"So this is what you're like when sky Daddy isn't watching?" I ask, closing the gap of my mouth about to give him another teasing suck, but he moves too fast, slipping his digits past my tonsils, putting my gag reflex to the test.

"Oh, he's watching... I just don't care anymore."

The combination of his words mixed with his fingers grazing the back of my throat both shock and excite me all in the same breath.

I like what he's saying. Fuck. I've been wanting to hear this forever. To hear the pastor's son, my stepbrother, lay down his morals, which have always been questionable, just waiting for an invitation to be toyed with, and admit he doesn't care. But what fun would it be if I don't use this as an opportunity to not only test his limits, but to completely *shatter* them?

I tease his fingers with the edge of my teeth. Applying just the right amount of pressure that he feels like I'm on the verge of breaking skin, but leaving him wondering if I will actually do it.

"You don't believe me, do you?"

I shake my head no.

A challenge.

An invitation for him to do his worst. To prove to me he doesn't care about anything but sinning— even if he burns —with me.

Nine

Araceli

Harlan pulls his hand from my mouth abruptly, bringing it to my head. His callouses scratch and tangle my hair as he pushes me to my knees.

"Well, don't just stare at it," he groans. "Show me that burn you keep promising me. You can start by wrapping those pretty lips around this." He jolts his hips forward, his concealed cock knocks into my face.

Skimming my greedy hands to his pants, I begin to lower his zipper, though it's not fast enough for him. Harlan takes a step back, brushing my hands away, so he can unzip his pants himself.

A loud moan from the side of us distracts me. Just as Harlan lowers his pants, I turn my head wanting to see the actions that match the carnal screams filling the air.

"Eyes over here," he roars, slapping my cheek before bringing his hands to my cheeks, hollowing them.

Another growl sounds from Harlan. His hand is now pinching my chin as he tries to force my attention to him.

His grip intensifies, and my eyes bulge in response.

"Don't look so afraid. Isn't this what you wanted? A big brother to look up to?"

Yes.

"Isn't it?"

"Yes," I say this time out loud.

I don't know what has overcome Harlan but I'll take it. I salivate at the sight of the pre-cum dripping from his tip.

"Good." He takes a step forward, closing the gap between us. Fisting his cock, he lines it up to my lips. "Time to take your punishment before it's too late," he says, sadistic and unrecognizable. Those words might have leaked from his mouth, but, that voice, it wasn't him. It's *not* him. It has to be the drugs or the influence of the scene around us.

With both hands on my head, he breaks the barrier between my lips. "That's it," he mewls, increasing the pressure on my head, shoving himself to the back of my throat.

My eyes water on impact, and a warmth fills my mouth. His cock is burning hot, and the more he thrusts himself between my lips, the more it builds until the heat spreads down my throat, tightening it.

"Fuck. Your mouth feels so... so ... good," Harlan pants. His breath, a warm current, tickling the top of my head.

My hollowed cheeks take all of him. Sucking him in like he really is punishing my mouth. *Like I want to be punished.*

I continue gliding my mouth up and down his shaft. Maintaining suction on him, I flick my tongue, back and forth, playing with the bulging vein that protrudes from his impressive length.

He pulls my hair, and I can feel his release nearing. I close my eyes to brace myself for him to spill down my throat, though as I my lids close, the heat from before increases. This time moving past my throat. It spreads violently down across my shoulder, trickling down my spine, until it whips its fiery burn at my thighs before finding solace in my aching center.

"I'm almost there," Harlan announces. I open my eyes and the inferno dissipates. Through watery eyes, I peer up at him. His head is thrown back, and his body relaxed.

I increase suction around his thick, long cock, humming as I draw him in deeper. My hands lift to his balls, massaging them.

"Don't stop," he mewls, shoving my head as far as it can go, choking me with his cock as he spills down my throat.

A breath hitches in my throat, trapped there, as an abundant load fills my mouth. I keep still, swallowing every warm drop. His cock continues to twitch as he pours into me.

Harlan's boot knocks into my knee as he takes a step closer, and my jaw acts on instinct, hollowing around his length, even though he's finished coming.

"The initiation has begun," a stranger shouts in the distance, but as I flick my gaze over to my side, a hooded figure appears, staring at me before running off.

"Get up," Harlan instructs, pulling himself from my mouth.

A solid drop of his cum leaks onto my chin as I rise to my feet. He catches it with his finger, swiping his thumb in a short horizontal line first before dragging it down my chin.

"There isn't much time," he deadpans. Not exactly what I was expecting after he just fucked my goddamn throat.

Insulted, I stare at him. "You're welcome, dick. What's the rush?"

He ignores me, pulling up his pants. I peer into the dark-rimmed slits of his mask, waiting for him to say something, but we remain in tense silence until another chant breaks through, stealing both our attention. It's not one word like all the others have been. It's three words strung together consecutively over and over.

"Fatum enim eligimus."

"Fatum enim eligimus."

"Fatum..."

"... enim."

"... eligimus."

Over and over on repeat. I know I've heard that before, but my brain feels scrambled.

A growl erupts from his throat as he rips off his mask, tossing it to the ground, and the disappointed pout on my lips is a stark contrast to his chest heaving with excitement.

"Boo," I shout playfully. "I liked you better with the mask on, remember?"

Once again, he charges me, this time tossing me over his shoulder.

"I think you'll like me better when I can use my mouth to show you how much I don't care if *He* is watching. Let Him. I want to put on a show with you, little sister. I want you to christen my tongue."

Harlan moves with speed throughout the crowd. People bump into us as he brings us closer to the fire. A dizzy rush floats over my body when he places me onto a hay barrel that holds one of the many crosses around the flames.

"Hold still," he instructs, lifting one of my wrists up to the horizontal stalk. He fastens it with a piece of rope that hangs down from the stalk before repeating the same with the other wrist.

"Such an obedient sinner," he praises. "So willing to do whatever your big brother says."

Yes. Yes, I fucking am.

The air is thick, drenched with as much anticipation as it is in darkness. I feel Harlan's body heat mixing with mine as my corset rips slightly from the tight grip he has on it, the frayed fabric disintegrating in his palms.

A cloaked stranger holding a bucket walks over to us, tapping Harlan on the shoulder. "Here. Take some." The stranger offers Harlan the bucket, and without hesitation, Harlan dips his hand into it—surprising me—before the stranger walks off. Rivulets of crimson fall from his hand as he brings it back in front of me. His fingertips still for a moment. I can't tell if he's having second thoughts or what, but a tormented look fills his irises.

He locks eyes with mine, and without saying a word, he drives his free hand to my corset, and rips it completely off me in one shot. I let out a gasp as my tits bounce from the impact, and the remaining sweat-soaked drugs fall to the ground. Harlan brings his mouth to my chest, licking my sticky, sweaty skin before taking my nipple in his mouth and sucking.

"Fuck!" he exclaims. "You taste so fucking good, and I've barely gotten started." His words surprise me, and I remain absolutely transfixed by him, as he uses his fingers as a paintbrush. Circling them repeatedly at my chest before he does the same to my sternum, and then my belly so that there's three consecutive circles in a straight line on my skin.

I don't know why he did it. I don't care, but all I know is that once he does, everything around me begins to spin. I close my eyes, but they open the second his gravelly voice cuts in the air.

"I lied."

"About?" I swallow, fighting the urge again to close my eyes fully.

"My biggest fear."

"Okay?" My tone drags impatiently.

"It's *you*. You're my biggest fear, and tonight I'm going to conquer it. You." His cryptic words like music to my ears, giving me the strength to keep my eyes open. Thank fuck I do. I witness him fall to his knees, aligning his face with my waiting pussy.

"You have no idea how long I've wanted this," he hums, shimmying my skirt down my thighs, guiding each ankle out of it.

"Show me," I breathe, desperate for him. "Show me how bad you've wanted to sin with me, church boy."

His fingers crawl up my leg, tangling themselves in my fishnets until he reaches the apex of my thighs and stops. He spanks my thigh. The sting is heightened by the drugs wreaking sweet havoc on my body. "Stop calling me that," he groans.

"Then show me you're corruptible," I challenge him by draping one leg over his shoulder, and then the other, resting my weight on his shoulders, locking him into place. "Let me feel what that bitch felt when you ate her pussy pretending it was *mine*." I push my pussy into his face. I'm making it so easy for him. He already tore the crotch of my fishnets, so all he has to do is slip his tongue in and I'm his to consume.

"You sound jealous," he murmurs.

I am.

"I like how jealousy sounds on you." He inhales me like a starved man, and the groan that follows vibrates my entire pussy and my spine. "Jesus. Fucking. Christ." He moans. "You smell so sweet."

"I taste even sweeter," I hum. "Go ahead and—"

He buries his face at my center, silencing me. With an attentive stroke he drags his tongue slow and steady from my ass, up to my pussy until he captures my clit between his teeth. Kneading it with the perfect amount of pressure, he sucks my sensitive bud relentlessly, eliciting a moan that I didn't know I was capable of.

My thighs squeeze around his head, wanting more of what he's giving me. I want him deeper. So deep that he doesn't just consume me, but becomes a part of me.

I roll my hips forward, riding and grinding against his face. My head bangs against the bone on the cross he tied me to as he crawls his hand up my body, through the blood, before settling on the pentagram necklace dangling from my neck.

I jerk my neck forward, giving him more of the pentagram to pull, hoping he chokes me with it.

Like a good boy, he does just that. Wrapping the chain around his hand and twisting, I gasp as the cool silver tightens around my throat. Stars line my vision from the pressure he's placing on my windpipe. "Fuck yes," I mewl.

"Mmm," he bellows into my center before rolling his entire face in and around my wet pussy, coating it in my arousal.

"Har—" I begin to pant his name when a cloaked figure on stilts towers above me.

Harlan doesn't seem to notice, or if he does, he's too lost in licking me to care.

The person moves closer and beneath the hood, I can see they're wearing Harlan's mask—the one he tossed on the ground.

They wobble on the stilts as they near me.

"Harlan." I mean to say his name with the intention of

getting his attention, but it comes out as a breathy whimper. Which the person hovering above us doesn't seem to like, apparently. They're now leaning over and right in front of my face. The mask, somehow filthier than it was just a few moments before, scratches my face as it scrapes against my forehead.

I turn my head in the opposite direction, but a gloved hand wraps around my jaw, twisting my neck to face them.

"Harlan." I cry.

The masked person nods their head. A mechanical voice follows. "That's it."

"Rainey." I say without thought.

"Keep going," they encourage me, standing up straight, yet still hovering over us. My heart rate accelerates as red drips from the eyeholes of the mask. Rivulets of blood pour and stain the cracked and dirty plaster.

"Harlan!" I shout, thrashing my wrists, trying to undo the ties. Adrenaline on my side, the restraints break, falling to the ground.

"Harlan," I repeat his name again, this time taking my hand to his head, trying to shake him for his attention. It doesn't work. I take my hand and bring it to the mound above my pussy, trying to wiggle my way to his mouth to break the seal, but all he does is lick and bite at my fingers, still too busy licking me.

The masked figure meanwhile watches, now moving closer, as their head tilts to a ninety-degree angle, their concealed face inching closer to mine.

Nausea fills my mouth as the smell of rot invades my every sense.

"What do you want?!" I yell out.

"Sing for him," it says, as cryptic as can be. "Sing for him and let him *sail*."

"Who?" I cry. "What?"

The stranger straightens their spine, towering over us again, but this time it raises an arm. A gloved hand opens, and dirt pours over us, causing me to cough, my lungs burning on impact.

"Sing for him and let him sail," it repeats. "Sing," it whispers as it walks backward and away from us.

My lips move, but I hear no sound.

All I know is as my clit pulses like a drum, I'm about to come, and I can feel everything, but hear nothing.

Harlan

My whole body is on fire. I'm not sure what's sweat and what's her arousal anymore. I can't tell the difference—everything is warm and wet. Well, everything but my mouth. I don't know how it's possible. She's so wet—sloppy, fucking wet, but somehow the more I dip my tongue in her, the dryer my mouth becomes. It continues with every stroke, mystifying me.

She squeals, drawing my attention up to her. Blotches of red diluted by sweat mar her abdomen as she claws at her skin.

I lift my hand to move hers, so she stops hurting herself, but she slaps it away.

Wait. How is she swatting at me? I thought her hands were tied.

I peer up and over at the cross, but broken strands of rope hang off either side—she broke through them.

"Lick," she instructs. Cold. Sinister.

With one hand on my head, she guides my head to her pussy. "I said lick." She seals her demand with a harsh smack. Pain ricochets from my cheek to my core.

"Harlan," she mewls.

That's it, sister, say my name.

Desperate to taste more of her, and for her cum to coat my tongue again, I drag it up her slit. I feel something rough; it tastes bitter. I ignore the dry powdery substance falling on my head and filtering into my mouth, robbing my taste buds, and continue to lick up her release.

She mumbles something to herself, her voice somewhat distorted. I can't tell what, though, from the euphoria her pussy is giving me. Every sound she makes is not clear, just vibrating through me.

The first syllable of my name falls from her lips, but she doesn't follow through. She does this again, over and over.

"Ha—" she pants. Each time not finishing.

"Ha. Ha. Ha. Ha."

The beginning of my name is reminiscent of a laugh, and she does it over and over again as she locks my head in a chokehold with her thighs.

She says something else, but all I can focus on is how loud her wetness slaps against my tongue, and the closer she is to coming.

She thrashes against me.

"Has to die. Blood for blood. Eye for an eye," she mewls as she comes undone on my face.

My heart stalls in my chest. Its beat, slowing down each time she repeats the last part of her song.

"Eye for an eye. Eye for an eye. Eye for an eye. Eye for an eye. Eye for an eye."

What is she talking about?

It's the drugs.

I have to be hallucinating.

I pull away from her, gasping for air, but the blood in my veins runs cold when the night air doesn't meet my eyes.

Daylight does.

How fucking long have we been here?

The amber hues of dawn in autumn mixed with red and blue flashing lights consume my vision. A shiver runs down my spine because there's no one here.

No fire.

No naked people.

No one fucking.

No. One. Is. Here.

No one.

Except us and whoever has come here to help us.

"I want to come again." I hear her whisper, but it's impossible because when I turn to look at her, she's just laying there naked... unconscious. Dried, bloody symbols written all over her body that's slumped over the hay barrel.

"Brother, I want to come again. Make me come again. Make me come here again. Come. Here. Again..."

"Stop!" I scream. "Stop it! Stop it!" I throw my hands up to my ears but guilt washes over me, because she's not okay. I need to make sure she's okay.

I keep hearing her voice. Begging me to make her come. Taunting me.

This isn't how tonight is supposed to go.

This isn't right.

I throw myself onto her.

Relief, though fleeting, claws at my mind.

I can feel her heart beating.

She's still here with me.

She's here.

She's okay.

We're okay.

"Two possible overdoses, I need assistance!" a voice calls out, but everything becomes fuzzy.

I see Araceli being strapped to a stretcher and taken to an ambulance in the distance.

Fuck. Dad is going to kill us when he finds out.

My eyelids feel heavy. I want to close them, but a hooded figure kneels next to me. The patch on their sleeve—or I think it's their sleeve—matches one of the emblems on the sheet of acid we took.

"You didn't pay." It says.

"What?" I manage, but barely.

"You didn't *pay*," it repeats.

"Didn't pay for what?" I argue.

"To get in. You'll sink if you don't pay."

I grab onto the man's cloak, shaking him.

A radio scratches at my ear. I blink for just a second and the fabric I'm yanking on isn't black or a cloak. It's blue with a medic's patch sewn on.

"We're going to need backup, one is aggressive," the paramedic speaks into the radio before turning his attention back to me. "It's okay, you can rest now. We're going to transport you to the hospital." The paramedic's voice adjusts. Deep and eerie. "You didn't pay. We have to take you there."

Pay for what? I ask internally, unable to move my lips as sleep finds me. Ready for the nap that Araceli says is the best part of the crash.

Ten
Harlan

"Shh," a familiar voice whispers in my ear, slowly waking me up, though my eyes remain closed. The thought of opening them is a task I don't have the energy for. My eyes and my entire body feel too weak to move or do anything but lay here.

"Just like that." The voice sounds again. Soft, feminine... *familiar*.

Another string of words leaks from who I can only assume, judging from the subtle notes of cinnamon and pumpkin present in the air, is Araceli. I hear the murmuring of her voice, but I can't focus on what else she's saying. I'm too distracted by the *relief* I feel.

She's okay.

We're okay.

An unexpected surge of adrenaline ignites within my veins, and I fight the weakening current lingering over my skin by lifting one hand and then the other.

A slow, slurred motion takes my palms hostage, but I fight it, curling them.

Open, then shut.

Open, then shut.

Open then...

Unable to shut my hand fully, another hand slithers its way into mine. Fingers weaving their way into the vacant crevices between each of my fingers. Closing the gap with a hold that is anything but delicate. It's possessive. Overpowering.

Even in my out of it state, there's no mistaking the incessant, yet dull, beep of machinery grating at my ear drums every few seconds.

We're at the hospital.

What I'm laying on is a hospital bed.

That heaviness weighing down my limbs isn't solely from the web of wires hooked up to said beeping machines. It's my body's way of coming down from the high that the drugs—and Araceli—gave me at Heathen's Cross.

Dread finds me, attaching to my every vertebrae. I'm thankful to be alive, but the shit storm that will await me—meaning my dad—is going to put to the test how worth it this was.

Another hushed whisper sounds, from what feels to be Araceli's lips hovering over mine. Her breath sends coils of warm air to my skin. My mouth still feels like I've been chewing on cotton balls, just like it did before I remember the paramedics wheeling us away.

I wonder if hers feels that way, too.

My lips go to part, but something is already lodged between them, obstructing my ability to move them further.

"I'm almost there," she coos, stealing my hands and tossing them, wires and all, over my head, in a death grip.

How the hell does she have the energy to be out of bed?

To be... on top of me?

Warmth meets my groin.

Tight, wet, *warmth*.

Fuck.

I try to open my eyes, but still they don't budge. I'm too tired. Not that I need to have them open to confirm what I feel.

Araceli.

My stepsister.

Riding my cock with her sloppy wet pussy... in a fucking hospital bed.

Doing what no one has ever done to me before.

Well, at least with their pussy. I've only ever had oral sex. Not this kind of sex. This feels better than any mouth slobbering on my cock ever could, because it's her, taking what she wants —from me.

Christ, she feels so fucking good.

Even in this shitty state, my body knows how much I want her—my painfully hard cock is a dead giveaway.

"I'm coming for—"

Hinges squeal, and the air grows silent. Eerily so, until another familiar voice—my *father's*—pokes at the euphoric bubble Araceli placed us in. Like a needle to a balloon, bursting it.

"Get off of him, you fucking bitch!" he screams.

Though she doesn't get off me and from the way her already tight cunt grows tighter...

Oh, she's about to get off Dad... on me.

"I'm so close," she lets out as her breathing becomes ragged.

"Oh, no, you're not!" Dad's footsteps stomp across the room.

"Get off of him, you crazy fucking bitch!" Dad shouts again and once again, she doesn't listen.

"I'm almost—" she gasps. "I'm al—" a stutter, her voice weakening, "... almost there," she mewls, faint, but it's there.

Shouting fills the room, competing with the chaotic melody of Araceli's panting and the machines beeping. Every part of this room, and my body as well as hers, is going absolutely haywire.

My eyes finally open, barely, but enough to see the chaos unfolding.

Two security guards barge in, multiple nurses follow, but all I see is Araceli in a hospital gown on top of me, straddling my body. Standing her ground with my dick still inside her, she fights off the hands clawing at her to get off me.

She looks so sad. The usual golden hue of her skin, robbed by a ghastly white. The wig she got from the Halloween shop, split down the middle with the competing shades of black and blonde, still rests on her head. Tilted slightly but there. The blonde side, however, is covered in the red liquid spewing from her wrists as she tries to fight everyone off her.

Strength like I've never seen before overcomes her, breaking through the stronghold of however many sets of hands there are trying to get her to get away from me.

She lunges forward, and the blood follows, dripping onto my hospital gown, causing the fabric to become drenched and stick to my skin.

Not paying any mind to the doctor trying to fight his way to her with a syringe in his hand, her lips find my ears. "I'm coming back for you," she whispers. "Don't believe his lies. I'm not leaving you."

Araceli is pulled off of me, our physical connection lost on impact. My cock bobs free of her warmth, but I can still feel her release coating it.

"Get off me!" she shouts. A security guard now holds her arms back, and the doctor looks hesitantly at my dad.

"It's your call," he says, monotone, waiting for him to give the order to inject Araceli with the syringe.

Her eyes lock onto mine for a moment before she looks at the hospital staff. "Where was all this help when I called for you after *he* did this to me?!" she screams, pointing at Dad, deep sorrow and anger coating her words.

Dad clears his throat. "She's a liar. A deviant with a drug addiction. Do not listen to her," he says with arrogance. "You heard the song she's been singing since the paramedics found them. She kept singing it here just now. She's trying to kill him!"

"Look!" She manages to wiggle one hand free. Circular burns line her skin. They look fresh. They look almost identical to the ones he used to leave on me before I learned that obedience means survival in a tyrant's home. Same as the ones I found on her back the other night.

"Do it!" Dad instructs the doctor, who begrudgingly listens

and pumps the fluid filled syringe in Araceli's arm while the guards pin her down.

She thrashes about in their hold before her eyes eventually glaze over. As her eyes finally close, mine close with her in solidarity—I want to scream. To tell her it's okay, but what I now realize is that a breathing tube in my mouth makes that impossible.

The shiver that attacks my spine doesn't stay put for long. It crawls onto my shoulder, crashing its violence onto my jaw. My entire body is cold and clammy in the same breath. Shivering. Shaking uncontrollably.

A nurse runs over. "He's going through withdrawal," she announces, messing with what I think is the bag that's hanging from the IV drip.

Another nurse comes over. "This will help him."

Warmth finds my veins as the lingering scent of tobacco wafts its way to my nostrils. It's as overpowering as the urgency, now competing with my exhaustion to stay awake.

My dad's tongue clicks and his fingers snap, causing my eyes to pry open and weakly glance in his direction.

"Please. Leave me and my son alone for a few moments."

The nurses nod and file out, leaving me and my father alone as he approaches the side of my hospital bed.

He remains silent until the door slams and when it does, it's not his words that break the air, it's the jingling of keys.

"I warned you to stay away from her. I warned you that she was trouble, but you didn't listen. No one ever listens to me," he pauses, and laughter follows. Loud and sinister, hair-raising laughter. "No one ever fucking listens," he grits, repeating himself, "until it's too late, but don't you worry my son." He reaches for my hand and the black sleeves of his jacket brush against my wrist first before he squeezes my hand. His entire body trembling from anger. His dark eyes bore into me, scaring me, but I'm too weak to move anything. I haven't seen this look on him since the first and last time I disobeyed him. He clears his throat, lowering his mouth to my ear, breathing out a cryptic warning. "She's getting what's coming to her, but lucky for you, I know how to make this mess go away."

The keys in his other hand jingle.

"It may take a bit more creativity."

Whatever medicine the nurse administered to me has pulled my eyes shut. Soft tingles of warmth burn through my veins.

"But I've done it before."

My hearing dulls and though I'm aware of the anger ripe within my father's words, it sounds like he's speaking into a funnel. He continues to talk, but I go in and out of being able to focus. My head is pounding and my mouth feels so fucking dry.

"... don't worry, he'll be here in a minute and walk you through what needs to be done. I never wanted it this way, but you need to understand that I have an image to protect."

The last word hangs on my conscience.

He said his image.

What the actual fuck?

Not his son or his family. His fucking *image*.

My father places his hand on my chest, and it aches upon contact. It feels so fucking sore. Emotion grips him for a moment as he sniffles. "I can't believe she did this to you. She won't get away with this. I'll see to it."

I mull internally over what he's saying. Araceli would never... I don't think.

He's lying.

Just like she said he would.

"I'll see you, son," he whispers before leaving the room. The hinges squeal, and a soft murmur is exchanged, but the door never closes. Footsteps filter through the room. These are slow and not as urgent as the ones from the nurses and security guards from before.

A warm hand grips my arm, squeezing it.

"Your father sent me here to..." the man pauses, "take care of things."

My eyes fight my need to sleep, peering down instead at my chest. Bandages cover my skin. Blood seeping from most of them. Fuck. My dad really wasn't lying.

I blink for a second and see Araceli, bloody and smiling at me with a knife in her hand. "Fatum enim eligimus brother, you understand," she says, repeating the chant from the haunt. I blink once more, but the memory fades. Reality hits me all over again that I'm here in the hospital. All because I didn't listen to my instincts. All because I let her tempt me.

The man clears his throat. "Quite the mess you and her made." He stares at my bandages. "You're lucky. Those wounds will heal, but it's this one." He stops to point at his chest. "Those inner wounds that will take some time. If you need someone to talk to about what happened, so you can better understand, don't hesitate to reach out." The man drops a card on the small table to my side.

I nod. Not taking any of this to heart. I'm too tired. My eyes close. Falling asleep with the taste of Araceli's essence on my lips.

I hear the man's footsteps move to the door, but he stops dramatically and my lids jolt open.

"I wouldn't wait too long. That invitation is good for a limited time. If I don't hear from you, I will upgrade it to a request."

A final message breaks through my dwindling conscience as sleep begins to consume me.

"You can't expect to attend Heathen's Cross unscathed. No one leaves as they came in. You either become a member or you become a sacrifice. Take care, Mr. Rainey. We'll be in touch."

What the fuck did she do to me?

PART II

PRESENT DAY

"Home is the place where, when you have to go there, they have to take you in." — Robert Frost

Eleven

Harlan

"Good evening and Happy Halloween Eve..."

The radio announcer doesn't finish their sentence before I'm transported elsewhere. No longer in the driver's seat, but back to the last time I felt something. Back to when I wasn't sitting in a car but laying in a hospital bed in a hideous hospital gown. When I woke up with a tube in my throat and my step sister straddling me, sinking that black hole of a cunt down on my cock.

Tomorrow will be the thirteen-year anniversary of my corruption, and oh, what an interesting thirteen years it has been. So much has changed. For one, I'm no longer bound to the cross I used to wear around my neck. Something my father detests, but he got over it, he had no choice. With Araceli conveniently out of the picture, it left me to contend with Dad. First, with his anger for what her, and I did that night at Heathen's Cross, and then with his illness to take care. He learned real quick that if he didn't come to accept the man I've become, he'd be completely alone with no one to take care of him.

Slipknot's *Bone Church* infects the air leaking through the speakers, and the carnivalesque intro only adds to the fury of twisted thoughts I have swirling in my head. The lyrics drive a sledgehammer to my heart.

"... And my heart is a memory of the pain. I don't need a miracle. Prayers will not save me again."

Ain't that the fucking truth. Prayers. Time. Nothing will save me or her ever again. Not after the oath we began years ago that she still hasn't fulfilled.

Black and gray ink flashes before my eyes as I lift my hand to the radio dial, twisting it so fast, the round knob lifts from the stereo and nearly falls off. "Ahh!" I yell out, and the hand that was just turning off the radio is now curled into a fist. I'd like nothing more than to slam into something other than the leather steering wheel.

I can't do that, though. The horn will sound, and that will make my presence too obvious.

It's not that I don't want Araceli to know I'm here.

Just not yet.

This veil of selective numbness can only stay put for so long before it lifts, needing a certain someone to help me feel something other than hatred and resentment.

The bitterness that has lodged itself in the very fabric of my being has become as potent as the drugs that were flowing through our veins that night. The high might have worn off, but the memory and carnal desire—steeped in a resentment so strong it's changed me to my very core—hasn't lessened, but grown stronger. So strong that if I don't have a taste. A lick. Fucking something, *anything* that gives me a piece of her, I might combust.

I swear, every time I breathe in through my nose, I can still smell the blood that poured like a faucet from her wrists as she rode my half-conscious body, to what I can only assume was an orgasm. I wouldn't know the specifics of our encounter in the hospital. It's not like the bitch stayed around to talk to me after she almost tried to kill me, not once, but twice that night. At least the second time she had the fucking dignity to get my dick wet instead of having her cunt smothered by my entire face. Dad was right about her. She's nothing, but a broken and greedy fucking whore who deserves to be punished, except Dad's idea of punishment aligns with the idea of redemption. Something I don't believe in. Not anymore.

I turn the ignition off, and the envelope crumpled in my hand makes my decision for me.

I'm here because she finally, all this time later, wants to make amends. In her own half assed shitty way. It's why she had this note, hand delivered to the house with my name on it. I guess she finally decided that thirteen years is a bit excessive to go without so much as a word or visit to the place she used to call home. Sure, it was broken, but it was our home. *Ours.*

Whatever happens once I leave this car is because of her.

It's all her fault.

I lean back and catch my reflection in the rearview. My hair is a fucking mess. I've been so preoccupied with it being almost Halloween, and all the not so lovely reminders that come with it, that I can't remember the last time I ran a comb through it. It's longer than she's used to me keeping it. Darker too. Still blonde, but the shade has morphed into a deeper, more earthy hue. Once she gets a look at how the years have made me, the perfect archetype of the nightmares she writes about, she'll feel even more regret than I know she already does, buried deep in that soulless body of hers.

I break the seal of the envelope, slipping the thick folded stationery out.

Her cursive fills my vision. Overdone and almost illegible. I dive into it, ready for whatever sorry excuse she has for running away from me for this long.

Harlan,

I've been thinking about you lately. Actually, that's a lie. I haven't been able to stop thinking about you since that night, but I've been too afraid to see you again. Afraid of what would happen if you and I saw each other and what it would mean, since the details of that night were fuzzy at best. But I know that you felt it too. That connection we share. The one that your dad used to punish you for, before I became his new favorite punching bag. I took a lot of his hatred for the both of us. I know it doesn't make up for what I did when I left, but the hell I went through living in that house should count for something. Or at the very least, make you hate me a little less. Either way, with Halloween being around the corner it brings me back to that night. It makes me miss you. Whether you believe it or not, I do miss you and I'd love to see you again. I know you're probably still mad at me, but if you find it in your heart to see me again, you know where to find me.

Yours,
Araceli

I crumple the note and toss it on the passenger side floor. Well, she got two things right. I do know where to find her. The house that she inherited from her paternal grandparents that took her in when my dad kicked her out. The second being the 'yours' part. She's right. She's *mine*. Always has been and always will be.

I head out of her car, careful not to slam the door. I want my presence tonight to be a surprise. Slipping my black hood onto my head, I use the dark night air as my cover as I move from the driveway to the porch.

A creak betrays the silence I'm trying to maintain beneath my boot, and another follows the next step I take. I pause for a moment, trying to hear any noise on the other side of the sheetrock to see if she heard me.

Nothing but the faint trickle of running water meets my ears. Coming from the other side of the porch that I'm standing on.

Memories of the last time I saw her in the bathtub, before the night at the haunt, fill my mind.

Fuck it.

She wanted me here. She said it herself in her note. Granted, she didn't know that I was planning on paying her a visit since it's been long enough before I opened her letter, but this is what she wanted, so I might as well give it to her.

Embracing the symphony of creaks and groans that sound with each step, I continue until I'm standing in front of the open window. A flutter erupts in my chest seeing her.

Fuck.

It's been so long.

Too fucking long.

Thirteen long and agonizing years.

Yet all that time has done—aside from tormenting me with conflicted feelings of longing and disdain for the very person who gave me freedom and gifted me hell simultaneously—is make her more picturesque than she already was.

The scene before me is like watching a goddamn Staind song unfold. Candles line the floor around the bathtub. Their dim light offers an ominous glow to a very naked and very unconscious Araceli.

How many pills did you take this time, sister?

Clearly not enough, because even with the minimal light I can detect breathing. Shallow and staggered, but it's there and relief only finds me because I know that's not what she wants, and what I want is the opposite of her desires.

I want her to suffer for how she left me. If she wants to end it on her own, I hope each time she comes up empty-handed. Her time will come, not when God says so, but when *I* say so.

As I crouch down to get a grip on the window so I can go inside, something strange dawns on me.

The water... there is none.

I heard water running, yet there isn't any.

Slipping through the window, I navigate around the candles. My vision, glued to the floor, to make sure I don't knock one over by accident.

The closer I move to the tub, large muddy footprints mar the tile floor. As I drag my gaze to Araceli's bare body, the mud continues its trail onto her skin. Painting her like a canvas. Muddying her curves and making her look filthy... *desirable*.

That desire quickly morphs into intrigue when I close the gap between me and the tub where she lay.

Despite her consciousness hanging by a thread, her hand remains firm on something as equally filthy as her. Something that she shouldn't have access to. Not anymore. Dad made sure of that with the additional security measure he's taken to keep the property free of her grubby hands... or so he thought.

"Would you look at that?" The rasp of my own voice breaks the silence, my hands reaching for hers. The undeniable spark our fingertips make brushing against each other is hard to ignore, but I need to see what she's doing with that notebook—*her* notebook —the one my dad made a point of burying on our property. Same property I now live on, and the one I thought she'd never return to, but it looks like I was wrong.

Which angers me more because that means she came home and didn't have the fucking decency to go see me. Nothing. All she wanted was that creepy book. As if this thing holds the key to what she needs in life.

I take it from her hand and a shiver runs down my spine as I touch it. The image from years ago, of the bloodshed, the absolute mayhem, back at the forefront of my mind. When I flip the page it isn't there, well, a picture is there, but it's no longer the horrific scene that I remember. It's calm. Serene even. A depiction of a man holding his hand out, placing a coin in a woman's mouth. Suddenly, the beauty that Araceli spoke of that day in the bathroom at home rings true. It's not the horrid scene I remember it being. This is beautiful, but what isn't beautiful are the words written next to it.

I lower myself beside the bathtub and rest on my knees. Licking my lips, I ready myself to read out loud.

"... with features defined by scars and dried up blood. A horror to others but a savior to me."

Anger seeps into my veins, clouding my head with delusional fantasies that I want nothing more than to fulfill.

I lift my head from her notebook, her bare breasts tempting me. I reach a hand out, squeezing one into my grip. Her erect nipple now caught beneath my thumb. Becoming one with the dirt and grime that covers her skin, my fingers trail her sternum, taking their sweet time until they graze the mound above her pussy.

Her legs are already bent at the knee, spread wide and waiting for me.

It'd be so easy to slip one, maybe two... or possibly three fingers in. Too easy.

She'd like that. Having my fingers in her while she's off in druggie dreamland.

She'd love waking up with a satisfied yet aching cunt, courtesy of her big brother that she's too good for.

Fuck that.

I leave my hand hovering on her slit and reach over to the pen on the floor, scribbling down a message for her below this piss-poor story she's writing. By hand too. Who does that anymore?

"You can run from the truth, but you can't run from me."

Leaving the book open, I carefully place it on her pussy and remove my hand, which is now slick with her wetness.

She stirs at the impact, a faint hum leaks from her lips. The blonde side of her hair shifts ever so slightly, falling from overtop her breast, revealing her precious pentagram necklace with a new addition to it.

Sitting alongside the pendant that belongs to her is one that belongs to *me*.

You bitch, taking things that don't belong to you.

My fingers act before I can think or stop it. Yanking at the necklace, breaking the chain. It falls off her neck and into my possession as I rise to my feet.

Now hovering over her, I slip the necklace carrying our pendants in my pocket. An inescapable grin smears on my face thinking of how pissed she'll be when she wakes up realizing they're missing.

I bend at the waist, pressing a kiss to the crown of her head.

Fuck.

Cinnamon and pumpkins... that signature scent again, although this time it's mixed with an overpowering stench of desperation.

I lower my mouth to her ear, knowing that her subconscious will do the legwork. Recalling everything I'm about to say to her and relay the message when she comes to. Taunting her with my presence. Reminding her how close she was to having me—and my cock—but also how I just left her here tonight with scraps of me.

"Stop running from me. Come home to me. I've been lonely waiting for you. I promise I won't bite."

But I can't promise it won't hurt when you see me again.

Twelve

Araceli

The next day...

"STAY STILL, YOU FUCKING BITCH!" The harsh cement floor digs into my knees, scratching at my flattened palms as I flatten my back. Remaining still like a fucking dog or in this case a human ash tray. "Just like that."

Despite wanting to spring up and stab the motherfucker with the knife I brought with me, I flatten my back and hold still. Not out of respect or fear, but out of convenience. If I obey by playing along one last time, he'll be convinced that it's because I've finally conceded. He'll never see what I have planned for him the second my opportunity strikes.

Smoke coils around me, notes of tobacco and menthol drench the air. The smell turns my stomach, but it's the motivator I need. The reminder of why I'm here and what I need and will do this time.

"You burn like a sinner," the delusional man observes, digging the tip of his cigarette into the nape of my neck.

A shiver runs down my spine. It hurts, but not as much as the knife I tucked in my boot. It's in there loosely so I can gain easy access to it when needed, but its positioning by my Achilles and is close to slicing it if I don't hurry the fuck up.

"*You hear me, pecadora?*"

Sinner.

I mumble a half-assed 'yes' but the questions continue. I tune them out. My focus glued to the sliver of steel beckoning me to grab the handle and end this.

"*I wonder if I can fuck the sinner out of you?*"

The 'again' part is left out. It always is. Delusional fuck. Every time I'm down here, it's under the guise of it being the first time. Every time it's the same. The same torture, the same pain, always the fucking same. What won't be the same this time is what I do next.

"*Stand up!*"

My heart rate elevates, driving my pulse to my ears. I ignore the command. Adrenaline taking over every cell as I rehearse the scene in my head of what I'm about to do.

"*You're going to pay for the lies you've spread, you whore. You're going to pay for what you've done.*" Another set of hollow words do little to affect me. I wait until the belt buckle jingles and it's tossed on the floor for me to make my move. Time slows as I spring up, retrieving the knife.

"Fuck you," I spew, charging the monster dressed in human flesh. With a clenched fist and my eye on the prize, I break the barrier of skin concealing his vital artery. Blood spills down his neck, slowly. Too slow for my liking. I need more. I need him to suffer more. I tear the blade from inside him and stab again...and again...and again. With every strike, I scream 'fuck you' louder and angrier. Reveling in the blood splatter painting my skin, the floor, and most importantly—him. To my surprise, he doesn't put up a fight. Then again, when the first place you've stabbed is the carotid, the brain connection starts to get a bit fuzzy.

He falls to the floor. A loud, messy pool of pierced flesh and crimson.

Breathless, I try to collect myself. My work isn't done yet, it's just beginning. Staring at the bloodbath before me, I try figuring out what will be the easiest way to gather the blood to fill the tub *upstairs. A large bucket catches my attention, as does the broom in the corner of the basement. I gather both because it's time to collect. El Barquero should be here any minute, and if I don't hurry, I'll miss my opportunity to join him.*

Using a mop, I maneuver the blood of the sacrifice into the bucket, filling it up to the brim, and then walking the overflowing bucket to the bathroom to pour into the tub. Time passes, unaware of how long this process takes, but with each step closer, I hear a voice in my head, trying to throw me off guard.

"It's not too late, hija, you can change your mind." The voice now morphs into my mother's, taunting me as I drag the overflowing bucket to the bathroom.

"No, I can't." I won't.

Adrenaline continues to fuel me, but only until I make it upstairs to the bathroom. I feel the crash coming. I need to push through only a few moments more. Dropping the bucket, I use both hands to open the door. The hinges fight me tooth and nail, but my stubbornness prevails, determined to win. To finish what I came here for.

Finally, the door opens and I retrieve the bucket, dragging it on the tiled floor, and placing it beside the porcelain of the already full clawfoot tub centered in the bathroom. I lean forward, my reflection in the still water both comforting and horrifying. I swallow a lump of saliva in my dry throat, the equivalent of a dozen knives stabbing me as I take off my clothes.

Using all the strength I'm clinging to with everything I have left, I bend at the knees, cupping the overflowing bucket of blood in my grip. Slowly, I ascend from my bent position and dump the blood into the water.

It slaps against the water's edge. First a faint shade of pink before it spirals and spreads in a slow, concentrated dance, morphing into an opaque hue of crimson. It's then and only then, when the water no longer looks like water but a bath full of blood, that I enter it. The voice from before returns. This time joined by others, all chanting a verse I've heard many times before.

"For the life of a creature is in the blood, and I have given it to you to make atonement for yourselves on the altar; it is the blood that makes atonement for one's life."

"Shut the fuck up!" The tip of my nose brushes against the murky water. My eyes move to the reflection of the open window in the mirror on the wall in front of me. A sadistic cackle erupts, leaking through it, traveling to my core.

"There you are," he announces, cryptic and amused.

El Barquero.

I inch upward. Just enough that my nose is lifted and my mouth is able to speak without taking in the water.

"Here I am," I mumble to the rotting God outside the half-open window of the bathroom. His face is riddled in decay and dirt, with features defined by scars and dried up blood. A horror to others but a savior to me. "As promised, I brought you a gift. Come in, the water is just how you like it... bloody."

He accepts the invitation, curling his filthy fingers at the window's edge, lifting it. Slithering his way from the window, he moves with the agility of a serpent, until he stops by the tub hovering over it.

"Are you sure?" his low and rough baritone asks.

I nod.

His rough hand tips my chin as he studies my face.

"Once fed, there's no escaping el Barquero," he warns.

I nod again. This time with the vibrant addition of a smile, remembering the steel knife I hid in the tub.

Keeping my eyes on him, I discreetly curl my fingers as his tongue nears mine. As the token of my commitment to the sacrifice is transferred from my mouth to his, I use the sadistic communion as my opportunity to secure the knife's handle in my palm and drive it into his throat.

Blood streams from the wound, the look of betrayal ripe within his irises as he slumps over me and into the tub.

"You're wrong," I spit on his slumped body. "Tell el Barquero there's no escaping me."

"That was amazing!" Applause fills my ear. My agent, Beth, on the other line claps away, but her rehearsed excitement does little to distract from the hesitation that permeates from her breath.

A long-winded sigh escapes my mouth, knowing she has more to say.

"Go on. What's wrong with it?"

"Well, it's just so, so, I don't know," Beth hesitates.

I rise to my feet and the wheeled chair I was just sitting on rolls all the way behind me, hitting the bookshelf behind my desk. "Beth," I say sternly. "Spit it the fuck out."

A phony scoff of surprise muffles the earpiece with her overdone surprised act. She should be used to me by now. She's been around long enough to know that I don't mince words, agent or otherwise. Considering the shit sleep I got last night, what I said to her versus what I could've said to her, is on the tame side. I used to love this time of year, but the dreams—or rather nightmares—that I have every goddamn year become too much. The one I had last night was the most vivid one that I've had in a long time, or ever.

"I loved it, Char." I wince at the nickname. An abbreviation of my pen name, A.H. Charon, and the only name she knows me by. Her voice trails. "But..."

My eyes roll. There's always a 'but'. Hesitation injects itself into the air before she starts yelling at someone, honking her horn.

"Sorry, I'm back. I swear to fuck people can't drive here."

I laugh. "It's Halloween in New York. What do you expect today of all days? Plus, they're always rushing."

"True, but this is the burbs, not the city."

My brow furrows. Beth is a city girl through and through. She rarely ever leaves the comfort of the concrete jungle.

"What the fuck are you doing in the burbs?"

"My mom has been sick and hasn't been able to take care of my dad. You know how he's been since the accident. She needs my help. Trust me, I'm not thrilled about it either." Her throat clears as she redirects the conversation. "Anyway, listen, Char. I love the intensity, but this is the last book in the Ferryman series. Your readers want, and quite frankly, deserve, a neater ending."

I pace my home office. "First of all, it's horror. Since when does a horror ending need to be neat or wrapped up in a pretty bow? Horror should creep into the reader's mind. It should linger and fester and make the person think. I'm not going to spell it out for them. I still have the—"

She cuts me off. "Let me guess. An epilogue, because God forbid, you write anything without an epilogue." The annoyance in her tone is rubbing me the wrong way. What the fuck does it matter if I *always* have to write an epilogue? It's my style, and they're arguably my favorite thing to write since it signifies the end. Everyone deserves a good ending, the same applies to books.

"Well, yes, I have an epilogue. Maybe even two for this one." I stick it back to her.

"Just hurry up. The publisher wants me to give it to them next week. I don't know what you're waiting for. All of your other stories you've handed in before the deadline."

I interrupt her.

"Calm your tits. Have I ever missed a deadline?"

A scoff disguised as a giggle sounds from her.

"Have I?"

Now a sigh sounds, probably because she realizes I'm right. "Well. No."

"Exactly."

"Fine," she concedes. "Just make sure it's done on time."

Walking out of my office and to the bedroom, I go to grab my notebook, since I wrote the rest of the chapter by hand before bed. "Will do. Besides, whoever said I wasn't done? You know what they say when you assume. You make an ass out of you and—"

"Me," she finishes my sentence. "Yes, I know."

"I just stopped reading from my computer. I wrote the rest by hand."

Now Beth scoffs. "By hand? Jesus—" she interrupts herself. "I meant to say, who does that anymore?"

Me, that's fucking who.

"By the way, do we have a title yet for this story?"

I round the corner to my bedroom about to walk down the hall. The bathroom on the main level, the one that I never use because the water pressure sucks, grabs my attention. Stopping me in my tracks, and a gasp that bellows from my mouth feels like an out-of-body experience.

"Char," Beth says my name and a bunch of other things that I can't focus on.

My notebook is on the floor. Not on my nightstand where I know I left it.

Carefully, I navigate the bathroom. Shattered glass and lumps of hardened wax line the tile by the tub.

"Char," Beth repeats my name. "Are you okay?"

No.

No. I'm not fucking okay.

I'm the opposite of okay.

I'm in shock.

As I bend to retrieve my notebook. I see the part of the story I started in bed, not in the bathroom, above handwriting that does not belong to me.

"You can run from the truth, but you can't run from me."

My blood turns cold.

No. He couldn't have been here.

I look to the window, the only glass that isn't shattered in the entire bathroom.

If he were here last night, that means that my dream wasn't a dream... and that the pills are losing their magic. They aren't helping me like they used to.

But why now?

What the fuck does he want from me?

Why can't he let what happened go?

I have.

Why. Can't. He?

Still trying to process this, I reach for my necklace, but as my fingertips graze my neck, all I feel is fire. Ripples of flames dancing like they did the night of the haunt. Thirteen years ago. On Halloween. I close my eyes, taking a deep breath in, but my feelings have now escalated to a vision of Harlan on his knees. Licking me. Fucking consuming me. His tongue so deep inside of me that he was practically choking.

My pussy pulses at the memory.

No.

I can't do this.

I reach for my chain, needing to feel the pentagram in my grip, but my palm is empty. My lids jolt open, I peer down, and there's no pendant... no necklace to be found.

You motherfucker.

He not only broke in, he ruined my bathroom and took the only thing I have left of my mother.

Finally entering the conversation, I interrupt Beth's spiral.

"I need to go. I'll be in touch, okay? I need to go home."

She hesitates, confused. "Home? I thought you were home."

No, and that's the fucking problem.

"Are you...?" Beth begins, but I hang up the phone and go to grab my car keys from the kitchen.

As I reach for them on the countertop, I see an aged newspaper article next to the bowl I keep my keys in. My stomach drops the closer I inch towards it. Its headline glaring at me.

"Local haunt closed after multiple reports of... "

I stop reading, taking the article and crumpling it though as I do, something sticky and red steals my attention on the backside. Slowly, I turn it over and flatten the scrunched paper.

Another message. This one undeniably Harlan's doing. Clearly, he took the olive branch I tried to extend to him and saw it as a sign to mess with me. Something my church boy would never do, but I suppose, as much as it pains me to admit, his dad got one thing right in his Devil's Night service all those years ago.

"All it takes is one moment of temptation. Just one taste of what the enemy has to offer and even the best of men can be transformed into the evil incarnate."

I was the enemy. The taste Harlan needed to take all that was good in him and throw it all away. Not to be like me... to be worse.

I throw the newspaper article in a ball to the ground, becoming incensed all over again. This is not what I had in mind when I wrote him that letter. I reached out to put an end to the divide that has grown with each passing year. I don't understand why he's still so angry. Did he seriously think that because we shared a moment, a fucking hot one at that, that I would be his forever?

That night at Heathen's Cross, the drugs, all of it, was just a temporary escape. I didn't literally mean that I would escape with him like he wanted forever. At least for me, the one silver lining is that his dad offered me a way out, to go live with my grandparents, and now that they've passed this house I've built my life in alone, is mine.

I don't need him.

I don't want him.

What I do want is my necklace, and to get back home to finish my deadline, so I can finally do what I haven't been able to do for so fucking long. Rest.

With my book clutched against my chest, I storm out of my house, locking the door behind me. Turning, I walk down the steps and past the rows of pumpkins that line the footpath in front of my house. All of them have different—yet equally fucked up—faces carved into them, reflecting my mood this time of year.

As my feet reach the last pumpkin, a gust of wind crashes into me, knocking the book out of my hands and into the dirt. The breeze quickly picks up, displacing my hair. Though only the side of my part that has the bleach blonde moves, whipping me in the eye causing it to water. I tuck my hair behind my ear and snatch the notebook up. Fallen leaves and twigs drag around me as the wind continues its relentless howl, making it clear a storm is near. I love storms, but right now this feels more like a sinister omen, than it does just another October night storm.

As I head towards my car, I brace myself, readying my nerves to go back to the hell I used to call *'home'*. Hunger strikes at my core, processing the anger I feel right now for Harlan. Though above all, the sense of fear he has elicited from me feels the most striking, because the thought of seeing Harlan, after all these years, feels somehow scarier than any of the horrors I've written or the ones I've endured. Most of which are loosely based on moments in my life I've had no one to tell but the paper or screen in front of me. Harlan and me, we're a tragedy with no end in sight. The kind of horror that lingers before it festers and rots.... before it kills.

Thirteen

Araceli

I slow the car to a stop. My foot hovers on the pedal and the exhaust hacks away as I take in the tall iron gates in front of my windshield, dumbfounded by its presence. "Well, this is new," I grumble to myself... and definitely wasn't here the last time. Throwing the car in park, I sit and try to figure out my options since I can't plow through it how I'd like without risking an injury to myself or this already shitty car. I reach in the glove box, grabbing my pocket knife and two strips of Listerine from the pack I keep in there. I was so frazzled leaving my house this morning after the mess I was left with, I forgot to brush my teeth. Not like bad breath would be the worst of my problems, considering that once I get past this obstacle, I'll be faced with another, much angrier one. *Harlan.*

The car door slams as I leave it behind me, exchanging it for the unpaved driveway. It's a stark contrast to the intricacy of the gate where ornate slats of wrought iron tower over me. Every detail is grand and obnoxious and nothing that would be expected to be on a pastor's property.

My hands wrap around one of the iron rods, shaking it, but of course it doesn't budge. I look at either side of the locked gate, trying to see if there's magically another way around it or in. It's useless. Bricks stacked higher than the expansive gate span as far as my eye can see, wrapping around the property in a protective hug, separating me from it.

"Fuck!" I yell, stomping my boot on the ground. Gravel kicks up as a dust cloud forms. Every loose particle clinging onto my black clothing.

Maybe this is the sign I've needed to put the hell of living as a Rainey on this hellish property to rest. A warning from the universe, giving me one last opportunity to just get in my car and drive away for good. To forget about what happened last night and forget getting my necklace back. Even though Frida always told me to keep my pentagram on me for protection, and considering how far it seems Harlan has plummeted, he'll likely taunt me and I can use all the protection I can get.

Who knows, maybe seeing each other—that is, when we're both aware of it—will give us the closure we need, and we can both move on in peace. Or, at the very least, one of us can move under the other, finish what I tried to start in the hospital bed before his dad ruined that for us, too.

A flush of heat spreads to my cheeks from that image of me straddling Harlan while he slept that day. I should feel guilty, but I don't. That's the problem. I don't feel anything anymore. I'm incapable. I'm just so...

"Can I help you?" a voice calls out, disrupting my internal battle. I turn my attention to the uniformed security guard running towards me from a small shed. I somehow missed it being off to the side and in front of the closed gates.

I look at him, studying his plain features, trying to determine if I've seen him before. Given that the gate is new since I've been here last, let alone having the property guarded, I think it's safe to say that he's just another addition since I've left... with the intention of keeping me out.

Inching closer, I try to think on the fly, since I know for a fact that I'm banned from the property. It's only a matter of time before he pieces that together.

"Sorry, I'm a friend of—"

"Holy shit," he interrupts me. "You're..." He pauses, looking me over, up and down. A combination of uncertainty and intrigue consume his brown stare.

Panic strikes. In the years that I've spent living away from the Rainey property, I've changed in appearance. My hair, no longer solid black, but split down the middle. One side is my natural black and the other, a shade of pale blonde that teeters on white. Some Botox has helped define my features more, as well. I look different, sure, but not unrecognizable. All it'd take is him pulling up a picture of me from a couple years ago and he'd connect the dots real fast.

"Trying to see Mr. Rainey." I finish his sentence for him, hoping it will be enough to disrupt whatever thought process he's been stewing.

"Hold up." Excitement claws at his tone. Taking his eyes off me, the gun and taser holstered to his belt beckon my attention. Fuck, my puny pocketknife is no match for either of those.

I try to maintain an even keeled demeanor, but it's slipping the more I watch in horror as he mulls over what to grab from his belt.

My lips part, words about to spew from my mouth like vomit, because I have no idea what I'm about to say. I just know I need to say something.

"Shit, it's not here. Give me a second. I gotta go get it."

I latch onto the calm that seems to have washed over him as he jogs back to the security shed. Not sure what he's getting, but hoping—as naive as it may seem—that it's not a weapon since he already has an exhaustive arsenal of them attached to his person. I stand and wait.

A few moments later, he runs over, out of breath, with a book in his hands.

Fuck, I would've preferred a grenade thrown at my feet over this, but here we are.

Excitement clicks his tongue. "I knew you looked familiar. You're A.H. Charon."

Extra fuck.

A reader.

Of course, this would be my luck.

His accuracy sends a surge of annoyance down my spine, especially now that he's flipped to the back of the book. He's pointing his finger at the picture I told Beth to make sure was *not* included in my author bio.

"You got me." I force a smile and a shrug. It's meant to be playful, but if it's coming off to him like it feels to me—stiff and irritated—then I've failed.

He flips to the front of the book, now pointing at the title page, *Masks We Keep*. "Can I get your signature? I fucking love your Ferryman series."

"Thank you." I say plainly, appreciating the support even though this couldn't be at a worse time. "But I'm afraid I don't have a pen with me."

Disgust riddles his face unexpectedly. "What kind of author travels without a pen?"

The kind who would rather travel with a pocketknife than a pen, apparently.

I touch my pockets again, giving off the illusion that I'm double checking. I shrug, "Sorry."

"Well, that's disappointing." He places the book into his jacket pocket. "So, what can I do for you?" The shift in his demeanor is undeniable. No longer an eager reader and right back to what I expected when I saw him emerge from his post, a stoic guard.

"Like I said, I'm here to see Pastor Rainey," I lie. I'm definitely not in the mood to see my stepdad. Never again, but since Harlan hasn't spread his wings past this hellhole, I have no choice but to see the two of them to get my necklace back.

Once again, he eyes me up and down. Probably wondering if I'm here for an exorcism with the way I'm dressed. Not that anyone would think twice about the thigh high Petrine cross socks I'm wearing over my all-black bodysuit and full body harness, given that it's Halloween. Except this isn't my costume. This is how I dress daily, whether or not I have to see good ol' Pastor Rainey.

His gaze lingers on my harness and his eyes squint at the portion where I slid my knife in. Thankfully, the all-black ensemble and pocketknife make it difficult for him to see what's what.

"Ummm," is all he can manage, sounding nervous. He looks back to the security shed he emerged from. A poster with red writing and picture beneath it well within view.

Shit. I didn't want it to come to this, but if I need to work my charm to get my way, so fucking be it.

I soften my tone, waltzing over to him with an exaggerated sway of my hips. But he takes a step back and then another, forcing me to morph from a seductive stride to a leaping stomp.

"Lady, you're coming too close." His hand nears his duty belt again.

"And you're in my way," I mutter, but he doesn't hear me. The static on his radio piercing the air. A muffled voice sounds from the other side, but the connection is poor, making it impossible to decipher who is talking or what is being said.

His boots scuff against the gravel as he continues backing away from me. "I'm going to need you to get back in your car." He retrieves the baton from his side. "No one is supposed to be here tonight."

Figures, now Daddy decides to no longer hold Holy Harvest. Where was that consideration when I lived here?

Slamming his hand down, the steel of the baton extends, but all I can focus on is the tattoo on his wrist. A cross with a crushed snake beneath it. Just like I remember from that night at Heathen's Cross on the patches. No wait, on the blotter sheet. My forehead scrunches in confusion. I can't remember now. Everything about that night feels so fuzzy. I just know I've seen it before. Continuing to stare, I swear I can see the ink slither on his hand. My mind is clearly playing tricks on me.

Ignoring the weapon in his hand—knowing it's out as a scare tactic, and that he's too pussy to use it—I slide the cuff of his jacket up to get a better look at his ink. I shake my head, trying to rid myself of the illusion. Sure enough, the tattooed snake stops moving but the voices start up again.

"Let him sail. Blood for blood. Eye for an..."

I groan in desperation for it to stop. The guard's eyes watching me in understandable fear. He flinches from my touch, but I grip him tighter, wanting to look away but unable to.

"Get off me or I will..."

I squeeze tighter. "Oh, please. If you were going to use that, you would have already," I interrupt him. "What made you get this?"

"I don't know. I just liked it." He pries himself from my grip with success.

"Sorry," I try to compose myself, but it's difficult. The last time I saw that symbol was at Heathen's Cross. Suddenly, all the memories that I'm still trying to piece together from that night flood me. Each one is as confusing as it was that night.

Especially the blood. There was so much blood. Buckets of it and it didn't end when we left. It followed us to the hospital, and every so often it still finds me when I close my eyes.

"Whatever." He turns down the volume on his radio. A man's voice is on the other side. A familiar voice that has captured my attention, making everything he's muttering irrelevant to my attention. With a snap of a finger, he summons my attention back to him, but barely. "Listen, it was cool and fucking unexpected to see you of all people here at this shithole, but I'm afraid I'm going to have to tell you to get back in your car and head home. The boss doesn't like anyone snooping around here. Especially on Halloween night."

I roll my eyes. "Of course he doesn't. God! Fucking forbid something threatens his fortress of lies."

Fucking holy prick.

The guard says nothing to me as a mystified face warps his features.

I need to get to the other side of this gate. I need to see him. To end this drawn-out game between us.

Desperation infects my ability to think straight. "You don't understand. This is my home," I blurt, regretting every fucking syllable.

"Your home?" The confusion in his voice is quickly overshadowed by him piecing together the puzzle I so foolishly helped him with.

He takes another step back, looking more scared than anything. "Holy shit. I know I smoked before my shift, but how could I be so stupid? It's *you*." The baton falls to the ground as he nervously fumbles around his belt, trying to grab his gun, but I lunge towards him, beating him to it. "You're Pastor Rainey's daughter," he stutters, making my blood boil at the realization and having to be reminded that at one time I was, in fact, his stepdaughter. But I lost that title the second I lost connection to this place and to him.

The pistol grip of his Glock practically magnetizes to my hand. I lift my hand, driving his gun down on his face, hitting him with the side of the barrel. He winces in pain, but not enough for my liking, so I wind up once again and slam down on his face harder. A shrill cry of pain leaks from his mouth this time. *Much better.*

Keeping the edge of the barrel at his bloody temple, I bring myself to his ear. "Stepdaughter," I correct him.

"Don't shoot me," he pleads.

"Of course not," I giggle, digging the tip further into his temple. I reach over, grabbing his knife from the leather holder on his belt. "That'd be too loud, and we don't want to draw any unwanted attention."

Confusion mars his face, but it's quickly replaced by stunned agony as the tip of his own blade glides across his throat with the ease of a bow on a finely tuned violin.

Spit gurgles and bubbles in his mouth as blood leaks from the open wound.

"Shh." Annoyed with his noises, I guide his mouth shut with the bloodied tip of the knife, unintentionally nicking his lips. Oops.

Stepping back, not wanting to get any of his mess on me, he falls face down in a violent thud on the ground.

"Sorry, it was nothing personal. It's just important that I get to the other side." I nudge my head to the gate.

I'm about to get up to go to the control panel to press the button, but my book pokes out and the guilt trickles in. I kneel beside him, taking my book out from where it's tucked in his jacket. Opening it to the title page, I dip my finger into his slit neck, just enough to get some of his blood on it so I can sign my name. "I know you would've preferred a pen," I say to his lifeless body, "but I would've preferred you let me in the first time I asked. Well, now you have one of a kind. I don't think anyone can say they've had one of my books signed in their own blood before." I slam the book shut, tucking it back into his jacket. "Lucky you."

But I'm not lucky. Before I open the gate, I have to figure out what the fuck to do with him. I look over at the security shed he was in. That would be easy if it wasn't the first thing people who drive by will see, so of course that won't work. I preemptively roll my eyes, knowing that the only feasible option is my trunk. So much for not getting dirty.

Holstering my grip on both his wrists, I drag his body over to the trunk. I open it and it's not a pretty sight. In fact, it's damn near laughable as I bend and maneuver his body into the trunk, but I succeed.

Slamming the trunk closed, the next order of business is opening the gate. I walk over to the control panel in the security booth. My finger hovers the button, not able to press down on it just yet; already knowing what's on the other side won't be pretty.

You've come this far. Press the fucking button, Araceli.

My lids pinch closed, bracing myself for when my finger crashes down on the button. I work up the courage to do so and on cue, the gates crank open. Though the more their iron separates, the more anxious I feel, but I've gotten this far. Hell, I just killed someone, and a fan no less, to make it to the other side of this hellhole I used to call home. I can't turn back now. Not if I want to write my perfect ending and get my necklace back... even if it will likely result in blood.

Before I leave the security booth, I flip the lock on the door before closing it so no one can get in. Knowing my stepdad, he has surveillance on the property and the last thing I need is a nosy wanderer stumbling across the empty booth, scrounging around, and discovering the footage.

I take a deep inhale, readying myself for what lays ahead as I drive through the open gates. As soon as I break the threshold, I look in the rearview mirror at the gates closing me in. I drive down the long stretch of gravel before heading to the main part of the property. A fork in the road presents itself with the graveyard in the middle. If I go left, I will pass the church—which has a path that leads straight to the house—but if I go right, I'd have to pass through a stretch of the graveyard.

I opt to go right down the wider, more scenic path, through the tombstones that line the unkempt grass. The uneven terrain doing a number on my tires, the guard's body bumping in the trunk. Every thud and thump grates at my nerves more than the last, forcing me to slam on my brakes to make it stop.

Fuck this. I chose this way so I could avoid the nausea seeing the church gives me, but this is becoming too much. I get out of the car, walking around to the trunk, making sure it's locked.

"I'll be back for you later." I pat the trunk before walking through the remainder of tombstones that lead the way to the house.

Weeds gnaw at my legs with each step as the sharp, overgrown grass blades prick at my skin through my pants. Last I heard, my stepdad wasn't doing too well, but he's always maintained the grounds himself, or had people to do it for him, so this is unexpected. But not as unexpected as the view of the front porch that has me stopping dead in my tracks.

Rows of carved pumpkins consume my vision. Jagged lines compromise hollowed out holes for eyes and an equally jagged and sinister line forms a smile on each, highlighted by a flickering candle inside. All misshapen, yet beautiful in their own way. I move closer, in awe since I've never seen the house like this... *ever*. Especially since the exterior of the house looks about as cared for as the property. Which is not at all.

Distracted by the scene before me, I brace myself for what will happen the moment I walk up those steps and knock on that door. The beauty before me will vanish and reality will set in. No amount of pumpkins on a fucking porch can, or will, erase that.

A few deep breaths in and out are what I need to give myself the nudge to head to the door. The porch steps still creak, same as they used to, but the music that vibrates beneath my feet, that flows loudly from inside to where I'm standing outside, isn't what I expected. Harsh drums and even harsher lyrics leak through the barrier of siding, and it doesn't sound anything like the usual hymns my stepdad was accustomed to poisoning our ears with growing up.

Intrigued still, I lift my hand to the doorbell, wondering if the chime will be heard over the music. Though, before I can ring the bell, the door swings open. The music now clear, Bone Church by Slipknot slaps me in the face with its blaring sound.

"Is that fake?" a rough, masculine voice asks but I can't make eye contact with him. Instead, my gaze lowers to the blood saturating the dark fabric of my bodysuit.

Thinking quickly on my feet, I fake a cool smile. My lids close for a second as my words lead the way. "Yes, it's fake blood." I scoff. *I lie.* "It's Halloween, Ha..." A breath hitches in my throat as I open my eyes, not prepared for the blue irises boring into mine. Not prepared for any of what stares back at me. Time has changed him into someone I don't recognize. Long gone is the lean, tall, blonde teen I knew Harlan to be, and in his place is a tall, muscular, tattooed man. With his dirty blonde hair that's now long enough to be slicked back, but not too long that it hides the gauges in his ears or the spiked barbells that line each cartilage.

"Harlan." I finish my sentence, as striking lines of black and gray drawn to look like a skeleton hand capture my attention as he lifts his inked hand to the doorway. Securing one hand in place, he takes the other to my body. Without asking, he brushes his fingers on my torso, swirling the blood I told him is fake onto his digits, without faltering his gaze away from mine. Goosebumps line my spine as the hairs raise on my arm from his touch. I can't read his expression. It teeters somewhere between blank and amused. After another pass of his fingers, he finally retracts them from me, and I inhale. Rubbing his index and middle fingers against his thumb, he breaks eye contact, studying the crimson that coats his fingertips.

"Right," he says, unconvinced. His eyes flick back to mine.

Fuck, this isn't good. "What... are you going to tell on me, church boy?" I make a jab at him by calling him the nickname he hated so much, but that's what I do when I'm trying to deflect, whether it be emotions, blame, or the *truth*.

To my surprise, he ignores the jab instead by taking his hand coated in the guard's blood to his blonde locks. He runs his inked hand through the loose strands and his bent elbow shows off another tattoo. It's hard to make out completely from this angle, but it looks like an oar with a flower surrounding it.

Time has been kind to him. It's done wonders, actually. He looks so different from when I saw him last. Not only has he grown more muscular, which compliments the ink now drawn on his skin, but he's kept with the style I had him wear that night. Covered head to toe in darkness, which suits him more than light ever could. Though, as much as my eyes like how the man staring back at me looks, I can't help but feel jealous. How nice it must be for him to have also been involved in whatever ritual we stumbled into that night, and took drugs just like I did, yet he got to remain here. While I got kicked out. Banned from the property with nothing but the clothes on my back. If anything, he was able to come back here *renewed*. A true version of who, and what, he was destined to be, and his father clearly hasn't put up a fuss about it. Meanwhile, the blame, as it always does, falls on me.

Must be nice being an archetype for hypocrisy. That's a privilege I never had.

He shoots a smug look my way, forcing my gaze to his ocean blue eyes and not gawking over his ink. "Well, are you planning on coming in, or did you go through all that trouble just to stand and stare at me all night?"

My stomach drops. I can't tell if he knows what I did to the security guard, or if he's just trying to rattle me for all I've done to him that I know he'll never forgive me for.

"That depends."

His brows arch, waiting for me to continue.

"Do you promise to give back what you took from me?"

Harlan inches backward. His inked hand motioning for me to come in. The smug expression on his face lingers, now amplified by the moonlight casting a luminous beam on his irises.

"Well," I drag my tone. "Do you?"

He scoffs at my question.

"Pretty, little, thickheaded sister. I know your whore ass did not come all this way to discuss a fucking necklace."

Indignance motivates my next move. My boot stomps on the porch and my arms cross in front of me.

He laughs, and I hate that the natural rasp of his voice makes his condescension sound more alluring than it should be.

He stifles a sigh, now grinning ear to ear. "Goddamn, your tits look great when you get all huffy like that." He's mocking me. Crossing his arms like mine, except jokes on him, because he is right. My tits look great when they're forced to jut forward with the pressure my crossed arms put on them.

"It's not just a necklace, Harlan," I correct, disgust holding my voice hostage when forced to say his name.

"You're right, it's not," he snaps, cold and brutal, like he has become. "Now you have two options. You can either strut that plump ass back to that piece of shit car you drove here in. Nice, and slow, of course, so I can enjoy the view of you leaving me... again."

Oh my god, Harlan, get the fuck over it.

"Or you can get over yourself and come inside to get what you drove all this way for."

A lump lodges itself in my throat at his harshness. I shouldn't admit this, not even to myself, but I like him like this. Assertive and to the point, everything I once wished he could be.

I don't answer him. I let my booted feet lead the way.

"That's what I thought," he hisses as I walk past him. "You're right. It's never just a *book*," he says through a whisper.

I pause my steps, my hair flipping as I turn back to him. His words eerily similar to Frida's that night I got the book—the one he fucking took the liberty to write in last night. But I'm not here for my book, I have it already. I'm here for my necklace. He knows that. He literally just acknowledged that seconds before.

"What did you say?" My eyes narrow.

His hand curls on the doorknob. "You're right, it's not just a necklace," he says so nonchalantly it makes me wonder if I'm hearing things... again. Wouldn't be the first time. "Your mom left it for you. It means everything to you. It's the only way I knew how to get you here."

It's just in your head, Araceli. Focus. You're so close.

"Awww," I echo his condescending nature. "How cute. Someone missed their little sister, didn't they?" I pout.

My words rob him of his brief moment of vulnerability. In an instant, his demeanor shifts. The warm sentiment of why he stole the necklace, gone, and in its place a much colder version of

Harlan that I'm not sure I can get used to, stands before me. Tempting me to play. Enticing me with his newfound darkness.

He closes—or rather *slams*—the door shut, locking us in, and I could've sworn I heard him mumble, "It's how I'm going to keep you here." Though, as I look at the monster that my big, *fuckable,* brother has become, his mouth is shut and it's my body doing all the talking. Begging me to not be so stubborn and open up to him like he deserves. Like an apologetic whore. *His apologetic whore.*

Fourteen

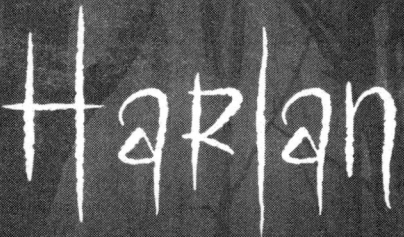

Harlan

SHE'S BACK. *I knew she'd be.*

Disappointment rattles me as I stare at her plump ass—that she somehow managed to secure in those tight pants—jiggling with each step she takes past me. Not that the view isn't delicious. At least she didn't run away this time, so we're off to a good start.

Fuck, I've waited so fucking long to be able to have her at my disposal and I can touch her. Tease her. Sink my fucking hands so deep inside her that she'll pray to a god she doesn't believe in— that neither of us do—all because she's so terrified of what I've become because of her betrayal. She opened my eyes to what life could be without the confines of religion being shoved down my throat. If anything, I should thank her for unleashing my inner demon, for letting him roam free and allow me to be who I've always wanted. A lost, wandering soul content with his brokenness, not in the market to have it patched up for some sky Daddy's ego.

Though this isn't how I envisioned our reunion going. Yeah, I figured she'd be pissed I stole her necklace, but it worked. I got her attention. However, this act of indifference she has is insulting. Despite me being able to smell the arousal leaking onto—from what my eyes can manage with the visible panty lines centered on her bottom in between two of the roundest ass cheeks I've ever seen outside of a fucking porno—her thong.

Has she not missed me like I have missed her?

Did our night at the haunt, when she was practically suffocating me with her pussy like a feral fucking whore, mean nothing to her?

Or when she fucking rode my dick in the hospital?

Did it all mean... nothing?

Seething, I slam the door. Part of me wants to tell her to lose the act. I know what she did. I watched it all. It's all on tape. What she did yesterday before I paid her a visit and now what she did tonight, killing Fred, the security guard. I can't believe she did that to him without what looked like a second thought or an ounce of remorse.

My fists clench into a ball still lingering on the doorknob, but all my gaze can focus on is the blood. Fred's blood, now on my hands, competing with the ink that paints my flesh.

The crimson becoming a catalyst to that night at Heathen's Cross. Buckets of it. Being poured on us both.

Fuck.

Why...

How...

How the fuck can blood suit her like that and make my dick so fucking hard like it is right now?

How...

How...

Ho—

My internal rumblings cut off from her voice, cutting into the air. Even with my inner spiraling, there was such peace in the air before she came here and infected it once again with her presence.

I pivot my stance and my vision is consumed once more by her. With no other choice, I drink her like the poison she is as my steps trail hers. Except her toxicity isn't the kind that kills. Not right away, at least. It takes its sweet fucking time, infusing its deadly potion slowly into the bloodstream with diabolical precision... just like her.

"I like what you've done with the place."

She isn't lying. She's probably wet over the fact that this place —*our home*—has gone to shit. Ever since Dad became too sick to maintain it and the burden fell on me, I decided I no longer give a fuck about keeping up appearances. I let the earth do what it does best to things no longer worthy of tender loving care...rot.

Where white molding used to define the tall ceiling, it now is a spider's playground. The floral wallpaper glued to the walls is now a backdrop to the abundant and thick cobwebs that drape over them. So many, in fact, that it gives the illusion that I went to the Halloween shop—like the one we went to years ago—and put them up on purpose, but I didn't. They are as real as my hatred for her and as tangible as the blood rushing to my cock as I watch her take in the wreckage I've lived in, waiting for her to return to me.

"Thanks," I deadpan. Impatience doing a number on my body, already growing bored of this drawn-out act.

"Is he home?" she asks, referring to my dad. Her question, full of disgust.

"Fuck you, Araceli," I spit and finally her attention is where I want it...back on me.

"Excuse me?" She snaps her words as her neck follows suit. Bobbing her head causing her split-colored hair to sway, and the past does what it does best, haunts me with muses from the past.

"Look, hermano, it's me and you. The saint and the sinner."

Except I'm not the saint anymore. No one here is.

"You don't give a fuck about him. So cut the small talk." I remind her.

A smile tugs at her lips. "He's dead, isn't he?" she asks with fucking glee, a level of excitement that should scare me, and it would if she were capable of scaring me anymore. That privilege died the moment she made me realize she's no better than my father.

She's a manipulator, just like him. Only difference is the words she twists are her own, not written for her to recite, and she has the audacity to call her lies art.

"He has to be." Her voice trails off, as if she's trying to put pieces of the puzzle she isn't fully equipped to put together in place. "He would've never let you keep the place like this. It looks *abandoned*." She pauses, and the inflection in her voice on the word abandoned is impossible to ignore. She sounds, dare I say, aroused?

There she is. Brother's gruesome little whore.

Gathering her wits about her, she continues. "What finally got him? Karma?" she asks sarcastically. She knows that he doesn't believe in karma. *Sky Daddy* would never allow such a concept to exist. It'll ruin his story.

I'm about to burst her bubble with the sad fact that Dad is still alive, but the sadistic part of me that she is just starting to meet wants to play with her some more. Tease her some more. What's one more lie after we've been plagued with endless ones?

Fuck it.

"Heart attack."

She laughs. Maniacal and sultry... and it travels right to my fucking cock.

Lifting her hand to the wall to her right, she finally pauses to play with the cobwebs scattered on the walls. "Was that before or after he saw the way you desecrated his house?" Araceli turns her head, the white-blonde side of her hair facing me.

"Before," I say in a growl.

You'd know that if you didn't fucking leave. If you didn't fucking abandon me.

"Right," her voice drags, sounding unconvinced.

Unable to stand the distance between us any longer. I demolish it. Charging at her, I don't stop until I'm towering over her, with her body pinned to the wall, and those delicate fucking wrists of hers that I could easily squeeze and snap in fucking half up and over her head, locked in my possessive grip.

"Harlan," she breathes.

I transfer her wrists to one hand, now taking my free one to her lips. First running an outstretched finger to her lips, silencing her, or trying to. Ignoring me and the power she and I both know I have over her, she fights me, moving her lips to speak instead of obeying my one-time warning to shut the fuck up.

My finger leaves her lips, but only for a second. Just enough time that it can meet the rest of my fingers as I wind up and smack her cheek before pinching my hand at her face, pressing her cheek into my hand.

A moan slips her mouth and her chest heaves violently. Up and down in rapid succession. Her quickening pulse ricocheting beneath my touch is a gift, granting me the invisible checkmate I was seeking.

I win. You lose, little sister.

"You look nervous," I point out, which is something that I'm not used to making her feel, and something she most certainly is not used to feeling because of me. Her gaze is as polarizing and hypnotic as she is, but I can't give in and lose the persona I've worked so hard to maintain...just for her.

Curious how she's going to spin the truth this time. I let her go. She takes a step forward but doesn't run...like she should.

"You look *really* nervous."

"I'm fine," she clips as she shakes her head, mumbling something to herself. "This was a mistake."

"Aw, don't say that," I pout sadistically. "You can't mean that coming to see me after I stole from you is a mistake? No, no. That can't be it. You're growing wetter by the second since you've infected my airwaves. I can smell that needy cunt from here. So that can't be it. It *has* to be something else." I begin to circle her. Picking up speed with each orbit I make around her body, hoping to make her dizzy. Throw her off even more. "Hmm, now what can it be that has that moral compass you buried so long ago rise to the surface of your equally broken conscience?"

She doesn't answer. Caught between a tidal wave of fear and arousal, she looks down at the floor.

I stop circling her, stomping my foot onto the ground. Demanding her attention, but still the stubborn bitch keeps her eyes off me. Insulting me with her lack of attention.

I lunge at her again, snatching her chin into my grip, and she loses her footing a bit.

There it is again. Her shaking her fucking head.

"You're fucking crazy, Harlan," she spits. Literally. A splash of warm and scattered saliva sprinkles onto my face.

My grip sears into her face harder.

"Stop talking about yourself that way, Araceli." I taunt, but she doesn't budge, remaining incensed and stubborn.

"Go ahead. Make it tighter." She brings her hands to mine, her gaze unwavering as it bores into mine. "Matter of fact, slap me again, church boy." Again, my hold tightens, and it's a wonder I haven't broken her skin. Though somehow, even with her cheeks hollowed from my touch, her stubbornness prevails and the ability for her to speak penetrates the air. "Go ahead, you fucking—"

Abruptly, I let go of her.

She catches her breath.

"That's what I fucking thought."

"Did you, now? Is that what you think? That, because I took my hands off you, you're suddenly exempt from my wrath?"

She cackles, and it's the equivalent to nails on a chalkboard.

"Wrath? Really? Fuck, you've been listening to too many of your daddy's sermons. You aren't capable of wrath."

Frustration fills my veins, raising them to my skin's surface. But for some reason, the anger I feel—towards her refusal to be honest for once in her fucked up life—has me laughing. Cackling actually. Loud and eerie. Uncontrollably, so.

"What's so funny?" The scoff at the end of her question is as infuriating as it is cute.

"You." I increase my steps towards her and by default she

moves hers back, this time propelling her deeper into the house and down the hallway.

Her feistiness withers before my eyes, as does the delusional assumption she had that made her think she has one up on me, vanishes.

"You know what, just forget it. Forget I was ever even here." She shakes her head, trying to move past me.

Oh, no you fucking don't. Not this time.

I mirror her movements. Stomping every which way, she attempts to sneak past me. Frustrated, she lets out a growl before locking her gaze on my face. My tongue clicks before extending my newly split tongue out past my lips, and just like the little whore she is, she stops in her tracks, entranced by it.

"Harlan," she gasps. "You're so... so..."

Say it.

"... different," she breathes.

I close the space between us more. "Yep," I hiss.

"Fuck," she lets out, exasperated, from her anger and need, toying with her. Her hand sears itself to her forehead as she slaps it. "This isn't happening," she mutters, now shaking her head back and forth.

"What's the matter? Am I scaring you?" I laugh, stomping closer to her.

Her hands fall to her harness, probably about to reach for the knife she thinks I didn't clock the second she walked on the porch.

"Cat got your tongue? What? Is my little sister too much of a whore for the fear that she can't think straight? Are you too consumed by the need to spread your fucking legs for me, and let me finish what I teased you with in the bathroom of your house last night? While you were unconscious, no less. Fucking druggie whore."

She growls, loud this time. Stomping her feet. So fucking flustered that she abandons the mission she was just on to grab her knife.

What a forgetful little thing.
How pathetic, yet fortunate for me.

"Harlan, I swear to—"

I click my tongue, interrupting her. A phony, overdone shiver runs down my spine. "Don't say," my voice lowers as my finger points to the ceiling, "Him." I shake my head violently. "He doesn't live here anymore. Not in my heart or this house. Calling on Him won't save you now," I taunt.

Her eyes narrow to slits, shocked by the words coming out of my mouth. "Fine, you fucking psycho."

Fuck. The degradation is just too delicious coming from her mouth.

Go on, sis. Tell me how psycho I've become so I can act on it and prove you wrong.

"I swear. If you don't move out of my way, I'm going to—" She reaches for her back pocket, but my next words interrupt her.

"Stab me like Fred?"

Her brows furrow. "Who the fuck is Fred?"

I laugh. "Of course, you only remember the names of characters you kill off, not people." I stop, letting her marinate on my vague words.

"I don't know what you're talking about," she deflects.

"Fred is the security guard you killed," I remind her.

Shock lines her irises. There it is. The truth is written all over her face, but as her lips part, she does what she does best…lie.

"I don't know what you're talking about," she repeats, sounding like she's trying to convince herself. "I told you the blood was—"

She stops as I bring my hand that touched the very real blood on her body to my mouth. Sucking in the iron tang that covered it, humming around my finger.

"Fuck," she breathes. Shocked and aroused by the scene before it.

I moan as I suck in the blood before popping my finger out of my mouth.

"It's a bit bitter. At least way more bitter than I would imagine your blood tasting. Well, no, that's a lie. Let me rephrase. It tastes more bitter than how I *remember* your blood tasting, but then again, that was so long ago when you," I pause, clearing my throat to raise my volume, "fucked me with your blood spewing all over me while I slept, you fucking crazy whore!" I shout.

"Oh, my fuck! When will you get over it? I didn't do anything to you that you didn't like or want, you self-righteous prick! When will you get over it?!"

"Never," I deadpan. The nonchalance of my response shocks her, just as my ability to calmly dive back into what I was saying before about our dearly departed friend, and one of her readers, no less—Fred.

"Lie all you want to me, but I got it all on camera." My steps quicken. Hers mirroring mine.

"Yeah, okay, whatever. Fuck this and fuck you!" Araceli's split colored hair waves as she stomps to the left, then right, and I block her every time.

"Well, if you stick around, that is what I'd like to do. Fuck you."

Reaching for the knife in her harness, a wave of confidence falls over her shoulders. "Of course, that's what will make you happy. My pussy wetting that stale dick of yours."

She presses on the button and the blade retracts, but I'm too fast for her. I swat at the blade, cutting myself in the process before it falls.

"Give me my fucking knife!" She shouts as she plunges to the ground to retrieve it, but I follow after her.

God damn it. Here I was thinking the view I had of her ass was hot from before? That was nothing compared to the view I have of her on all fours, thinking she's going to get her knife back and get away from me.

I claw at her ankles, yanking her towards me, but she fights it. Back and forth, we fight each other for dominance.

"You're not leaving. Accept it. You can't leave unless you want me to leak the tape."

With both hands on her ankles, I drag her further from the knife.

"Please. No amount of ink or body modifications you've made can give you that level of balls. You don't have it in you."

"That's where you're wrong." I yank her so hard that her body skids against the floor with ease. I continue to pull her where I want her. Pinned to the ground so she can remember where her place is in the new pecking order I've established for our family... beneath me. Where she belongs.

"Do you know what it was like after you left? No? Well I'll tell you." Spit falls unintentionally to her mouth and disgust mars her face. Infuriating me more. "He was ruthless. The sermons were nonstop. So were the punishments. He blamed me for what you did that night. He took it out on me until he finally got what he deserved."

"Harlan," she pants my name, "you're scaring me."

I lower my lips to hers, teasing her trembling mouth. "I don't care."

"You're hurting me." But the inflection in her voice says anything but pain. She sounds excited. Needy. Like this is a game she is about to win by getting me just how she's craved.

"Good," I seethe, taking her hands in one of mine, bringing them above her head while the other wraps around the slender column of her throat. She gasps, fighting for air... for the ability to move, but I grant her neither. "What's the matter, all that snarky, stubborn, sass suddenly gone? How fucking sad." I squeeze tighter. Spitting again, but this time it's intentional.

Keeping my hand on her throat, I creep my index and middle fingers up to her mouth.

"When I tell you to suck, I want you to suck on them."

Confusion lines her brow and she pinches her lips closed.

She hums a 'no', but I don't listen, breaking the barrier of her lips, anyway. Who the fuck is she kidding? Her tongue is swirling around them, probably wishing it were my cock as she takes me deeper into my mouth.

"Who's a good little whore?" I taunt her, letting go of her wrists, I fish my free hand to my pocket, grabbing the syringe. I don't bother hiding it and she doesn't bother pretending that she doesn't see it.

Still, I brace myself, expecting her to flinch and fight, but she does neither. She wants it. I shouldn't be surprised. Whatever she took before driving to see me is likely wearing off by this point, and reality is probably too strong for her. She would rather be numbed, and lucky for her, I have what it takes to do just that.

She rolls her head, exposing her neck to me, and my fingers fall from her mouth.

"Do it," she begs. "Just punish me and get it over with."

I flick the syringe, but her skin beckons me to taste first. Lowering my lips to her neck, extending the split muscle of my tongue, I tease her with just the tip. Licking a soft trail up and down her now pebbled skin.

"Welcome home, little sister." I murmur, bringing the needle to her neck, exchanging my tongue with its tip, and tease her with that instead.

She scoffs. "This isn't home, it's Hell," she grits as I lower my lips near hers. She's staring at me with nothing but hatred spewing from her every pore, yet it doesn't stop her from puckering her lips. The misplaced expectation that she's going to get a kiss from me. Laughable.

I extend my tongue, the torn flesh playing with her septum piercing, before I yank it. Hard.

"Same thing," I hiss.

Her stubbornness prevails as her jaw clenches, making the veins in her neck lift and throw me off. But I won't let her win, not this time. Determined, I break the barrier of her skin with the loaded syringe and inject her with it.

As I retract the needle from her neck, her lids fall shut, and for a moment, I am in disbelief that I've fallen this far from the person I once was.

It's not too late, I can just behave myself and wait until she wakes up, and take her back home. But, if I do that, and spare her from the wrath she thinks I'm not capable of, who wins? Who loses?

Blood rushes violently to my cock the more I stare at her still body. She's breathing. Unfortunately. Still my mind drifts to a dark place that it's found solace in over the years, wondering, fantasizing about how beautiful she would look if she were dead.

Fuck, I could come just at the thought of how peaceful my life would become if she didn't live anymore.

It'd be so easy, too.

She's already passed out. She wouldn't feel a thing.

But that's the problem. I don't want her to get off easy.

I want her to suffer for what she's done.

I want to remind her that I am who I am now because of her.

Shit, I should thank her... and thank her I fucking will.

This is all her fault. She shouldn't have come back here.

Not tonight.

Not last night and *all* the nights before. All of which she'll deny, but time stamped videos don't lie.

She's the one who foolishly fell into my trap. So fucking easily. All I had to do was dangle the bait in front of her and she came crawling—cunt dripping and all—like the needy fucking whore she is. All so she can kneel at big brother's cock. If only it were that easy. Tonight, she's my victim. Tonight, she's my prey. Tonight, she will have no choice but to succumb to my undying need to punish her.

When she wakes, I'll give her a crash course on what happens when the church boy sells his soul to the devil.

Fifteen

Araceli

"I TOLD YOU TO STAY AWAY!" My stepfather shouts, as his angry hands latch onto my ankles. The contact alone is enough to make me want to vomit. I hate when he touches me. I hate when he's near me. I. Hate. Him.

"You get over here right now," he mutters, still yanking at my limbs.

Still insistent that I need to be punished... again.

He grumbles some more, this time with an array of colorful obscenities. I bet none of his congregants would ever believe he is capable of saying such filth, but I can't focus on what he's saying—the stench is too overpowering.

"Fight me all you want, but you're not going to find what you're looking for in there. You good for nothing—" I somehow manage to wiggle my foot just enough that it loosens his grip on one of my ankles, and I kick at him. "Bitch!" he yells, trying to grab at me again. I use this as my opportunity to try to submerge myself deeper into the trenches of the decay and rot I feared would be hidden here.

I sneak a quick inhale through my mouth, hoping to spare my nostrils the burden of taking in the potent aroma that lay thick all around me.

My bent knees glide forward and every hair on my body raises, *as a cool, slimy texture slithers onto my skin. Coiling its way around my leg, causing a lump so harsh to form in my throat, it feels like I've swallowed glass.*

A boisterous rumble, angrier than I've ever heard from him before, erupts. The force he applies to my limbs, pulling me back to him—to where I don't want to be—matches his tone.

"Get. Over. Here."

"No!" *I shriek.* "No. No. No." *My breathing becomes as erratic as my heart, beating a mile a minute.* "Just let me go! Let me see for myself!" *I beg.*

But it all falls on deaf ears. He's already made up his mind.

"I know you burn like a sinner, but I wonder—" *his voice trails, the belt buckle clinking as it comes undone and falls to the ground.* "Hmmm," *he groans,* "hmm, I wonder if I can fuck the sinner out of you."

"I'm sorry," *I cry, pinching my eyelids shut.* "I didn't mean to find out."

My pleas are too late.

"Shh pecadora, this will only hurt if you fight me. Don't worry, He isn't watching. This is your fault, though. You've steered too far off the narrow path. But don't you worry, after I use my God given parts to exercise the demon out of you, He'll care again, and He'll watch over you."

"I don't want Him or you. You sick fuck!"

"I know, but it's why I have to do this."

I gasp, startling myself awake, but my eyelids remain shut, afraid that the nightmare will follow. Air burns my lungs upon inhaling. A dryness I can't explain settling over my lips, trickling its way into my mouth. It increases with every staggered inhale I take as it's exacerbated by the cool, slimy sensation taking hold of my airways.

"Araceli." Harlan coos my name, encouraging yet sadistic. His deep baritone forms a blanket over my body, summoning goosebumps to rise to the surface of my skin. They continue to prickle my flesh, making me painfully aware that something is physically choking me—or trying to—and it's not Harlan's hands.

I open my eyes, and a dizzying rush consumes my head. I take in not only Harlan's broad frame hovering mine, straddling me, but the abundance of scales—slimy fucking scales—taunting me.

As quick as I opened my eyes, I'm already pinching them shut, or at least I try to, but Harlan clicks his snake-like tongue—that I'm now wondering if he had modified to mess with me, since he knows I don't like snakes—before laying a not so gentle tap to my cheek.

"Eyes up here," he commands, and as tempting as the directive is, especially coming from Harlan of all people, I don't obey. Instead, I grant myself the vapid veil of serenity my eyelids provide me when shut. That way I can pretend there isn't a snake making its rounds on my décolletage, and that my stepbrother hasn't fallen farther than even I'm willing to go to help him.

"He won't hurt you," Harlan attempts to reassure me, but the snake's hiss indicates otherwise. "Not if you cooperate, that is."

I scoff internally, still not able to muster up the energy I need to fight him or this damn snake off me. Not yet, at least.

"What did you give me? I feel..." I pause, trying to determine how I actually feel. Aside from the very real fear I have of snakes—which Harlan clearly made note when we dropped acid before Heathen's Cross—I surprisingly feel rested. Something I haven't felt since, well, that night or since I stepped foot in this godforsaken house for the first time.

"You feel relaxed, don't you? I, myself, love a light sedative every once in a while. It works quicker than melatonin and doesn't have all those nasty side effects like the concoctions you usually flock to." He sounds so sure of himself. Like there isn't even the faintest of inklings in his subconscious that what he's doing to me is wrong.

He's sick... and it's all *my* fault. The old Harlan would never do this. He would never do anything to cause me pain, let alone enjoy doing it.

He continues on, "I just wanted you to get some rest. We still have a long night ahead of us." The cheshire grin on his face unveils more sinister intent. Something that usually would entice me, though now, coming from him, I feel an immense unease that won't dissipate.

"No. We. Don't." My words are choppy. The tension in my jaw is mounting.

Harlan laughs at me, and with a snap of his fingers, the snake is practically charmed away.

Thank fuck.

"Oh. Yes. We. Do." He corrects me. "You should be thanking me, by the way." He spits, and a strand of saliva drips onto my cheek, only adding to the swarm of goosebumps already plaguing my skin. If it were anyone else, I would be disgusted. However, his warm, slippery spit transports me back to when he fucking devoured me like I was his last meal; when his spit became lost in the wetness he created at my center.

"How else are we going to finish what you started?" The cryptic nature of his question pulls me from reminiscing.

My neck twists, eyes now on his. "What the fuck are you talking—"

He waves his inked finger my way, retrieving a notebook from his back pocket. My eyes widen. That's *my* notebook.

"Where did you get that?" My accusatory tone causes him to laugh, arrogantly so.

"I found it."

"Liar!" I spit at him, but all my saliva does is spew droplets onto my face.

I flinch upward, but he scoots forward and onto my chest, trapping my arms under him before he lowers his mouth to my face, licking up my spit. Humming as he does it, so every stroke of his tongue vibrates my skin, distracting me.

"You—" I begin, but my voice isn't angry, it's breathy. I push through the current of twisted intrigue his new persona evokes throughout my entire body. Trying to ignore that his tongue's modification reminds me of a serpent's, or how badly I want to take his gauged lobes to my lips and sink my teeth into them. "You stole it," I manage, through a half pant, though it's not enough that my statement is mooted.

His tongue skims my cheek before he rolls and flicks the wet muscle over to my chin. He takes his time there, circling the edge of my chin in alternating jabs with either side of his tongue, before he drags it to the column of my throat. This teasing dance continues, with my laying motionless to the spell he's put on my body until he's satisfied with the wanton need he's creating inside me. It's then, as a whimper betrays my silence, that he decides to retract his tongue from my skin—leaving me high and dry.

"Asshole," I mutter.

"Come again?" He lifts his brows. "Oh, that's right, you can't," he singsongs before his voice drops to a dangerously low and seductive octave. "I won't let you."

My eyes roll. Hating that every word he's spewing my way is slowly breaking through the strong front I need to maintain if I want to get what I came here for. Which, at this point, feels so futile. The necklace I came for, that he took, it's supposed to protect me, though looking at what he's become, I'm starting to think that's impossible.

I should've never come back.

This was a mistake.

He lifts the notebook up. Pages shuffle, wafting the musky aroma of aged paper my way until he lands on a random spot. "Here we go." His throat clears, but he doesn't dive right in. Instead, he looks over the book, boring those ocean blue eyes that are so deceivingly peaceful looking my way. "You should've never opened the can of worms you did when you wrote me that bullshit letter. I was going to leave you alone. I had every intention of letting you slip away from my memory, even if it left me eternally lost and aching to be inside that tight cunt forever. But you just had to interject yourself, once again, into something bigger than you."

My lips part, about to ask what the fuck he means by something bigger than me. What, to apologize? I wrote to him to apologize for the time that's slipped us by.

"Shh," he coos. Let me read."

'His body, already bloodied and beaten, hangs on the cross. The same cross he made us look at as he punished us for our sins. Now the only punishment that will be heard in this room is in the echoes of a wailing man, not a god or a descendant of him, begging for a life that neither of us deem worthy of saving. His cries fill the room, though with each one, my patience grows thin as does the fleeting compassion I once had for a man so innately rotten and so unbelievably volatile.

"Are you ready, hermano?" I ask, as he hammers a nail into his father's hand.

"Why?" his dad, our victim, croaks. "Why are you doing this?"

I step in front of my brother, demanding that the ultimate sinner look at me. Not for who he wants me to be in his story, but for who I am.

His penance.

His damnation.

"Hammer," I instruct, leaving my outstretched hand out, waiting for the wooden handle to graze my palm.

"What are you going to do to me?" he pleads.

"Payback," I deadpan as I strike my clenched hammer-wielding fist down onto the top of his head.

His skull breaks with ease. The only simple thing that's ever come from him. But I don't want to only injure him—I want to annihilate him. For what he did to us, to them, and all the ones before.

Blood drips onto his forehead, staining his skin, begging me to continue, and I do. One strike after another. Blood for blood. Eye for an eye.'

Harlan slams the book closed and I flinch. "You know, for someone who claims to write fiction, I find it rather convenient or, I don't know, ironic, that everything you write has some truth to it. Some, of course, more than others."

This is ridiculous. "I don't know what you're talking about." The cross part, yes, there is some truth to that. I mean, it was inspired by the first and last night that Harlan and I shared, but the torture scene he just read, that's purely fictional.

He clenches his jaw. A notable knot forms in response as he shakes his head in disbelief. "I bet you believe that, don't you? Tell me then, if it's all fictional, then when are you going to tell me this isn't the first night you've returned to the very property you swore you'd never return to?"

As I marinate on what he's saying, all I can think of is what he's conveniently forgetting. I never swore not to return. I was kicked out. Threatened to never return. There's a difference. That's not something he'd ever have to contend with, though. He partook in the same things I did that night at Heathen's Cross, yet the consequences that I suffered were not the same as his. His father allowed him to exist while I was the one who was shunned. Not Harlan.

"This is the first time." I defend myself because it's the truth.

Harlan tosses the book on the floor and dust lifts from the soiled floorboards. Who knows when the last time this place was cleaned? Probably around the same time Harlan was who I remember him to be, an angel with an unsteady halo. It was always waiting to fall, but never did I think it'd shatter quite like his has.

"When were you going to tell me?" His question is full of venom.

I lift my brows at him, signaling for him to continue. I'm so confused. I'm so tired. I don't know what he wants me to say, or what I can say to convince him that whatever he's conjured himself into believing, isn't true.

"Don't play stupid with me. When were you going to tell me what you started and were too chicken shit to finish? Were you going to leave another mess for me to clean up when you do what you do best and disappear?"

What the fuck is he talking about?

He groans, increasingly aggravated. "Fuck, Araceli, don't make me show you the camera footage."

Sixteen

Araceli

What the actual fuck is he talking about?

Apparently, my stunned silence is too much for him to bear. Either that or the vexation that's been festering in him is in need of a release because his hand is practically clawing at his belt buckle, undoing it. "Unbelievable," he groans, now slipping the belt through the loopholes of his pants, with such speed, the leather audibly whips at the still air. "I don't know if I should be impressed by your acting skills or insulted by them. Playing dumb isn't a good look on you. I mean, I'd still fuck, but come on. Work with me here. I thought you were better than this? I always thought you were smarter than this somehow, but if you insist on acting like a stupid fucking brat, I think I have something that will get you talking." His zipper sounds as he lowers it. "Or at the very least, this will get you to open your mouth."

He laughs.

Well, time may have made him hotter, but this is pathetic. All this to get me to suck his dick.

Sure enough, the head of his cock meets my lips, forcefully parting them as he does, good on his promise to fill my mouth since I refuse to talk to him. Slowly, he stuffs my mouth with his cock. His shaft is so smooth; all of it except the unexpected barbell that presses against the roof of my mouth and onto my tongue. Mouth full of him, robbing me of my opportunity to speak, he holds himself in place, waiting for me to make a move.

The intense need to suck him in, and give him a taste of what I should've given him that night, floods me. Making me weak.

"You're pathetic," I mumble around his girth.

"No, no, no," he clicks his tongue, thrusting his hips forward. Controlling the tempo he has fucking my mouth. With every thrust he makes in my mouth, I'm finding the will to not hollow my cheeks around him more and more difficult. "You, my beautiful, slutty, little sister, are the pathetic one," he practically hisses. With each drive of his length in and out of my mouth, a dry sensation overtakes my mouth. It's gritty. Rough. "You've wanted my cock since the day you laid eyes on me," he continues as my mouth accepts its fate. The warm, wet hole he needs to get off with—and the one I want him to get off in. My eyes fall shut, and he continues to fuck my mouth. Though now with my submission hanging in the balance, every stroke of his cock elicits a response that feels almost out of body. The story he was just reading lays vivid in my mind.

The cross.

The blood.

So much fucking blood.

It all plays in my head like a movie, the pace of the carnage quickening as he pumps himself in me. "That's it. You see it, don't you?"

Yes.

Yes. I see it. But why?

What the fuck did he give me?

I flinch, but he fights me, shoving himself deeper into my throat as his hand strokes my forehead, tucking a piece of hair behind my ear. "Look at us, reunited, the sinner and the saint," he says with twisted glee.

I open my eyes and for a split second I don't see Harlan; I see his father. I know it's not him, but the intrusive thought is too strong to deny, and the image both terrifies and haunts me.

"It's okay, pecadora," he calls me. Just like his father used to.

With a snap of his fingers, the snake from before slithers his way back over to me, coiling around my throat, weaving its scales over and under my neck, through my hair, and back around again. Not tight enough to suffocate me, but snug enough that my lungs are burning with anticipation... and fear.

Harlan removes himself from my mouth and buckles his pants while I lay down frozen with the snake on top of me.

A satisfied groan erupts from Harlan's mouth. "Fuck. Fear looks good on you. But, that's the thing, I'm tired of looking." He stops, taking a blotter sheet out from his back pocket. Placing it in view, he rips a square off and then another.

A square with the same emblem on it as the ones we took all those years before flashes before my eyes.

"Open." I ignore his command and his hand finds my cheeks, prying my mouth open. He places the square on the tip of one of the torn muscles of his tongue and gingerly brings it to my mouth. I try to squirm beneath his touch, but he's too strong. Success lines his movements as the paper settles on my tongue as he closes my mouth, placing his hand over it. "Seeing you come alive from the dance terror performs on your flesh can only do so much."

Settling his mouth at my ear, he whispers, "I want to feel your pain," before cooing, "I want to *bathe* in it. Now swallow." His command is firm and demanding as he tightens the hold of his hand over my mouth. "I said swallow." His hand spreads to my nostrils, as he attempts to cut off my air.

With no fucking choice, and sadly craving the high this will give me, I oblige his request. That's all it takes to have him remove his hand, still leaving the snake in place. The drugs mix with the ones in my system and it's the only reason I'm not screaming. My body is too buzzed, my senses fooling me.

Harlan takes his knife, and without hesitation, slices the fabric between my legs, exposing my pussy to him.

"So wet." He hums in approval. "So fucking wet when you're scared." His split tongue dances at my entrance until the competing flesh finds a synchronized rhythm, each end taking turns dipping into my arousal before he unites the torn muscle and has it crash into me all at once. "I wonder how wet you'll be when the fear no longer excites you, but kills you," he groans and with his mouth pressed so firmly against my center, the words vibrate through me, making me want his wrath more than I should. I squeeze my legs, wanting to suffocate him, but the slap he places on my skin is so intense, it throws me off.

The lights above me mesh into a kaleidoscope of colors. I've never felt this high before. So alive.

"What did you give me?" I pant, writhing my hips at his face, but he moves back, standing up. I watch as he goes back to grab another book from the shelf, except he doesn't take this one off. He pulls it just enough that the floor moves, and I fall like I'm sinking into the ground.

I stare up as I hear his boots stomp across the floor, nearing me.

He looks down at me.

"An escape." Those two words are the equivalent to a time machine. Mocking me as they transport me back to when I was the one slipping him the drugs, and he was nervous. I told him the exact thing, to soften the blow of what I made him take. Of what I forced on him.

"Get up," he instructs. His command hits my system like a whip. Harsh with an undeniable sting, yet it heightens my senses, and the knife in his grip becomes the main focus of my periphery.

He repeats his instruction, and the patience that's already been dwindling reaches a crescendo of annoyance, so I listen.

As I do so, I try playing it cool so he doesn't catch on that I noticed his knife, and that I have every intention of grabbing it.

I rise to my feet, and the blood rushes to my head, causing a dark flash over my eyes before it dissipates in the form of white dots, fuzzing my vision, before I can regain it. This feeling of giving up control, and waiting for the rug to be pulled from underneath me with whatever path the drugs will put me on, feels like home. It always does. It shouldn't, but it gives my mind a comfort that it can't seek on its own. I feel just like I did the last time we split the blotter sheet. Loopy. Happy. *Hopeful.*

"Walk," he points to the small cutout door nestled in the wall. *No. No. No No. I'm not going back there.* My inner thoughts try to break through. I know I don't want to go back there, but I don't know why. I giggle instead of crying, like I think I want to. I'm not sure anymore. Everything feels off.

"Yes, you are," he boasts as if he can read my thoughts.

"No," my lips move, trying to win the war of my dwindling conscience.

"Yes. You. Are." Harlan grabs hold of my arms, trying to strong arm me, and guides me to the door I now recognize as the beginning to the crawl space that leads from the house all the way to church.

"He's going to kill you." Frida's warning from years ago rings in my ears, giving me the strength I need to fight his touch off, no matter how damning or good it feels.

A surge of strength ignites within me, one that I've only ever known myself capable of mentally, but never physically, and I squirm my way from his hold.

The room spins with me as I turn back to face him. My gaze zoning in on the knife. I charge him and snatch it from him. An electrical current of adrenaline renders me prisoner to it, but it gives me the strength I need to fight him off, and maintain possession of the knife. Curling my fingers around the handle, I lift it in the air for barely a second before my hand, now tingling and feeling weightless as ever, plunges into his midsection.

He yelps on impact. Blade still in him, I stare down at the fresh puncture wound. It's high enough and off to the side that I likely got him in his ribcage.

"What the—" he mewls, but I plunge the knife in deeper. Just for good measure.

The smug grin on his face is so fucking punchable. Too punchable to ignore. Taking a step forward, I rotate my wrist side to side, deepening his wound, but all he does is laugh. Giving me no choice but to take his sadistic laugh and raise him with a punch to the face. His high cheekbones sting my knuckles as I lay a clenched fist down onto his skin.

"You're a real fucking bitch, you know that?" Blood falls from his lip and small droplets gather, highlighting the bone white shade of his teeth.

"So are you," I retort, yanking my knife out of him as rivulets of crimson stain the floor on impact.

Harlan doesn't bother wiping the blood from his mouth, nor does he seem phased by the sizable wound to his abdomen.

With a quick shrug of his shoulders, his bent elbows highlight his lifted hands, motioning for me to come back and give him some more.

"I've been waiting a long time for this. That can't be all you got," he taunts.

Not sure how I want to play this. I assess the room, looking for a way that I can escape. Though of course, I can't. He's bolted the door, and the windows are all boarded up. The only way out is through the crawl space.

He claps his hands, taking a sick amount of enjoyment in the fact that he has me cornered.

"Like I told you before, you can run from the truth, but you can't run from me. Go ahead, I'll catch up with you." He nudges his chin to the crawl space door as he stands there eerily still, as though he was not stabbed with a very sharp four-inch blade.

Knowing that staying in this room with him isn't an option, I keep my head turned in his direction to keep an eye on him. I make my way to the crawl space, but my speed is slowed down as I try to keep my jaw from falling to the floor at what I see. Harlan takes his hand to his open wound, dipping his fingers in. Swirling and gathering the blood, he brings it to his mouth.

I begin to enter the crawl space backwards, one foot in the confined hellhole, and the other out still on the floor. I watch him dip his blood-soaked fingers deep into his mouth. He groans, humming around his slick fingers before releasing them.

"For this is my blood of the covenant, which is poured out for many for the forgiveness of sins. Matthew 26:28," he recites, unwavering in his eye contact with me. "The man upstairs said it himself. Forgiveness only comes from bloodshed. When I catch you, and make no mistake, I will catch you, you will bleed for me. It's the path to forgiveness. It's the only way I'll let you—"

I don't wait around to let him finish. I contort my body to face forward into the blackened entry of the crawl space and slam the door behind me.

I miss the old Harlan. I miss who he used to be before he scared me as much as he turns me on.

Now I have no choice but to run on my hands and knees from the monster I've created, and hope that when he catches me, I can survive a darkness that far surpasses my own.

Seventeen

I'M NAUSEOUS. Absolutely fucking sick over the fact that those verses, that used to play in my head like a record stuck on repeat *still* find a way to penetrate the truth I've come to accept. That none of what my father held dear, or tried to manipulate us with, is as real as the nightmare Araceli has catapulted us into. However, that verse in particular that fled from my lips without even so much as a hesitating breath, can be applicable to the situation we find ourselves in today, for once. Araceli has made me bleed on a metaphorical level and now a physical one. There's no stopping the levels she will stoop to, to make everyone but herself suffer.

Voices whisper to me from within. The same ones that did when I was younger. The same ones that stopped for a while until Araceli resurrected them unintentionally.

I swallow them down, ignoring their warning.

They're trying to get me to forget her.

Impossible.

They're pleading with me to move on without her.

Another implausibility.

As much as I hate to see her go. Truly, I do. The view... *oh, the fucking view.* Her scurrying into that crawl space—that I know is scaring her more than she is showing—well, that is almost as sweet as the lie I'm allowing her to believe. That I could ever possibly let her go.

I mean, considering how she left me high and fucking dry with my father's wrath to contend with—*alone*—I think I'm being more than gracious by giving her a head start. An escape other than the one the drugs provide isn't an option. Not anymore. Not since the dominoes are beginning to fall in a perfect line, and the inevitable is as inescapable as the gift her and I share.

Swiping my hand at my mouth, I capture the spilled blood she drew with that impressive sucker punch of hers. I don't know what does it for me more, her fear, or her violence. My fingers now coated in more blood, but this time hers. I can't help but have another taste, so I slip them into my mouth again.

Fuck. What has she done to me? Even through the metallic tang encasing my tastebuds, her scent penetrates it. Making me instantly fiend for more of it.

Entranced as ever from whatever remnants she gives me of herself, I become so distracted that I almost miss the buzz of my phone.

I already miss the taste of her betrayal as I'm forced to pop my fingers out of my mouth to retrieve my phone and read the incoming text.

It's Frida.

Unlocking my phone, I walk to the closet off to the side of the crawl space entrance. I laugh to myself as I stare at the door that's shut from Araceli's doing.

Ever the fool, that one. All she's doing is creating another obstacle that I will demolish. Yet another barrier I'll gladly break through to get to her.

Frida: We hear her coming.

Me: That's because she's on her way.

> Frida: Excellent.

> Me: Is my old man still tied up?

> Frida: Yes.

Perfect. Just how she left him.

I toss my phone onto the floor. The service isn't great anyway on the other side of the crawl space. It'll be useless to me. What I do need, however, is her notebook. Her glorified diary. It'll make her initiation into Heathen's Cross go smoother and how it's intended to be.

As the entrance to the crawl space burns in my periphery, beckoning me to it, I first pick up Araceli's book, then finish making my way to the closet. There's something I need to get, to help set the mood and hopefully help jog Araceli's memory of the details of what it really means to be an attendee at Heathen's Cross, since they seem to have become fuzzy to her over time.

The musky scent of mothballs overpowers my senses as I sift through the hangers until I settle on the item I've been searching for.

An all-black jacket, long with a brimmed hood, stares back at me. Excitement burrowing in my fingertips as I slip it on and lift the hood onto my head.

"Fatum enim eligimus," I chant. Anticipation flows through my veins. My whole being practically buzzing as I stomp my boots forward to the crawl space.

This passageway that leads to where I gave Araceli a head start has become both a playground and a safe space. But not any longer. That ends tonight.

My knees bend to begin the trek and immediately become dirty from years of neglect. The smell, the air, all of it, is putrid.

But there's unfinished business to attend to.

A score that was promised and not yet settled.

I wouldn't let the very real reminder of death that lingers in the crawl space my father used for years as his personal dumping ground, to hide the sins, get in my way.

I'll do anything to give Araceli what she deserves.

My punishment.

My revenge.

A second chance to do what she promised me years ago, and still hasn't been able to do... kill for me.

It's only fair since I've killed the person I once was, all so she can look up to her big brother—preferably from her knees—and beam with pride at the monster I've become. The perfect archetype of her demented fantasies.

This sacrifice, I and the others, will force her to participate in merely settles the score.

Let her go?

What a fucking joke.

Never.

Never could I ever let her go.

I've waited too long to have someone as broken as I am.

I've plummeted too far not to make her pussy mine for all eternity... and then some.

Blood for blood. Eye for an eye, right?

It's the Heathen's Cross way. A cause I swore my allegiance to thirteen years ago to the day. The Cross saved me. Not like my dad would've hoped. But submitting to the initiation we unknowingly embarked upon that night did me good. Now, Dad will see that for himself and now, so will she.

Eighteen

Araceli

Just keep moving.
 Do.
 Not.
 Look.
 Back.

I tell myself. Fighting the very real urge I have to stop crawling. To stop trying to fight him and let him do to me what he's wanted to since we parted ways. Make me face the truth I've been unwilling to accept. That I'm not in control. He is. So he can make me feel as discarded as I've made him feel. It'll hurt. Fuck, will it ever, but a part of me wants his punishment, because all of me knows that I deserve it. Maybe then, if I let him win and have this, I can allow my true fears to rise to the surface. To not numb them, but let them free. Let *me* free.

My movements are guesswork. The blanket of darkness I'm entrenched in has propelled my senses to a painstaking level of hyper awareness. As the air becomes denser, my airways trick me into thinking they're being constricted. Each attempt at bringing new air into my lungs feels like an attack from the sharp pain that radiates through my chest at every inhale.

It's so difficult to see what I'm moving toward... or on. I'm well aware of what soil feels like on the skin. It sometimes can be damp from moisture, but it's rarely slimy or spongy. It never feels or smells the way the soil I'm trekking through feels.

"Neither of you are allowed access to this crawl space. It's as old as the foundation. It isn't safe."

Warnings that hit like foreshadowing cloud my head as I hold my breath, indulging myself in the ignorant bliss that is believing that the uneven ground I'm crawling on, is just that, ground.

A collection of dirt with fragments of broken earth and not what I think it is, or what I know in my gut, is the truth.

A mound of torn flesh and bones that have surrendered their living conditions.

I muscle through, pretending that the stench is not what it smells like.

Rot—abundant piles of *rot*.

Bile flirts with my throat. An uncontrollable tang burns through my esophagus the deeper I plunge myself into the passageway below this house of nightmares.

What's worse is that the stench, and the lingering effect it has on my skin, as horrid as it is, feels familiar. It's as though each rotting scrap is clinging onto my limbs, trying to suck me in and jog my memory.

I shake my head. This isn't the time for this. I can't afford to stop and wonder *why* this looks familiar. I can only focus on *how* to get out.

It's just what he gave you, Araceli.

Your mind is playing tricks on you.

Get. It. Together. Just. Keep. Fucking. Moving. You stupid—

"Oh, sister," Harlan sneers off in the distance. Though the deep notes of his voice that echo in the cramped space are not as far off as I'd like them to be. He's getting closer and his voice, cold as he's become, is the jolt of energy I need to revitalize my limbs and motivate them to move. Fast.

Continuing forward, at lightning speed compared to how I was moving before, I can see the finish line in sight. Light finally breaks through the darkness. It's menial. Not bright. Crimson. It's the beacon I've been hoping for. I'm almost free and once I am, I'm never coming back here again. Never again.

Never.

Ever.

The thick air burns my lungs. I try to breathe, but it feels like the walls of my lungs are closing in, just as they always do when a panic attack takes over. I've made it this far, yet my mind—that tricky, fickle bitch—can't help but let the games linger. To manipulate me. To trick me. I can't trust my mind. I've never been able to. It's why I've always turned to drugs and alternate realities, whether written by others or my own. At least then I know that if I see something, it's because of an outside source other than the internal one that taunts me daily, when I'm sober as can be... myself.

More red light drips past the door that will be the exit of the crawl space. My eager fingers curl around the small knob, anticipating the fresh air.

A tongue clicks from behind me as it flicks into my exposed center.

Harlan.

I try to move and fight the current of pleasure and pain the competing muscle of his tongue is inflicting on me. He nibbles and bites his way on and around my sex, but he pulls me back with his hand and it only deepens the angle he can dart his tongue inside of me.

If I only knew then what a can of worms I'd open, exposing him to darkness, I would have never engaged with him. Pastor's son or not. He's his father's son above all, and knowing the damage his father has caused, it shouldn't surprise me that his own flesh and blood can do much worse.

"Let. Me." I begin to pant and grunt, but he snatches my waist into his hands. Pulling me back and deeper into his face. "Go!" I finish my plea.

"No," he hisses, burying his face between my ass cheeks. His words linger, vibrating me to my core.

My eyes roll both in annoyance... and pleasure.

"What's the use?" I drawl. "You aren't going to let me come."

"Yet." Another flick of his tongue at my pussy before he tugs at my folds, kneading my sex in his teeth, hard enough that the likeliness of blood being drawn is very real, yet it only adds to how good it feels.

Deciding not to fight it, I lean into his mouth, rolling my hips as I try to work with the erratic tempo of his split tongue. Though the more I grind on his face, the more he holds back, until his face abandons my center. I gasp from the absence of his mouth. The neediness in my breath echoes throughout the crawlspace, reminding me how weak Harlan makes me. In stillness, I wait for a command, or for him to say anything, but neither come. Instead, my wet and pulsing sex becomes home for something sharp.

"Shh," Harlan coos with sinister excitement laced within his breath. "You take it so well."

It?

What's it?

His dick?

Is he talking about his —

A ravenous moan breaks my own thought process as Harlan ups the tempo of whatever he's fucking me with. It's cold and sharp. The more he plunges it into me, I fear the pleasure is diluting my ability to think straight and fight him off.

My jaw tightens, my words gritted. "What are you doing to me?"

"Edging you, like you've edged me." Harlan seals his vague words with another violent thrust inside me. This one, harsher than the others but it gets me one step closer to finishing with whatever weapon he's chosen to punish me with.

"You're close aren't you?" he taunts.

Yes.

"Yeah, you are. I can feel you trembling. What a whore, begging to come on scraps."

"Scraps?" I pant.

"Scraps," he echoes.

I inhale and the putrid scent I've been able to ignore is back, whipping at my nostrils with a vengeance. The word scraps lingering in my psyche elevates the odor to a vomit inducing level.

"Fucking scraps, that's all I've given you and here you are, on all fours like a fucking beggar. Just begging for what big brother will give you."

Harlan laughs and the notes of his baritone rattle my eardrums. "So pathetic, and you're so close to escaping."

I look forward to the door.

"Let me go," I grit out.

Harlan surprisingly listens, withdrawing whatever he was playing with inside me. He inhales loud, sniffing the remnants of what I left on it.

"What was that?" I ask again.

"Who cares? Open it," he instructs. His lips make their way to my inner thigh. He clamps down and his bite feels harsher than the fucking. Hard enough to draw blood this time and with my senses still in hyper-drive from the drugs, I swear I can smell the iron tinge stifle the air.

With my hand already on the knob, I turn it. The light, no longer sneaking past the crevices of the crawl space door, is now burning in my view. The red I had mistaken it for is in fact a deep flickering rust accompanied with shades of burnt orange and amber riddled throughout.

This isn't right. No. This. Is. Not. Right.

This is impossible.

I glance back, past Harlan's eerily calm stare, to the darkened tunnel we just crawled through, to do a double take. Ready and desperate to blame what I just saw on the drugs. However, the heat from the open flames is as real as the sweat it's causing on my skin.

"Isn't it amazing?" Harlan's voice commands my attention.

I swallow thickly. Pushing down a wad of saliva that might as well be a shard of glass with how it tears at my esophagus.

"What is?" I whisper, still dealing with the assault my own throat is having on me.

"How a little truth dust can put it all into perspective."

My brows furrow at his vagueness.

"Harlan, what did you fucking give me?" I grit through a heavy and clenched jaw. This kind of feeling of being transported to another time, another place, has never happened with any of the numerous drug trips I've taken myself on. I should be impressed. This is what I've always wanted. An escape. However, this feels too real. Too frightening. Too much like a precursor to the protective and possibly ignorant wool about to be pulled from my eyes.

"What I gave you and what I'm about to give you are two different things. But what you are currently giving me is a fucking headache." He stops to move back into the dark pit, and for a second, I lose track of his movements. It's only as his foot emerges, pressing down on my body that I realize he's contorted himself once again, this time turning around and laying back, all so he can kick me, and nudge me forward. "Let's get a move on." He kicks me again. Harder this time, it forces me to turn my head and move fully out of the crawl space. The main line from the house that the crawl space provides goes from his room, under the ground of the cemetery, to the main sanctuary. It's been like that since the house was built well over a hundred years ago. Yet, what's staring back at me isn't another structure, it's the open air. A damn near perfect replica to where Harlan and I spent Halloween together…at Heathen's Cross.

As I rise to my feet, there's no missing the surplus of filth covering me. My hands, my arms, my shirt and what's left of my pants—since Harlan took it upon himself to tear them so he could have better access to me—are all covered. Stained in shades of red and inky black. Though, the blackness that steals the show is the fabric draped over Harlan's body as he slips out of the crawl space after me.

He rises to his feet, blood flirts with his skin, visibly staining his shirt yet he looks unaffected by the very open, very real wound I caused from stabbing him. None of it makes sense. Either Harlan has built an impenetrable pain tolerance —likely with the help of drugs—or his need to fuck with me surpasses him addressing his wounds... or reality. Though what really has me confused is what he's wearing. The very cloak the workers at Heathen's Cross wore. Which, now that I think of it, is the same thing the two men who met his dad after the Devil's Night service wore. Long, draping, all-black cloaks with brimming hoods, and the distinct patchwork on the sleeve of a slithering snake wrapped around a cross I thought was upright. Though, as I inch closer to Harlan's towering frame, I notice the cross is upside down.

I extend my hand out near his arm, wanting to touch the patchwork, but he flinches away before stepping in front of me, seemingly aggravated by my advance towards him.

"Why are you wearing that?" I ask.

His back now facing me as I turn around to where he stands, his shoulders stiffen in aggravation before he turns his head to me. "This is what we all wear on initiation night."

"Initiation night?"

"Yes," he huffs, clearly growing bored with my questions. "Now follow me." Harlan holds out his hand for me to take, but I don't take it. Not yet. I want to. *I have to.* However, that word—initiation—repeats in my head. Impatience trickles to his veins and the large, already protruding one that wraps from the top of his palm to his wrist bulges more. "We don't have much time," Harlan quips, pointing his inked hand to his open palm, condescendingly so I can grab hold of his hint. "Hand. Now."

"Will it hurt?" I ask another question that is the result of my mind running faster than my body can catch up.

"No," he responds, unconvincingly.

"Fine, then." I cross my arms, ignoring his invitation, or

rather, command to hold his hand, as I try to maintain some form of dignity that's clearly up for grabs this evening. "I'll follow you."

The old Harlan wouldn't have liked my refusal, but he would've accepted it. But this Harlan? The one who has taken the boy I knew, and turned him into a man I'm not sure if I want to fuck or kill... or both? He takes my refusal as an invitation to do what he wants, unapologetically.

He steps closer to me, taking my hand in his. "This way," he groans, yanking my arm as he leads the way through rows of hooded people sitting in pews similar to the ones in the sanctuary, but these are made of hay. They all look forward, not sparing us any looks, though the closer we get to the main cross that's centered in the hay, I notice it isn't empty. Silence that somehow speaks louder than words, or chanting, ever could, infects the air as we walk closer to the occupied cross. Flailing wrists adorn the coarse wood cross. The person's backside mirrors my own with deep round scars scattered throughout their naked skin. The only difference is that the number two is etched into their backside.

Panic unexpectedly trickles into my veins as adrenaline makes my hearing go dull. I move forward, needing to see, even though I don't want to. Rounding the cross, the naked, gagged person is none other than my stepfather. His naked front is just as bad as his backside...if not worse. Fresh cigarette burns mar his flaccid penis and they continue up his abdomen, in a distinct pattern that I've seen before.

Three large circles. Reminiscent of the ones Harlan painted in blood on my abdomen when it was me on that cross, and not his dad.

I turn back to Harlan. He stands hooded, looking like a dark god, staring at me with glee in his eyes.

My mouth moves faster than my mind can stop it. "What did you do to him?" I ask Harlan and even I'm shocked by the way my own voice is betraying me. It sounds...sad. *Disappointed* even.

Not waiting for a response, I jog over to my stepdad and yank the gag out of his mouth.

"Araceli," he breathes. I hate how my name always sounds like poison falling from his lips.

I swallow the disgust down.

This isn't the time. I need to get out of here.

I need to get past this.

"I knew you'd change your mind," he says, catching his breath, sounding relieved. "I knew you'd repent... for what you've done."

There it is again, that word, *repent*.

That's all he cares about. That everyone around him show remorse for their sins while he goes on living as a liar, a phony, a fucking wolf in sheep's clothing. The audacity. Even now, when it's so clear to anyone looking in at the conundrum he's found himself in, that I certainly couldn't be the cause of it. He still assumes I will take the blame as I always have.

Harlan steps behind me, and his father's gaze grows frantic in their weariness. Moving back and forth, up, and down, between where I stand in front of him, and where his son now has one hand on my neck and the other offering me an ice pick.

"You have repented, haven't you?" Harlan's father pleads.

"Don't listen to him," Harlan whispers in my ear, opening my clenched palm wide enough to slip a knife in. My digits adhere to the smooth handle as I keep my eyes on his dad.

"Oh, dear Lord," my stepdad begins, bellowing. "Araceli, please, no. Harlan—"

With the knife in my hand, I jolt forward, breaking the hold Harlan just had on me. The sharp tip flashes before my stepfather's eyes, silencing him.

"Stop," I command. "Stop your fucking blabbering, your lies, stop all of it!"

It's not lost on me that I should be reacting to this differently. That the sight before me, no matter how vile my stepfather was to me and Harlan, should evoke some sort of sadness in me. But, it doesn't. Even with the questions I have as to why Harlan has gone out of his way to recreate the setting of Heathen's Cross, and why he dressed like a member, I take this bizarre moment as an opportunity to grasp onto the karma that's been awaiting this man that's caused me more pain that any human should inflict on another. Let alone a pastor.

He peers at me confused. "I don't know how it got to this, Araceli. I loved you like a daughter."

My tongue clicks. "Liar."

"It's true," he lies, yet again.

I inch closer, causing his constrained body to flinch. The knife curled in my fist feels like a magnet. With each second that passes, the force intensifies, practically begging me to make contact with his skin and end him.

"You were like a—"

I cut him off. "A daughter. Yes, I know. Pardon me for missing the memo. I didn't realize using me as an ashtray, or a human punching bag, or a place to sink your, what was it? Oh yes," and I air quote, "'God given parts to exorcise the demon out of me'. Sorry, Pastor. Abuse and rape isn't how you show love."

The truth in my words does what I knew it would do. Take that demon that lays dormant in him and summon it to the surface. Gone is his pleading case, and here is the asshole I've always known him to be, for all the people around us to witness.

He laughs, dry and sarcastic. "You're irredeemable. Just like she was."

My hand trembles around the knife as he continues.

"Just like your disgusting mother," he spits, disdain and glee dancing in his expression.

Harlan, who I almost forgot has been standing behind me, places a kiss on my neck before he steps in front of me to confront his father.

"Is that why you had her killed? Huh, Dad? Is that why you had Mom, and Araceli's mom, and all the others who threatened your way of spinning God's truth into your own, all killed?"

Harlan's words stab at my heart. I always knew in my heart it was true. The evidence has always been mounting against

Harlan's dad. But his role in the community and his ties to law enforcement protected him. It helped him get away with murder.

"You can't deny it Dad, there's years worth of your extermination ploy rotting in that fucking house. I don't know how you didn't think I'd see it! Considering that you haven't let me fucking leave you in years!"

An empty, hollow grin becomes smeared on his father's face. Tears rim the pastor's eyes like he's hearing everything Harlan is saying, but he won't admit to himself it's true.

That he's the monster he's been preaching against.

The one I always knew he was... yet even I am in shock.

"It's all bullshit." His dad brushes off the accusations, barely even giving Harlan the time of fucking day. As usual, all his rage, misplaced as ever, is on me.

Why should I be surprised?

Why would now be any fucking different?

"Is it though?" I break my silence, interjecting myself in their conversation. "Is it all bullshit? Everything your own son is saying makes perfect sense. You took my mother's life, then claimed her death and ran with it. Making the people of our town think that the Devil himself was after us. That you were the first line of defense and protection we all needed to be able to escape the fate that found my mother... and Harlan's... and fuck knows how many more. You fabricated the truth to protect your own filthy lies."

A boisterous roar sounds from the crowd before a dull hum— a chanting hum—replaces it.

"You're fucking crazy. No one will believe you. Not after what you've done."

He keeps saying that. What exactly does he think I've done that could be worse than what he's done?

He looks at me with a new wave of confusion and shock, almost as though he is reading my mind and mirroring my own confusion. "You can't be serious, Araceli. You can't still be denying what you are and what you keep fucking doing. Now get with it and untie me... now!" He roars, and I'm in utter disbelief that this man is so thickheaded. He is so lost in the delusions he preaches about that even now, with his son dressed as the leader of a fucking cult for fuck's sake, he's blaming me for this—like he's always done.

"Araceli Rainey," he begins, saying my name in a reprimanding tone that I will not tolerate. Not from him. Not again, and certainly not now.

"Don't call me that," I mutter, charging him. The edge of the knife now within inches of his neck. Oh, how I want nothing more than to plow it through his neck. I could. Fuck, I should. But what's stopping me? Would turning to violence—the type of violence he has always mocked me for writing about—mean he's right somehow?

Harlan senses my inner turmoil and he walks back over to me, stationing himself at my ear, but doesn't say anything.

His father continues his taunting. "Rainey. Rainey. Rainey." He mocks me. "That's who you are now. A disgrace to my name, but a Rainey, nonetheless. At least when you die, your horror will overrule mine."

"Don't listen to him, sister." Harlan lifts his hands over his head to clap and the chanting intensifies.

"Shut up!" His dad yells but it only makes the chanting volume increase, yet every word Harlan is saying to me is clear as day.

"Tell him who you are," Harlan demands.

I freeze. Who am I anymore?

I know who I was before I encountered Pastor Rainey.

Happy.

I know what I've become.

Numb.

Tormented.

Anything but happy.

But who am I? At my core. I don't know anymore.

I don't know who or what I am, other than angry.

"Tell him," Harlan repeats, this time whispering something in my ear that makes my blood run cold. "Tell him that you're the daughter of Lucien Suárez."

My throat tightens at the mention of my father. I've spent years numbing myself after his loss. Wanting to pretend that it never happened to the point that I began to believe it.

"Tell him who you are and what you're going to do!" Harlan continues, sealing his demand with the drag of his tongue on my cheek, as he lifts my hand with the knife. "You are indebted to the Cross, to *Heathen's Cross*, you can't let him live. Tell him."

"Oh please," his dad bellows. "What are you going to do to me?"

"Payback," I deadpan, and a sense of déjà vu strikes me. Harlan hums in approval as he begins his descent down my back, planting soft kisses down my spine, lowering himself to the ground. His mouth presses against my center as his nose becomes swallowed by the swell of my ass. I feel his lips brush against my skin in a trail that moves around my side until he is positioned right in front of me on his knees. Another hum ignites my skin as he begins to recite something.

"Payback," I deadpan, as I strike my clenched hammer-wielding fist down onto the top of his head.

His skull breaks with ease. The only simple thing that's ever come from him. But I don't want to only injure him. I want to annihilate him. For what he did to us. To them and all the ones before.

Blood drips onto his forehead, staining his skin, begging me to continue, and I do. One strike after another. Blood for blood. Eye for an eye.

Harlan snaps his fingers, and just as he begins to dive into my pussy, a cloaked figure walks over to us with something in their hand. I try to turn my head to see what they are holding, but pleasure rids me of my ability to think straight. Harlan is devouring me just like he did at Heathen's Cross when I was the one hung up on the cross—and not his father.

None of this makes sense.

How we got here or how Heathen's Cross is here, in the fucking backyard.

It has to be the drugs.

"Why does this all feel so familiar?" I whisper through a pant.

Harlan lifts his lips from my sex only long enough to answer. "Because you started something you didn't finish."

As he continues licking me, the cloaked person slips something cool onto my neck.

"You don't lift a finger or that knife until I say so," Harlan commands. His voice soothes my skin. "My voice may sound muffled while I'm eating this sweet cunt of yours, so make sure you're paying attention."

I peer down at my chest, seeing my necklace back in its place. Looking at the pentagram, another pendant now sits beside it.

It's filthy.

It's a... *bone*.

Similar to the ones the people at Heathen's Cross wore, but theirs—although I don't remember the exact details—were different than this one. I lower my chin to my chest, trying to study it. The long single bone is bound by leather on one end and hanging vertically down my chest, before landing between my tits. From what I can see, it's wide at the top, tapering in on the sides towards the bottom and curved. It looks smooth except for the carvings. Three consecutive circles. I go to touch it, suddenly craving its cool edges on my fingertips, but Harlan slaps my thigh as he kneads the edges of his fingers to my skin, digging into them.

"Not yet," he commands, cool and cryptic. His voice vibrates on my skin as he speaks. "There will be time to discuss the mess you made that you now wear around your neck, but for now, I want you to listen to me. Wait for my command."

Nineteen

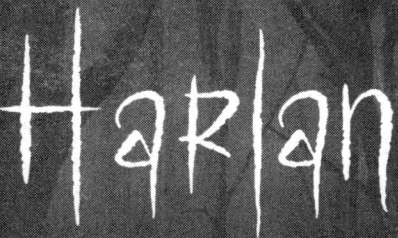

"Now," I murmur, keeping my lips stationed at her sex. Hovering her swollen lips close enough that I bet she'd burst with a single flick of one end of my tongue, but she doesn't move on my command. "I said now!" I repeat, this time shouting. The insult of her disobedience marinating in my veins. She remains still.

Why is she doing this now?

How is it that now, with the evidence mounting so blatantly high in front of her, even with me giving her the veritas serum —*truth serum*—that none of us receive until after initiation? *That I gifted her.* She still is unwavering in her defiance.

I rise to my feet, no longer interested in giving her the gift of my mutilated tongue. If she insists on being so thickheaded, then I'll match that energy... tenfold.

"Is there a problem?" I don't bother hiding the instigating tone in my voice.

"Why did you stop?" Her question directed to me as her back arches and her ass juts out, swaying left to right, just begging for me to lower to my knees again and devour her.

In due time, my gruesome sinner. In due time.

"I gave you a simple instruction. I told you to wait for my

command and in return, I'd give that greedy cunt what it's been always pining for."

Me. In my true form. No longer the suppressed, easily silenced pastor's son, but the heathen of her dreams.

She shakes her head, the knife in her hand coming dangerously close to her temple.

Closing the gap between us, I reach for her wrist, pulling it away from her head.

"You're not getting out of this that easy," I whisper. "Now finish what you started. Think of everything he's done to you." *To us.* "Let that motivate every strike." I instruct her and this time... she listens.

She unleashes on him. Stabbing his flesh like a pincushion, and the desire I had to punish her dwindles. Bloodshed. Revenge. All of it, present before my eyes, acts as an aphrodisiac more than it does a warning flare or deterrent.

"You lied!" she repeats. Her yelling, though bold, grows more distraught with each stab and the mayhem that ensues becomes her, just as much as it becomes more apparent that I need her violence as much as I need her.

I take a step back from her just enough that I have better access to her already torn pants and continue the job I started on them, shredding them until they are no longer on her body and tossed on the ground.

Keeping behind her, I reach around and over to her pussy, dipping all but my thumb—which I reserve for her clit—into her warmth.

She trembles upon contact. Arching her back enough that it forces my hand deeper.

I keep it there, working her as she exacts a revenge that's been written in the stars, waiting for her to seize.

"That's it. Let it all out," I encourage her. *Let it go.*

Just how it's meant to be.

Just like how she wrote about in her sick journal.

Lifting my free hand, I snap my fingers for one of the Cross members to see.

"Yes?" A member runs over to me, eager for instruction.

"Bring a bucket." He nods. "No," I stop to correct myself. "Make that multiple buckets." The eagerness increases as he instructs the others.

Seconds pass before cloaked members gather around us with buckets in hand. Two walk ahead of the others and place them in front of the man, who I was forced to call 'Dad', lays in the balance. The buckets are set down to form a V-shape in front of him, aimed to collect the splatter from different angles.

Araceli doesn't notice, she's lost in a trance. Too preoccupied with making him pay for everything he's done to her, and all those who are not here physically to fight for what was taken from them.

"You killed her! You're the killer! You killed all of them!" she pants.

My father. The pastor. The murderer.

The truth, which I've had more time to process than Araceli, still hits like a whip. All this time, he fooled people into thinking our town was under attack by the enemy. Yet the only enemy that existed was the one he worked so hard to keep hidden.

"That's it, little sister. Tell him the truth that he has denied. Gut. Him."

The heathens around me pick up on the last of my instructions, all chanting in unison.

Gut him.
Gut him.
Gut him.

Araceli starts to chant as well.

"Gut him," she breathes. Her pussy clenching around me as she says it.

She repeats it over again, growing closer to her orgasm as she says it. She's so close that I can practically feel it reaching the horizon, squeezing around the calloused fingers I have jammed inside her. So. Fucking. Close. Though I fear if I let her finish like this, she won't be able to finish the larger job. So I pull back, opting to watch instead.

We can't have that, not when we have a Ferryman to feed after all.

She mewls from the absence of my hands, but the betrayal of me leaving her hanging isn't enough to stop her. Her movements become more erratic. Drawing deep gashes into his bare chest like she is carving a pumpkin.

Like a twisted jack-o'-lantern getting ready to be lit on Halloween. The day he detested more than anything.

Oh, the irony.

Up, down, slide.

Up, down, slide.

The makings of a jagged grin form on his abdomen.

I peel my gaze from the bloodbath, registering the mouths moving around me, but I can't hear their words.

Too distracted by the rich smell of earthy incense and the click-clack of coins being dropped around me, my hearing becomes robbed.

A fellow heathen with a hood that protrudes more outward than any of ours walks over to my side. A soft, feminine voice follows, leaking into my ear. "She's doing so well. Adhering to what has been written."

I turn to face the woman I know to be Frida, but her cloak offers a veil of anonymity that my eyes can't penetrate.

"Shh," she breathes and her voice coils around me like a rope, securing me to her words and twisting my body in the direction of the cross.

"The initiation passage has begun."

Frida's wrinkled hands raise, one holding a key and the other holding two masks. Two familiar masks. Almost identical to the ones from the Halloween shop.

The Ferryman and the passenger.

"She left these with me the last time she came to see me." The woman takes it upon herself to lower my hood as she stretches the elastic band over my head, lowering the mask into place.

She hands me the key next. Another surge of eerie familiarity ripples through me. "He won't be needing this anymore." She tilts her head towards my father's lifeless body. "He's gone. Lost to the abyss he created. Now she's ready for you. Your perfect passenger with payment in tow. Go to her. Make her pay the toll. Let her sail. She can't escape you now."

I close my eyes for a second to blink, but the moment my eyes open she's gone and that horrid song starts replaying in my mind, infecting my brain. Even worse, my brain is reciting it in the same sinister singsong she did when I heard her sing it in the graveyard years ago.

"Harlan Rainey has to go. Has to go, so no one knows. Harlan Rainey has to die. Blood for blood. Eye for an eye."

"No, this isn't right," I mutter to myself as I look up to Araceli who is now exhausted on her knees in front of a very dead and gutted Pastor Harlan Rainey... *senior.*

The song should've stopped. He's dead. The sick and twisted melody infects my brain. The one from the graveyard, and the one she sang over and over again while she smothered me with her pussy, that undoubtedly belongs to me now.

Frida's voice sounds again. Whispering to me from deep within, but she's nowhere to be found. *"The song was never about your father. It was always about you. She wants you dead, Harlan. Kill her before she kills you."*

I know. She's right. It's nothing I haven't already known deep down.

It was always about me and her.

Little did she know that the last part of her song, the whole blood for blood and eye for eye bit, is part of the credo of the Heathen's. Being Lucian Suárez's daughter may mean she has Heathen in her blood, but it starts and ends there. To be a member of Heathen's Cross is to believe in fatum enim eligimus —*for we choose fate.* Except our fate is very seldom a solitary path.

Often people find a way into our stories and sometimes when they do, betrayals occur. That's where the credo comes in, that her father, Lucian Suárez, created when he founded Heathen's Cross, back when it was known as La Cruz De Los Paganos in Puerto Rico, before he moved stateside. Blood for blood, eye for an eye, adds a layer to choosing one's fate. It means deciding how to exact revenge when necessary. Granted, Lucien meant that part for enemies of his people and those who didn't respect their spiritual freedom like my father, and not his daughter. But what he doesn't know won't kill him... he's already dead.

Araceli rises from her knees. Blood stains her skin, only adding to her allure, but it's the knife in her hand that steals my attention. The way it's clutched in her grip. The way it shines beneath the moonlight as she moves it up and down with each step of her stride over to me. It reminds me that if I don't end her the way the ancestors of the cross wanted, she will finish me...for good.

I lift both my hands, snapping my fingers for my fellow Heathens to attend to my command.

"You," I point to one, "retrieve the bucket and bring it to me."

I turn and point at another random, yet willing, heathen, "And you, put this on her." I toss the mask over. I point to two hooded members, both built so broad and tall, they look as if they can be on stilts. They can handle her when she puts up the fight that I know she will start once she realizes what I'm making them place on her face. "You two. Make sure she doesn't go anywhere."

Araceli's gaze falls to the mask and horror blossomes on her face, dulling her natural glow. "No," she cries, trying to fight the two members approaching her. "I don't want it."

My loyal Heathen's ignore her. The two I instructed to hold her down, grab hold of her arms, holding her in place while the other stretches the mask over her face.

"I changed my mind!" she pleas.

A grin mars my face, stretching the mask over my head as I

approach her. "Too late, you started this and now you're going to finish it. But this time you'll finish it *with me*," I announce with sadistic glee.

I continue over to her. Relishing in the way the fear—the reminder—of that night with the masks and carnage is ripping her boldness away, making her putty in my hands. "You look beautiful," I lie. Though her body looks as fuckable as ever. The mask is hideous, but even so, its putrid state becomes her.

It's adorable how hard Araceli is trying to fight against the hold of the Heathen's I've tasked with keeping her still until I'm ready for her. "Let go of me!" she shouts, though the vigor in her voice is dwindling. The knife drops to the ground and I bend down to retrieve the weapon she used to kill my dad. I should feel remorse, but that emotion died a long time ago. For the man I was, I feel nothing, and that includes all those associated with me before my fall, my dad included.

He got what was coming to him.

Finally.

Now she will get what's coming to her.

"Why are you doing this, Harlan?"

I ignore her, snapping my fingers for one of my fellow Heathen's, who has what I'm looking for, to listen and bring me it. "Snake!" I call out. Even through the hideous mask on her face, there's no missing the disdain—the terror—ripe within her irises.

I take an additional step forward, teasing her with the edge of the knife while I wait for the bucket with the snake. I remember how much she hates them, but she should appreciate my reasoning behind making sure a snake is present. Despite our upbringing, which made us look at serpents as evil creatures who represent God's enemy, snakes are rich in symbolism. Something a writer such as herself should appreciate. Snakes represent many things. Such as transformation, renewed energy, and in some cases, *rebirth.*

A holy trinity of sorts.

A new beginning.

A new trifecta to become attached to.

The bucket with the snake now arrives in front of her, and one Heathen holds it in place while the other takes its contents out, guiding the poisonous snake onto Araceli's body.

"You—" she stammers, the snake taking its sweet time wrapping around her thigh. I lick my lips at the sight of the pebbled marks on her skin. "You've changed."

"I know. Isn't it great how time has molded me into the heathen you've always wanted, but can't have?"

"You disgust me."

I click my tongue as my lips fall into a pout. "You shouldn't talk like that. Your hatred does things to me." I stifle a moan, watching her center glisten as her body remains in place by the force of hands that are not my own, and by the snake that has managed to tie her legs together as if it were practicing shibari.

Closing the gap between us, I dip one finger into her cunt. The pulse and clench it makes around my finger is a pathetic cry for me—one that I will make her work for if she wants it bad enough. Quick as I dove my hand in, I retract it, and she growls in anger. "You're pathetic. I want nothing to do with you after this."

A laugh sneaks past my lips. "After this? Who the fuck says there will be an *after* this? Look around, this isn't the Holy Harvest. This is the meeting ground of Heathen's Cross."

She shakes her head in defiance... in denial.

"No, this is impossible. Heathen's Cross was never here. It was out of town. It was far from here."

"Was it though?" My question is purely rhetorical. "You keep choosing to believe that, but the fact remains that it's All Hallows Eve, and since we have all gathered here today, a sacrifice must be made."

Araceli fumbles her words. "I—I thought you said initiation."

"Initiation. Sacrifice. Same shit."

"No, it's fucking not!" Araceli screams.

"There she is," I mutter as I clap my hands. "Goddammit, you are such a bore when you get all whiny and confused. I like your mean side. It gives me something to work with. Don't look so sad, though. This is the end, sister, get excited."

Live a little... before you can't anymore.

"You're a fucking idiot. I made a sacrifice for you. That part is done."

"For that, I thank you. Sincerely, I am so grateful. You have no idea how long I've waited for him to croak. But, with the only law of three, it wouldn't have worked if I took the liberty of killing him myself."

Her head tilts ,and I pick up on her confusion, continuing on only to add to it more. "Three. You know, like the Holy Trinity. Except in order to achieve true initiation, three deaths need to occur tonight before midnight. That way, you have three tokens to feed the Ferryman. Since you so rudely skipped out on him before, this time he wants to be paid."

"No."

"Yes," I retort. "And since you already killed the guard, and then dear old Daddy, there's just one more death that has to occur to complete your initiation into Heathen's Cross."

"This isn't happening. You're taking what Heathen's Cross was, and you're manipulating it."

"Oh, so only you are able to manipulate the truth?" I challenge her, bringing the blade to her chin, grazing it with enough pressure that a thin red line forms on her flesh.

"See, you made your sacrifice, but I've yet to make mine." My voice ignites with excitement, thinking of how fun my sacrifice will be.

"This isn't who you are."

"Wrong. This isn't who you remember me being. But what was, and what is, are two different things. You should be thanking me. I've become who you've wanted me to be. What you've always wanted me to be—*free*."

"I hate you." She says that like she believes it.

"Fuck, there's that hatred again. You're so fucking sexy when you pretend that you hate me. Will it make that needy cunt of yours pulse and beg for me, if I say that I hate you too, sister? I bet you'd cream yourself right here and now if I told you that everything that has transpired tonight is your fault. That my downfall is your doing. That I no longer give a shit about making you feel anything other than what you made me feel. Which, in case you forgot, is like worthless, fuckable, disposable trash. At least this time I'll fuck you with more than just my tongue. Don't want to send you to your grave unsatisfied."

She's speechless. Too much truth to process at once. So, I continue. "Remember, you're the one who fantasized about my hatred pumping in and out of your cunt that you came back here under the guise of needing a stupid necklace back. What happens tonight is on you. I'm just a vessel for your punishment and you just so happen to be the wet hole worthy of the punishment only I can give you."

Araceli remains motionless, quiet and unsure.

"Lift her." I instruct. The snake remains knotted on her legs and the two heathens signal for more to help transport her. "It's time we really take her to *the last stop*."

Let's see if *she* sails this time.

Twenty

Araceli

Darkness. It's everywhere. It's in the starless sky hanging above me. It colors the fabric of the hooded people gathered around me. It has taken their eyes hostage. No matter the actual shade of their irises—whether blue, green, brown or some variant in between—darkness... bleak, robotic darkness is all that stares back at me. Everything feels as dark as Harlan's newfound soul... or lack thereof.

"Drop her there." Harlan's instruction is met with a synchronized, and rhythmic clapping from the members who seem to look at him as if he's their leader. An arguably confusing position and an extremely frightening concept to grasp. That Harlan, my once conflicted church boy, now stands with pride as an intricate part of Heathen's Cross. I thought it was just a haunt, but clearly it's so much more. It's a movement, and now it's my curse.

The wind picks up, and the already fallen leaves lift and scatter about as my body feels like it's floating. I can tell from the way the leaves shift and scrape that I'm being taken to the graveyard between the church and house. I've spent too many nights in this part of the property when I lived here, especially in autumn, to not recognize the sound foliage makes when fallen on uneven and rough limestone graves.

Without so much as a word or warning, the many hands that aided in my journey to the graveyard vanish from my body. A sinking feeling implodes in my gut as I crash to the uneven ground. My body aches in response to the fall and the pain makes me more aware of the snake still wrapped around my limbs. I wiggle myself around, trying to signal my arms to move, but they don't budge. Rendered motionless by the drugs mixed with fear, I'm unable to fight it like I should. He's winning. *He's fucking winning.*

Harlan stands over me, saying something to get everyone to leave us alone. Of course, they obey, all mumbling a familiar chant as they walk away.

"Fatum enim eligimus." They repeat in unison until they are out of hearing range.

"Finally, just me and you," Harlan announces as something mauve in color, wrapped around my legs, grips my attention.

I blink repeatedly, desperate for clarity. "Ewww, get it off me!" I cry, vomit rising to my mouth as I stare at the slimy, thick intestines wrapped around my legs. As sick as it is, I would've preferred the snakes.

"Shut up!" Harlan's boot lands on my rib cage before he flips me over onto my stomach. "Look!" He directs my head, twisting his hands that dig into my jaw beneath my mask. "Tell me what you see?"

"This isn't real," I breathe out, trying to believe the words I'm saying. Standing before me is The Last Stop, with its ornate windows and uneven *limestone* porch. But it isn't in town like I remember it, it's here. On the property... in the graveyard.

"How is it here?" I mutter my question. "I don't understand. How is this The Last Stop?" I again try to convince myself, but all I see is the shed to the graveyard that my stepdad kept locked once he found me snooping inside.

"No, sister, you wanted it to be *your* last stop. But each time you visited, you were denied access with only the crumbs of truth you had. You can't gain full entry until you learn the whole truth.

That's the only way blood for blood can be achieved. My dad tried so hard to keep the truth from you, he definitely didn't help matters much."

"What truth?" I ask in desperation, unable to determine what is true and what's not anymore.

"Here, let me," Harlan says, walking ahead of me, with a key in his hand.

He twists it and opens the stubborn door that never opened with ease for me. Once the door opens, familiar scents of incense and musk fill my senses, like I remember when I visited The Last Stop. Though all my memories are as shaky as my limbs. The foundation I thought I knew, crumbling before me. "You were so close to discovering the truth about who my dad was, and it scared him. Then, after we both landed in the hospital, he was afraid of what you began to unearth. So, he locked it. He took your notebook and everything you held dear, locked it inside the shed, just like he had done before. But just like the previous times when he locked it, you found the key. You always found that damn key. He hoped that you'd forget about it and move on. Truthfully, we all assumed that you did move on, considering how long it took you to come back here. Now I'll ask you once, why did you come back last night only to leave?"

"I didn't. The first time I've come back here since I left is tonight."

He sighs. "Fucking Christ, Araceli! Seriously? I know you make a living off lying on paper, but even now you're going to? Why did you come back to me last night, just to leave me again?"

"But I didn't." Tears begin to line my eyes.

He wags his finger at me. "Don't you dare cry, not yet. I only want your tears when I'm close enough to lick them off your face."

"I'm only going to repeat myself one more time. Why did you fucking come so close, yet leave me again? Again, Araceli! You left me again!"

"I don't," I fumble my words. "I don't," I repeat, but before I can say anything else, Harlan yanks my wrists, dragging me across the dirt until I'm at the entrance of the shed. He moves inside, leaving me on the ground and as he walks to retrieve something.

A few moments later, he reemerges, and the entirety of his cloak is filthy. Dirt mucks it everywhere. He stares up at the moon, seeing the cracks of daylight infiltrating the sky.

"We don't have much time," he says.

"For what?"

"The initiation to be complete." He deadpans, swiping at a small monitor in his hands. "Here we are. Look."

Time stamped in front of me, October 30th, 2024—*last night*—I'm met with the view of me, dirty, full of mud, walking through the graveyard, in an almost catatonic state. I watch in horror as I drop to the ground, clawing at the ground—*screaming*. He presses fast forward and the time lapses, but there I remain just digging my hands into the ground until I stop with something white in my hand.

"See!" he exclaims. "You *were* here. You got what you wanted, and then you left. You weren't supposed to leave. Tell me. What did you forget?" He roars his question.

"I don't know."

"Liar!" His words are like a whip.

"Since you are conveniently forgetting every-fucking-thing. Let me help jog your memory." He tosses the camera down, and his hands latch onto me, dragging me back through the tombstones. He doesn't stop, or let go until we near a loaded dump truck. The red buttons glare at me. "Look familiar?" Harlan asks.

"No. Not yet." I try to fight him, but Harlan holds me in place with his possessive grip. Forced to look at what he's showing me as he turns my head away from the truck, I now see a six-foot-deep hole in the ground. Paired with a temporary marker next to it with my name on it... written in blood.

I gasp, but my reaction is overruled as a sharp pain shoots into my thigh before a warm, wet sensation trails down, and my legs go weak. I peer down at the intestines only to see they aren't intestines at all—they're gone. Harlan's snake has laced himself around my legs, locking me in place. His fangs sinking deep in my thigh, pumping his venom into me. "Good boy," Harlan coos before clapping, and the snake leaves me as fast as it slithered onto me.

Harlan laughs. "You really thought those were intestines, didn't you? That's the drugs tricking you. Hallucinogens have a funny way of messing with the truth."

"I hate this place. It's fucking haunted," I breathe out. Relieved that the snake is off me, but now I have Harlan to contend with.

He shakes his head, mumbling a no. "It's not the house that's haunted, it's your heart."

Harlan reaches over to my neck and yanks my necklace. I watch, stunned, as Harlan pushes aside the pentagram pendant as his fingers graze the large, curved bone hanging low enough that it becomes lost between my breasts.

"Good choice," he praises, rubbing the bone, getting an unexpected level of arousal from it, judging from the primal grunt that just echoed from beneath his mask. "You should add actress to your repertoire. Pretending to come back for your 'necklace'. Clearly, you came back for *me*... and oh, have I been waiting for *you*."

Harlan reaches into his back pocket, taking out my journal from it. "We won't be needing this anymore. All that was written is, and will come to fruition." He grins, tossing it over my head. The thud on the ground impossible to ignore.

"You know what makes me hard, Araceli?"

I roll my eyes.

Bones and death, clearly.

"I don't know... anything with a pulse?" I blurt, my sarcasm reemerging.

"Wrong," he quips. "Your fear, because in it lies your truth, and I intend after tonight to exhume your truth as you have exhumed mine. I want to terrorize you until your screams turn your throat hoarse. I want to taunt you like putty in my hands. The same hands that will gladly strangle the life out of you, until that pulse that you think is the only prerequisite I have to get my dick hard withers away. *That's* what gets me rock fucking hard."

Without warning, Harlan moves his hands to my waist, lifting me high enough that he can push me into the open pit *I* stupidly dug in the ground.

Dust clouds form as my body crashes into the earth and he continues on. "That, and fantasizing of how pretty you'll look when the olive of your flesh morphs into a lifeless array of purple and blue. All while those pouty lips of yours remain on mine until they turn cold and lifeless."

He starts humming to himself as he turns around, "Blood for blood. Eye for an eye." His voice trails off and he moves for a moment, out of my sight.

I hear the faint rumble of machinery begin, but it's not loud enough that I can't hear his voice. "Oh, brujita," Harlan says, but it's not his voice I hear, it's Frida. "*I taught you better than this. Seeing isn't always believing. You knew what you did. You knew what you had to do. But you ran like all the scared ones do.*"

"Frida?" I call out, to which Harlan laughs manically.

"No, silly, it's me. But sometimes they have a habit of doing that. You'll learn soon enough. All that once was, has a tendency to linger. Whatever you heard, I wouldn't brush it off. Trust your gut. It's your gift. Well, our gift now. Fuck, Araceli, I could've given you the world. You know that? But you just had to tempt me. You had to insert me in your twisted fantasy. Now all that's left is to give you the end you deserve, plus I'm not wearing this mask for nothing. It's time to pay the Ferryman."

Just like in the book. My book. My destiny.

He's taking it for me. Ending it.

On instinct, thinking back to the picture in the journal Frida gifted me, I think of the Ferryman illustration. Remembering the woman with her mouth open to pay her debt. I need to pay my debt so he can finally forgive me, so I do just that, and I open my mouth.

"No. Boring. I already had your mouth. Now I want something else to warm my cock. Open your legs. Be brother's gruesome little whore and play one last time with me. I want to make good on my promise and take you to where the sun doesn't shine and never will again. Well, not for you at least."

He jumps into the hole, dirt spilling in at a rapid pace. He quickly undoes his belt buckle, freeing his cock, then sits on top of me—pinning me in place. Within seconds, the blade I used to kill his father is at my chin, teasing my skin.

It feels better than I care to admit. For the first time in a long time—if ever—I feel at peace. At one with my roots—with my destiny.

I look past his hovering head and up at the sky, and the hooded members with their black cloaks reemerge, all wearing the same Ferryman mask that he is.

"I don't know why I ever bothered trying to make you happy. Sorrow suits you...just like the blood I'm about to draw."

"Harlan, I'm sor —" I begin, but he silences me with a growl. Something burns in my chest. The knife falls from my chin to my chest.

"I don't want your apologies. I want to see how far you're willing to fight for your life so I can steal it from you. Do you have any fight left in you?"

No.

"I want to crush you like you've crushed me. I think that's fair, wouldn't you say?"

Yes. I answer internally. Knowing deep down there's no other way this can end... or should.

Every pass he makes across my skin, I feel the knife edge slice through my clothes, and it feels like it's cutting through me, opening me up further for him. As his frantic slices slow, I feel his other hand begin to trace circles, smearing my blood all over me, allowing the chilly night air to bite at my skin.

"A new holy trinity. Three deaths for one renewal," he hums.

A hiss sounds near my ear, followed by a slimy chill that slithers and wraps around my neck, robbing my air.

"He missed you," Harlan sneers, taking the snake's tail and gently pulling it towards him, increasing the pressure around my airway.

Dirt continues to fall, clouding the air around us and before I can say anything or scream from the pain, he guides his cock into me with such force that I can feel a ricochet of pain latch onto my spine. His thrusts hurt more than the blade did. Each slam of his hard cock is more violent than the last. Yet each time he pulls back only to give me more of him, I clench my walls around him in anticipation. Not wanting to let him go. Hoping that the next harsh blow to my center will not only grant me release, but will release me from the guilt I've held onto for so long. For hurting him like I did, and for being the reason he's become as cold as he has. I'm what made him like this. I'm responsible for taking something pure, and corrupting it so badly it turned him into a monster who's now fucking me better than anyone ever has, or ever will. I ruined him, and now it's his turn to ruin me.

He continues his punishing thrusts into my cunt. It hurts so bad yet the more he pumps into me, the wetter I become. I look up at him. Into the eye slits of his mask, and I can feel the hollowness in his stare. Suddenly, the mask he's been wearing doesn't look like a mask... it looks *real*. Strength ignites in my limbs and I lift my hand to his face. The decay, the jagged texture, the rot, all of it, is part of his skin. All of it is as real, and brutal, as the pounding I'm taking from him, willingly.

"Why?" I whimper.

"Because you made me who I am."

"A villain?" I pant through the escalating pain and bliss dancing through my senses. Tricking me into believing that this isn't the torment my mind knows it to be.

"No, little sister. The ending you deserve."

"But I don't want this to end." I beg, but the stars that line my vision let me know that this will be the last time I feel him like this.

"Tighter," Harlan mewls, and the snake follows his command. It slithers slowly under my neck, and back around, this time facing Harlan. "Me too," he commands it, and it springs forward, latching onto Harlan's shoulder. Taking its sweet time, it slinks its scales around his neck before nearing me again.

"Look." *Thrust.* "At." *Thrust.* "Us." *Thrust.* "So connected," Harlan grunts. "So fucking doomed." He laughs as he revs up the pace he's wreaking havoc on my insides.

I never thought he could hurt me like this. I never dreamed he could hurt me so fucking good. But I have to remember, this isn't him. It can't be.

I close my eyes, hoping I'll see him. The real him. Innocent. *Alive.* So eager to please me like he's doing now, except not in the form my mind created out of lust. Hoping it would overshadow my guilt with my fantasies.

I open my eyes, and the Harlan of my living nightmares is gone. No longer hovering over me. Stabbing my eyes with his vicious blue stare. He's gone. Really gone. Though I still feel the tempo of his cock pounding into me as he summons my impending release.

"Where are—"

"Shh," he whispers. "Close your eyes."

I do as he says and my lids fall shut. Suddenly, we aren't in a filling hole in the ground. We're back at Heathen's Cross, back to years ago.

His head is buried between my legs, but where my skin feels warm, his is cold. Ice cold.

"Araceli. I. Can't."

"Shut up!" I yell.

"Araceli. I. Can't. Breathe."

Just like brother's gruesome, greedy, and high off her ass whore. I heard him, but it didn't register. His tongue, in one piece, not split, felt so good, as did the high I was riding. His plea only made me squeeze my legs around him tighter. He licked me until he couldn't anymore. Until he began his descent into unconsciousness while buried in between my legs and I blacked out.

It all becomes blurry until I hear the sirens. All over again, just like that night. Except when I look down, I see my feet, and when I look up, it's Harlan tied and bound on the cross. Not me. Blood mars my hand. A voice whispering from deep within. Screaming at me. Telling me it's all my fault. I did this to him. I killed him.

I killed the wrong one.

"No!" I open my eyes, peering down at my center. My naked, blood-stained body is covered in dirt... so much dirt. But Harlan isn't there. It's just my hand and the bone from my necklace. Harlan's bone. The bone that I recovered, that I dug up, the night before... from his grave.

His fucking *grave*.

He's not here.

This can't be real.

"Except it is, little sister," Harlan hisses in my ears. His deep whisper sends a trail of raised bumps down my spine.

"How?" I cry out. Voice trembling. My lungs are burning from lack of oxygen. The pressure on my throat and the dirt filling the hole we're fucking in, it's too much. I don't know how much more I can take until *it* takes me.

A response doesn't speak to me. Not audibly, or from within. But my hand moves, accelerating to a dizzying speed. In and out, the curved edge of his rib bone scraping at my insides.

"How?" I repeat to myself, now staring up at the night sky expecting to see nothing but the stars... but he's there. I can see him. I can feel him. Fucking me. Punishing me with every violent thrust that may not look like him, but I know it's him.

"Because your heart is haunted, that's why. Keep going," he whispers. "You're so close." Encouraging me from beyond. "You'll learn the truth soon. Keep. Going. Don't. Stop. You're doing so well, taking my punishment in that greedy, dying cunt."

I do as he says. Taking my punishment —*my penance*.

"Thank you for remembering me this time," Harlan whispers, bringing his lips to mine. His tongue darts out of his mouth, breaking through the barrier of earth, filling my mouth with its suffocating promise.

The crest of my orgasm now, on the horizon. I pinch my eyes, bracing myself. A violent quiver explodes throughout my body as I give him what will surely be my last living burst of pleasure.

Ignoring the gritty mound of soil sneaking past my lips, expecting the split muscle of his tongue to war with my boring intact one, I keep my mouth open for him. As expected, a warmth emerges between my lips, but it's not his tongue. It's slimy, thick, and *serpentine*.

I gasp, folding my tongue forward, trying to fight it off, but it's relentless. My airway, as if it already couldn't stand a chance against the burial in progress, becomes blocked. Harlan laughs as he drives one final thrust inside me, as he steals my release.

"You're vile, little sister. I'll give you that. Vile and savage. What made you come harder, the memory of my cock or the dead serpent punching your tonsils?"

Dead?

It's dead too?

I peer down towards my chest, and somehow, through the earth that's engulfed me, I see a long strand of thin, curved bones jutting from my mouth.

Harlan cackles. "See, you're pathetic. You're so desperate for my scraps that you'd settle for anything to fill those gaping holes of yours."

Frida was right. Messing with one's destiny has consequences. His haunting presence and the pain he is inflicting on me is all one horrid consequence.

A lesson I'm not learning, too late.

The fragile bones push their way deeper into my mouth, some breaking as they plummet down my throat, scratching me the same way Harlan -or what's left of him- did to my pussy.

I want to scream in disgust, but all that comes out is a muffled cry of pleasure, as I come just in time for me to vanish into the abyss.

"Mark 16:18. They will pick up snakes with their hands; and when they drink deadly poison, it will not hurt them at all; they will place their hands on sick people, and they will get well." Harlan hums, and I feel the weight of this life lift from my bones as a sea of wet warmth engulfs my body.

"Not you though, little sister. Your heart is sick and meant to rot with mine. Thank you for breaking me. It's only right that I returned the favor." A final whisper breaks through my consciousness, and I'm no longer in the grave plot—the one I dug up to be with him—*one last time*. I'm standing, naked, on a small sailboat with the waves whipping up on the boat, splashing onto me from the rough current.

Harlan stands in his cloak, with an extra in one hand, while his other is held out for me. Waiting for me. Waiting to welcome me to what awaits me after life's burden finally lets me go.

A tall, ominous figure, also dressed in all-black, with a scythe in their hand, stands off in the distance. Though their face is difficult to distinguish from the hood draped over their head, they look angry.

Harlan pays the figure no mind as he helps me off the boat and drapes the familiar black fabric—the Heathen's Cross cloak—onto my naked, clean, and blood-free body.

I feel renewed. Whole.

"Ready to pay?" Harlan asks me, reaching for my hand that now carries two coins, each marked with three circles.

"Not yet." I answer Harlan, ignoring the cloaked figure waiting for payment to complete our passage just behind him.

Harlan waves over to him, signaling something with his hands, and the figure seems to agree. Nodding once before walking off.

"That'll buy us some time, but I promise he will be after us if we don't pay. I've dodged him as long as I can while waiting for you. I won't be able to journey with you much longer."

"It won't take long," I reassure him. Excitement blossoming in my new form.

"What do you have in mind?" Harlan asks. Excited. Full of Life.

"You'll see."

Harlan's ink drawn hand finds my neck. The skeletal design that was on top of his hand now has spread to the entirety of his arm. His grip sinks into my neck. Hard. But I feel nothing.

No pain.

Only pleasure.

A *lot* of it.

"Welcome home, little sister," he growls.

"This isn't home, it's Hell." *Remember.*

"Yes, but now you and I... we're free."

Yep, free to do what I should've done a long fucking time ago.

PART III

THE AFTERMATH

"You know, the only thing that matters is the ending. It's the most important part of the story, the ending. And this one... is very good. This one's perfect."
— Mort Rainey (The Secret Window)

EPILOGUE

"Good evening, I'm Joan Lantz, and thank you for tuning into Channel Seven News. With another Halloween behind us, it appears that our town can't seem to escape the curse that comes to us with each trick-or-treating season. Though with the tragic news we are about to report, we hope that if nothing else, the good people of Mort can finally put a closure to the tragedies that have plagued us for far too long at the hands of the Samhain Killer, who until this day, has not been named, but is about to be.

A grizzly scene unfolded in the early morning hours today, when local law enforcement received an anonymous tip from a concerned resident driving on Summerland Drive reporting hearing a harrowing mix of terrifying screams and crying off in the distance, in the direction of the gated Rainey property.

Shortly after the tip was called in, law enforcement along with the Mort Fire Department, arrived at 333 Summerland Drive, which as many of you are aware is the address to what once stood as a pinnacle of unity and faith for our small town, Sacred Promises Church, which is located on the six-acre lot owned and lived on by Pastor Harlan Rainey Sr. The property was once split into two, three-acre lots, with a cemetery that divided the two. Pastor Rainey obtained the rest of the property after the neighboring owner, Lucien

Suárez, passed away, leaving no will in place. However, after what we have learned about the events of last night, how Pastor Rainey came to own the full six-acres is as eerie as it is damning.

As most of you remember, it was on Halloween night, thirteen years ago that Pastor Harlan Rainey Sr.'s son, Harlan Rainey Jr., was found tied to a cross with unholy symbols covering his body as part of a sacrilegious ritual in the graveyard that sits on the Rainey property, just between the Rainey's farmhouse, and Sacred Promises Church on Summerland Drive. Upon paramedics finding Harlan Jr. unconscious due to a suspected drug overdose along with his stepsister, Araceli Rainey, both were rushed to the hospital. Sadly, Harlan Jr. was pronounced dead shortly after his arrival at Allan Memorial Hospital. Araceli Rainey, however, did survive, but has been missing after she reportedly fought hospital staff and escaped in nothing but her hospital gown, and hasn't been seen since. That is until the grizzly and unthinkable scene first responders were met with last night.

In the graveyard that once sat as a divider between the Suárez and Rainey portions of the Summerland property, authorities found an empty hydraulic trailer that appeared to refill the grave plot of Harlan Rainey Jr. After removing the newly poured dirt, Araceli Rainey was found, buried with the exhumed bones of her stepbrother, Harlan Jr. Araceli was found with multiple wounds on her body, so it is unclear if she died before or after attempting to bury herself alive.

Though the horror does not end there. Authorities also discovered Pastor Rainey, who was found dead on arrival. His body bludgeoned, covered in unholy symbols, and hung on a cross similar to how his son was found years ago. Nailed to Pastor Rainey's hand was a note confessing to the murder of his two wives. His first being Ella Rainey, who is Harlan Jr.'s mom, and his second wife, Frida Suárez Rainey, the biological mother of his stepdaughter, Araceli, and ex-wife to Pagan leader and founder of the once beloved Pagan retreat, Heathen's Cross that was once located on his portion of Summerland Drive, before Rainey Sr. took over the land.

There was also a list of others that Rainey Sr. admitted to killing. In an effort to protect the rights of the families involved, those names shall remain anonymous. Authorities do now have an open investigation to determine the legitimacy of these claims; however, with the amount of decomposition found in the crawl space that connects the Rainey farmhouse to Sacred Promises Church, I think it's safe to say that the Samhain Killer won't be hurting our town any longer."

"Such a tragedy, Joan."

"Yes it is, Victor. Yes, it is."

"Now in other less horrific news. We have started our holiday shopping guide early for all you eager shoppers..."

VICTORIA ELIZABETH

I stare at the television as I turn it off. The remote in my hand gets flung onto the couch as I sit in stunned silence, processing what I just heard.

Pastor Rainey. The pastor at Sacred Promises, the church I went to for years—that I used to be the secretary to for a brief time when my mom was sick—is the *Samhain killer*?

How can that be?

My head shakes back and forth in disbelief. The need to clutch onto my cross necklace becomes immense.

As if all of this news isn't shocking enough, hearing Harlan's name again feels just as painful as it did the day I learned of his passing. From drugs, of all things.

So tragic.

So.

Fucking.

Tragic.

Though somehow the tragedy of Harlan's death and the horrors that happened on 333 Summerland Drive pale in comparison to what I discovered last night. That Harlan's stepsister and *my* literary client, Araceli Rainey, just couldn't help herself, and had to go home to see him.

To see my Harlan.

She already had her night with him that Halloween night thirteen years ago and look where it got both of them? He died, no thanks to her influences, and she has been a shell of herself for years. Depressed. Writing the most grotesque, morally questionable stories that people freaking eat up.

At least working with her was lucrative, while it lasted. Which is the only reason I offered to be her agent. That's the beauty of the internet. I was able to pull from my full name, Victoria Elizabeth, and use the screen name Beth's Writing Palace for my business, and she had no fucking clue I was the Tori that Harlan used to hook up with before she corrupted him.

We never had to meet face-to-face. All correspondence was done through social media and emails, so the dumb bitch had no idea. Lucky for me, Harlan's passing weighed on her so heavily that whatever witchy garbage she used to read people failed her.

I may hate what she writes, but I suppose even I can admit that she is—or *was*—objectively talented. I mean she is—ah, fuck, *was*—delusional and most delusional creatives make the best stories. There is, or was, promise in her work and I knew if I supported her enough, she would make the delusional decision to leave her fortune she amassed in her career to me upon her passing. It'd be the perfect payback for all the destruction she unknowingly caused me. Of course, I didn't think it'd happen so soon. Especially not with the final installment of her Ferryman series set to come out.

Though lucky for me, I found the junky notebook she insisted on writing in. She loved it so much she tried burying herself with it. Well, she tried to. It never quite made it in the grave plot since I saw it in the graveyard and snatched it up. With the control I have over her estate—that she so foolishly gave to me—I own the rights to her notebook and its contents. Now that I

EPILOGUE

have it, I can have an editor piece it together and once published, I'll be rolling in the fucking money.

My hand lifts to my mouth as I stifle a yawn. Fuck, I'm so tired. It took forever getting back home from the Rainey property after I not only called in the tip, but I got what I needed before law enforcements swarmed the fucking place.

Walking from my living room, I take the filthy book and the other *souvenir* I got from my excursion last night, and head to the bathroom to run myself a bath before crashing.

I lay both the book and the necklace on the vanity before running the water, setting it to warm. I undress and as my clothes fall to the floor. I hear the doorbell ring, and my heart skips a beat. I live on a secluded lot, so it's a rare occurrence that I get any visitors, let alone so early in the morning. I decide to ignore it, but the bell keeps ringing.

"Hold on a second," I call out, reaching for my robe, and slipping it on so I can see who is so insistent at the door.

The doorbell continues to ring, this time with less time in between rings, causing me to hurry my steps.

"Jesus Christ, I'm coming," I mutter beneath my breath, though as my hand curls around the knob, I'm rendered motionless. My wrist goes to turn, but the frigid sensation on the brass knob feels paralyzing. Still, the doorbell persists, so I fight through the odd sensation and twist the knob, opening the door.

No more ringing of the doorbell.

There's no one there.

Anger invades me as I step out onto the porch, scanning it without a sign of anyone there.

"Halloween is over!" I shout. "Have to wait until next year for your pranks!"

Shaking my head, I head back into the house, though as I break the threshold of the doorway, a collection of muddy footprints trails a scattered line on my flooring.

"What the—" I interrupt myself, slamming and locking the door behind me.

This is my karma.
No, Beth.
Or Tori.
Whoever you want to be called.
You don't believe in Karma.
You're a good Christian woman.
Well... you were *a good Christian woman until that fucking succubus of a woman tempted your moral compass.*

I frantically look around the living room to see any sign of the intruder. But everything is still in place.

"Hello," I call out, feeling like a fool.

The house is still. So silent that you can hear a pin drop.

I inch forward and the floorboards creak beneath my feet. I peer down and more of the muddy footsteps are in my view. The longer I stare down at the floorboards, the more appear.

Suddenly, all the gusto I had dissipates, as I run towards my bible I keep on the end table by my couch.

With each frantic move I make, I try not to look at the floor, but it's impossible, as more seem to appear each time I blink my eyes.

Finally, standing in front of the end table, I extend my hand for my bible, but it slides on the wood surface. I inch forward, curling my hand this time for it, but it slides again. It continues to slide back and forth, and side to side until it is suspended midair.

A rush of faintness trickles into my head as the bible floats in front of me. Still, I try to fight through it even as a familiar voice emerges, breaking the silence.

"Looking for this," Harlan's voice coos in my ear.

"Har—Harlan," I say, relieved, though I shouldn't be.

He's not here.

It's impossible.

"*Har—Harlan.*" Another voice mocks in singsong.

Feminine.

Angry.

I turn my head to face the other voice. I make it about a half turn before the bible is no longer floating.

"Looking for this?" Araceli cackles as the bible slaps me in the face. "Yeah, me too." She hits me again just as something is injected into my spine and the room becomes as dark as my dwindling consciousness.

HARLAN

"Turn the water off," Araceli demands. Her naked body looks as delectable as ever, even as she holds Tori's bible in her possession. A book that she and I detest. "And for the love of—"

"Lucifer." Araceli cuts me off. The seductive grin on her face makes what we have to do feel impossible. But like the old saying goes, *"thy shall be done."*

"Put the bible down." I demand.

With a dramatic shiver and ample relief, she obeys, about to leave it on the floor and walk away. I click my tongue and Araceli's eyes flicker over to mine.

"Yes?" she asks, sounding intrigued.

"Open it," I instruct her.

"Ooh," she hums. In excited obedience and the eagerness in her voice, the way it hangs in the air before plummeting to my cock is intoxicating. I must say, death is very becoming of her. The level of obedience that took over the brattiness I grew used to in her living days is refreshing... and hot as hell.

"Good—" I begin, but I'm cut off by Araceli's red nails, flashing in my periphery as her hand lifts.

"Don't say it." She clicks her tongue. There's that feistiness coming out to play. So it's only half gone away. "Don't call me a good girl, it feels so," she drags her tone, searching for the right word.

"So deceiving?" I finish her sentence for her.

"Why, yes. Yes. It. Does." She agrees, opening the bible to a random page as she kneels on the floor. "It feels like how *she—*"

Araceli pauses, to look at Tori—or 'Beth' as she knew her—who sits trembling in the cold bath water. Araceli clears her throat. "It feels like something that would suit her more. Since we all know that good is subjective and most good girls are bad girls who don't have the courage to accept their demons. Isn't that right?" Araceli juts her chin in Tori's direction. Waiting for her to speak. To say anything to defend herself. Though the temperature of the water, mixed with the injection I gave her which still has her limbs partially numb, is too strong for her to mutter more than a breathy and broken "sorry."

"Shh," Araceli whispers. "There will be a time for your apologies, but for right now, I need to know what a good Christian woman like you is doing with this." Now on her feet, Araceli moves to the necklace with *my* rib bone on it. The rib bone that Araceli dug up from beneath the dirt of my grave. Snatching it in her grip, she lifts it up for emphasis before taking hold of her notebook.

"I thought you didn't believe in this kind of stuff. Were you having a moment of weakness and thinking for yourself for a change?" She asks without giving Tori a second to respond. "You are familiar with what a moment of weakness is, correct? Or are you so lost in the Jesus sauce that you aren't?"

Tori's mouth trembles as she begins muttering a response, but Araceli speaks over her. "Shut up. See, I know firsthand that you are not the ideal Christian woman in the making that my stepfather claimed you were. Don't worry, he was no prize either, I mean you heard the news reports. Which, might I add, was only a fraction of the atrocities he committed. Let's not forget how he used to use me and Harlan at differing points of our lives as ashtrays. And let's not forget what he tried to do to exorcise the 'demons', as he called them, out of me." Araceli pauses. "With his dick, Tori Beth. With his fucking disgusting dick."

It's nothing I didn't already know, but the anger that arises in me hearing that my father did that to Araceli. That he punished her by violating her. That he took something that didn't belong to him infuriates me.

"But I digress," Araceli continues. "My point is that you've had many moments of weakness. Like when you used to suck Harlan's dick in the church basement. Or when you snuck onto our property and watched Harlan and I in the bathroom, and stood there seething while you watched me ride his leg from the window as I begged him—and got my way—for him to break the rules and spend Halloween with me."

"Fuck," I groan, interrupting Araceli.

"What is it, big brother?" she pouts her lips as a devious grin curls her lips.

"You can't talk like that," I groan again, this time louder. Needier.

Her pout deepens. "Like what?"

"You know what you're doing to me. It makes me want to—"

"Sin?" Araceli lifts her eyebrows.

"No, fuck."

"Hmm," Araceli hums. "Soon, brother. Very soon."

She redirects her attention to Tori. "Anyway, let's not forget when you inserted yourself into my life as my fucking literary agent. Hmm. That covers it. But wait." Araceli lifts her finger in the air as if a light bulb just went off. "Oh, and then there is the pièce de résistance."

I move from behind Tori, kneeling on the floor to the side of the tub, my attention on Araceli, dying to hear what she has to say next. I already know, but I want to hear it. I need to. We all do. Especially Tori.

"Don't leave us in suspense." I motion for Araceli to continue, but she's too busy straddling herself on top of the open bible. Her arms stretch forward as her palm flattens, anchoring herself to the ground. Though her shoulders remain slightly hunched with her neck cranked down to read.

"Here it is." Araceli breaks the silence. "Proverbs 6:34. Jealousy makes a man," she interrupts herself, shooting her gaze over to Tori, "or woman," she adds before looking back down to finish reading the rest of the verse, "rage; he'll show no mercy on his day of revenge." Araceli's neck cranks up, settling her stare on me first, then Tori, who even with the drugs slowing her breathing, is still aware enough to grasp every word Araceli is about to say.

"Your bible speaks about jealousy. Quite a bit, actually. I got tired of skimming through all the bullshit in it, so I gave up counting after fifty. But either way, there are plenty of verses that you should know that speak about how jealousy is bad. How it can lead a person—even a godly person—to do bad things."

Bringing one hand to her clit, Araceli begins to rub herself as she arches her back in a circular motion, grinding her bare pussy on the open bible. Her arousal clings to the thin pages and a crinkling sound echoes the gyration of her hips.

A pant leaks from Araceli's mouth, then another as she picks up the speed she's fucking the spread pages.

"What she's trying to say is... fuck your bible. Isn't that right?" I ask Araceli, who nods a yes before she huffs out a sultry gust of air. Twirling her fingers at her clit, she stops only to dip them into her warmth. Her fingers become crushed from her gliding her sex up and down the pages.

Fuck. Speaking of jealousy, I've never been more jealous of a bible of all fucking things.

I can't believe how wet she's getting. The pages are visibly soaked from her arousal.

"Yes," Araceli pants. "Fuck. Your. Bible." An explosive orgasm is followed by her mewls, , one that I wish I could lick up from her dripping wet pussy, but I'm still waiting for how she will deliver the news to Tori. Plus, I have eternity to worship, consume, tear apart, and repent at her pussy. As torturous as not diving in now is, I can be a good boy and wait just a little longer.

Riding the waves of her release, Araceli skims her fingers onto the torn pages, clawing at them, she shreds them into her palm as she rises. The remnants of her orgasm, fresh on the paper, locked in her grip. She approaches the tub, with nothing but revenge oozing from her pores.

"And fuck you, too. Tori or Beth. Fuck you, for thinking I'm that much of a fucking pendeja that I wouldn't figure out it was you that gave us those drugs at the Halloween Shop, or that you laced them yourself. Well, only the snake portion of the sheet that you explicitly told me to take." Araceli now stands by the tub and snatches Tori's chin with one hand, slapping it before prying her mouth open with the other, stuffing the wet bible pages in it.

Tears stream down Tori's face and she chokes and gags on the pages.

Araceli looks over at me and holds her hand out for me to give her something. I pat my pockets, but I don't have anything to give her that would inflict the kind of pain she's hoping to place on her.

Her eyes scan the bathroom.

"Give me that," she tilts her head to the floor.

The bone.

My bone.

Covered in enough dirt that the glistening sheen from Araceli's arousal shouldn't be visible as it is. But it's still there and I can't wait to see what she does with it.

ARACELI

My palm remains outstretched and ready for Harlan to place the bone in as I bore my stare into Tori Beth's. She's trying so damn hard to spit out the pages stuffed into her mouth.

I pout my lips. "Aww, does my dead cunt not taste yummy to you? Here, let me help you with that." I take my other hand, guiding my fingers into the space between her parted lips, and push the paper in further.

A gagging sounds while she adjusts to the drenched paper grazing the back of her throat just as Harlan slips the bone in my hand. I can feel his excitement. It's practically bubbling over in his cold, lifeless veins.

"This," I mutter in anticipation as I straighten my spine. Holding onto the bone on either of its curved ends, I lift my hands, bracing myself and with all my might, I crash it down onto one knee, splitting it in half. Giving me two uneven and sharp weapons to use.

The symphony of gagging noises now replaced with an arguably more aggravating sound. Whimpering pleas. A last effort to be forgiven. But I'm not here to forgive. I'm here for revenge.

Blood for blood. An eye for an eye.

"You look scared," I state the obvious as I make my way close to her.

Her eyes move like a pendulum just staring at me as I approach her.

"Are you scared?" I ask.

Her gaze continues its frantic assessing of the broken bones I have clutched in both palms. The rib, a sacred bone to her in her convoluted faith. A bone symbolizing creation—while it spits in the face of logic and science, or believing in any other system besides the one she was taught is superior—is now a makeshift weapon.

"You are just as guilty for his death as I am. Just like I'm about to be guilty for yours," I threaten.

I look back and see Harlan staring. Waiting to be involved.

"This is a really nice tub. It's so big. Big enough for three people." The inflection in my voice, an obvious suggestion for Harlan to get his ass into the water that I'm now dipping both legs into.

"How—i—i—is—thi—?" Tori's teeth are chattering too much for her to form a coherent sentence.

I submerge my entire body into the tub. Water splashing, but barely so. Benefits of being a ghost. She likely can barely feel me straddling her lap. However, she'll feel when I locate two of her

EPILOGUE

carotid arteries on either side of her neck and pierce through them.

"How is this happening?" I finish her question for her. "Well, you see, I've been naughty."

Harlan, now behind me, settles his chin on my shoulder. "Yeah, she has." He spanks my ass and again the water barely even ripples. Scaring Tori Beth more.

"Since I believe in *fatum enim eligimus*. Choosing my own fate. I've decided that death isn't it for me. I'm not ready to be completely lost in the abyss. There's still so much I can do in this form. But I think the real question is. How can you see me?"

"Us" Harlan corrects.

I scoff. "Yes, us." I turn my head to look at him. "Which, by the way, we aren't a thing." I remind him.

Finding Harlan was about healing, not about love. Not feeding the Ferryman was always about using the freedom death has granted us and putting it to good use. Some, of course, would argue that existing in a perpetual purgatory isn't good use or wise, but those who say such things haven't had the privilege of experiencing it. I have. *I am*, and I don't want to let this go. Not yet.

Harlan juts his chin to the bone in my hand. "You keep telling yourself that, but your dead cunt sure likes my 'stale cock', as you like to put it. It was weeping all over it just this morning."

"Oh, please. You're a good fuck, but that's where it starts and ends."

He clicks his split tongue. "I'm also a good partner..."

"In crime," I finish for him. "Only."

A grin expands on his chiseled face. "You keep telling yourself that."

Ah, yawn. Clingy ex-virgin.

Turning my focus back on a very cold, very frightened Tori, I continue. "Don't mind him. I let him fuck me once. While he was sleeping no less, and here we are. He's still clingy as ever for what he never wanted from you. Now, don't feel too special. You are just a check off the list of people who have wronged us and will pay. But I did, however, want you to be my first." I grin, playful and seductive.

I lean forward, pressing my lips against hers. Even hanging in the balance of fear, and the sedatives working, her lips still manage to purse to kiss mine back.

My mouth remains near hers, but I move far enough back. "No, not that kind of first. I've been with girls before. But I wanted you to be my first kill in my new form. My free, lifeless, happy form." I press one last kiss to her trembling mouth as I lift both hands up at either side of her neck.

My hands hang in the balance, making her sweat it out.

"Oh, by the way, I made that deadline you were so worried about. Had it hand delivered to the publisher myself, since I knew you'd be *busy*. Oh, and I decided to change the title and publish under my real name."

Her gaze skates from side to side, terrified of both my clenched fists.

"What's wrong? Cat got your tongue? Too scared to recite the Lord's prayer? Afraid he won't be the one you see when I do this." I don't give her an opportunity to answer—not like she could—or fight it. With precise force I plunge the sharp bones down, crashing into either side of her neck. Her skin breaks on impact, and blood pools around the bone, staining it as I stare into her eyes, watching the life fade from them. I wonder what she'll see when her soul escapes her body. The construct she hopes for or the reality of what she fears. Either way, that's her problem, not mine.

Red fills the tub, diluting as it hits the water's edge. I skim my fingers in the mixture, trying to gather as much as I can.

A familiar song fills my head as I rub the crimson between my thumb and index finger.

Blood for blood. Eye for an eye.

The more the melody repeats, the more I want to do what it says. I hum it over again as I turn to face Harlan. His arms are

EPILOGUE

slumped over the tub and he stares at me with a wide grin on his face.

"You gonna share or what?" His gaze falls to the blood on my fingers.

"Come and get it." I entice him with my dripping fingers, curling for him to move closer.

Water splashes as he lunges forward, capturing my hand in his. He sucks my fingers into his mouth, feasting on the fresh blood.

"Revenge tastes good, doesn't it?"

Harlan nods as the suction of his mouth loosens on around my fingers. His split tongue sloppily licking it up. He's so eager to please me, now that I am in the same lifeless boat as him.

"Tell me, brother. When you took my book, what did you see?"

Harlan peers up at me, confusion ripe on his brow. "Huh?"

"What did you see?" I repeat, pulling my finger from his mouth, so he can answer me.

"Death." He deadpans.

I shake my head. "That's not all you saw. Tell me. What else did you see?"

Unease warps his expression, though he fights it. "I saw," he stutters, clearing his throat. "Death's anger."

"That's right, and how did it make you feel?" I ask, already knowing how frightened it made him.

"I felt nothing."

My tongue clicks. "You're lying." I turn my head to the hooded figure waiting for us. "It frightened you. I know it did. Don't lie to me." I glide my body over top of his, lifting one hand out to the side for the hooded figure watching us to hand me my journal already open to the illustration.

I show the page to Harlan. "Tell me, what do you see now?"

He smiles and pulls me closer, locking me in his grip. My bare pussy brushing on his bare cock.

"Our end," he groans, biting on his lip, distracted by my gliding up and down his length, teasing him.

"Our ending?" I begin in an exaggerated coo, "or yours?"

The hooded figure takes a step closer, its skeletal hand outstretched, awaiting payment.

Harlan turns his head to face it—the destiny he escaped to haunt me—but I move my bloody hand down to guide his stiff, dead cock.

"Eyes on me," I instruct him as I ride him, with death staring at us... waiting.

"Fuck, you feel like —"

"Shh," I silence Harlan.

The figure lowers their hood to my mouth and I cup my hands to it, whispering, not giving up the tempo I'm fucking Harlan. An item is exchanged between us discreetly before their spine stiffens, and they move towards Harlan.

"Araceli, what did you say to it?"

I ignore Harlan's question. My lips skim his as our foreheads brush and my mouth falls agape to recite a part of my story I always knew would have to happen in order to be truly free of anything, or anyone, that will hold me back from being myself. After all, this has all been written in the stars, just like Frida said, waiting for me to grasp it. To take the ending destined for me and run wild with it.

"Keeping my eyes on him, I discreetly curl my fingers as his tongue nears mine. And just as the token of my commitment to the sacrifice is transferred from my mouth to his, I use the sadistic communion as my opportunity to secure the knife's handle in my palm, and drive it into his throat."

"Araceli." He skids back in the tub, trying to get away from me, but he can't. He's about to come. So am I.

"Rivulets of blood stream from the wound, the look of betrayal ripe within his irises as he slumps over me and into the tub."

"Stop it now. Stop th—" Harlan's words are halted by the hooded figure reaching for his throat, about to lift him from the tub.

EPILOGUE

"You stop it!" I snap. Not at Harlan, but the impatient visitor, who is ruining me and Harlan's farewell fuck.

"Come for me, brother," I encourage Harlan, and through his fear, he obeys, spewing his dead seed into me. "That's a good boy. You came for me and someday, when I'm ready, I'll come for you... again."

"Araceli, what the fuck are you talking about--" Harlan is interrupted by the hooded figure lifting him by the throat, out of the tub.

"His payment." The figure roars as I rise to my feet, handing the figure the coin he gave me in exchange for a few more minutes of quality time with Harlan, for his destiny to be complete, and for mine to begin.

Frida's warning plays in my mind.

"It's important that you keep that to yourself. Your story is yours and yours alone. If anyone gains access to your path, consequences will arise."

Registering what's happening, or what's about to happen, Harlan becomes visibly angry. "You fucking bitch!" He spits out.

"Ssh." My lips pout. "Don't talk dirty to me. I like it. Don't worry, I'll meet up with you soon enough. You had your time in limbo. It's my time to shine. *Alone.*" I continue to recite the words as I pry Harlan's tense jaw open. The look of betrayal dances throughout his irises as the coin for passage nears his tongue. "Summoning you was my apology. Saying goodbye is my gift. See you soon, brother." It's true, I gathered what was left of him with the intention of experiencing the punishment I deserved for being the catalyst for his downfall. It was my guilt that drove me back to that house, but it's the freedom and peace that death has given me that has me greedy for more.

I watch his soul leave the room. Just as the voices told me to that night at Heathen's Cross, when they urged me to let him sail. His passage is now complete, while mine is now beginning. Just how I wrote it to be.

The hooded figure disappears. His debt paid and now the

bathroom is full of Heathen's Cross members, surrounding me in their cloaks. Fellow fallen souls that refuse to give into the idea of submitting one's will, even in death, to seek refuge in another realm.

"*Now*, my initiation is complete." I say out loud, before reciting the end of the excerpt to myself in silence.

"*You're wrong,*" I spit. "*Tell el Barquero, there's no escaping me.*"

I meant it when I said that I'd rather be cursed, or haunted, over being saved. Except now, I can do the haunting because *I* choose my fate.

"True horror is given life through the lies we tell to protect ourselves and it lives on through the tragedies that not only define us... but own us." — Araceli Suárez. *In Flames We Thrive.* New York: Charon Press, 2024.

THE END.

AFTERWORD

If you got this far... thank you! It was both nerve wracking and exciting to step out of my comfort zone to write a horror story. Psychological horrors/thrillers are my absolute favorite. I love stories that seem tame, until events start unraveling and your mind is left in pieces. I hope this book achieved that.

For anyone who cares, a few things inspired this book. One being my unending love for Nickelback. Are you surprised? If you're new here, I love Nickelback and their songs have acted as inspiration in some way, shape, or form in all of my books (and always end up on the playlist). Their *Coin for the Ferryman* song has stuck with me since the Feed The Machine album came out. I'm a nerd and love researching the meaning beyond lyrics and once I discovered that it is based on Charon in Greek mythology who is the Ferryman of the underworld, I knew I had to write something incorporating it. Another song, that heavily inspired the twists this book took is Slow Burn by Jack Valentine. After reading BTD if you listen to those two songs, so much of the plot (I hope) will make sense.

This idea has been marinating for awhile but once I watch an episode of the American Horror Anthology series titled "Necro" which I won't give spoilers to, but that ending stood with me and played a part in Beneath The Dirt (specifically it's title).

Thank you for venturing off the HEA/romance train with me! I can't promise how many more of these stories I will write, since I do love my suspense romances but this definitely won't be my last!

Also by N.J. Weeks

The Trick: A Dark Stalker Romance

The Trap: A Dark Romantic Thriller

Skulls and Stitches: A Nightmare Before Christmas Reimagining

Cuervo's Carnival: A MMF Poly Thriller

TIL' DEATH MY LOYAL HELLCATS...

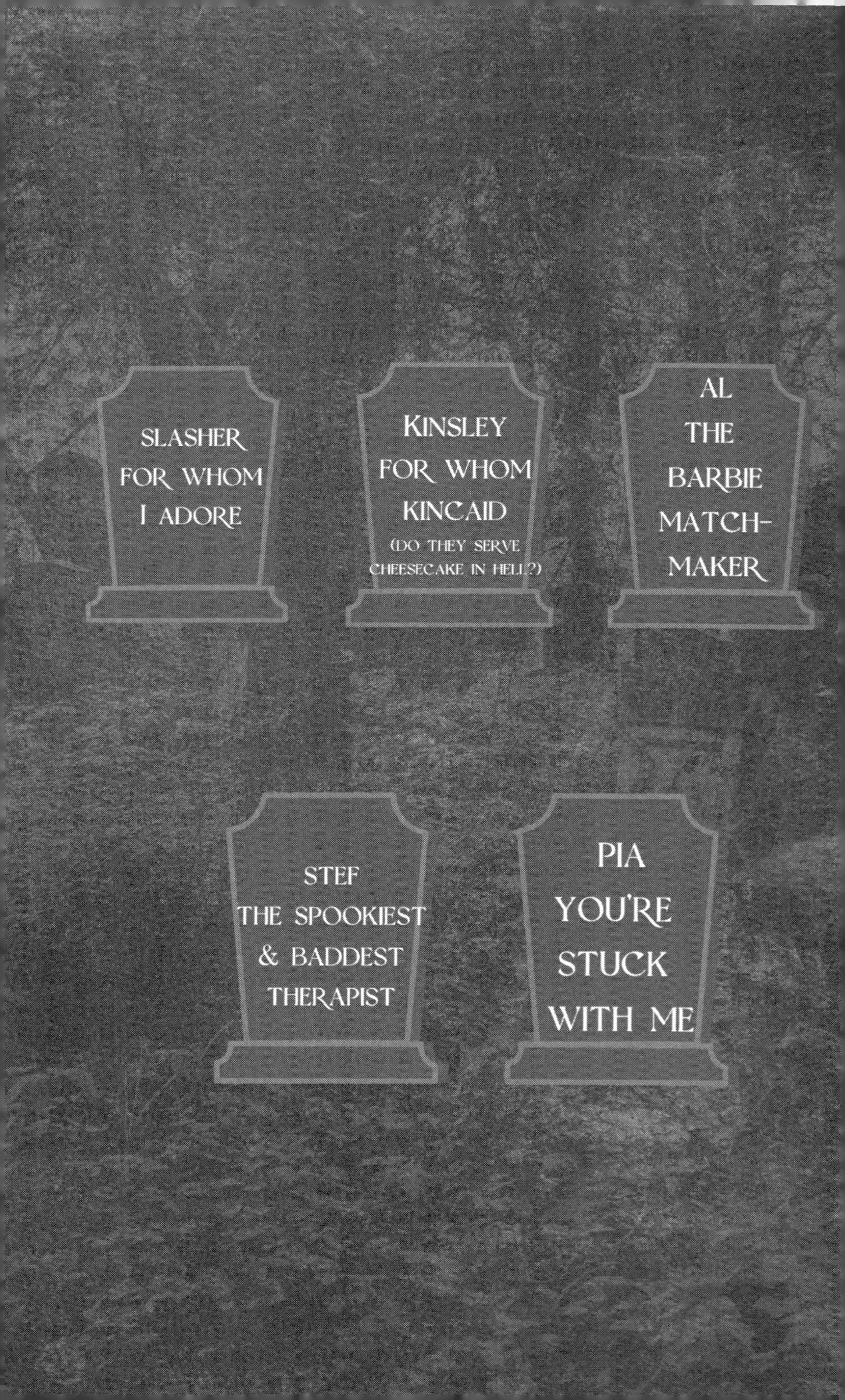

SLASHER
FOR WHOM
I ADORE

KINSLEY
FOR WHOM
KINCAID
(DO THEY SERVE
CHEESECAKE IN HELL?)

AL
THE
BARBIE
MATCH-
MAKER

STEF
THE SPOOKIEST
& BADDEST
THERAPIST

PIA
YOU'RE
STUCK
WITH ME

Wavel	Kiss My Ash	Onyx	Brim-stone
Geonna Marrae	Adri-anna	Misty Lynn Humphrey	Corrine
	Riggs & Lucy Chandler (buried together n death)	Stephanie Topp	

Jenn N	Kitten	Luralyn Castillo	Lisa Bob Hanhart
Mary Rose	Kayla G.	Kai	
Lucy Ghoulie	Michelle Montenegro	Emily Stellmar	Lauren Bowman

- Jennifer (Oogie Boogie Babe)
- Emily Cuen
- Amanda Jewell
- Michelle Partridge
- Tiffany Vera
- Katiee Comer
- Brandi Exline
- Kim Harney
- Amber Mack
- Sherri Boyat
- Cassie Mainella
- Chelsea Cardenas
- Ayden Perry
- Tyla

| Sam Webb | Melynda Allesandro | Adreanna Gonzalez | Tiva |

| Cat Crist | Zoe Tonks | Brittany Joy |

| Katiee Comer | Jenn (myspooky bookishlife) | Desiree |

Printed in Dunstable, United Kingdom